P9-CLB-877

Carnivore Diet

ALSO BY JULIA SLAVIN

*The Woman Who Cut Off Her Leg at the
Maidstone Club and Other Stories*

Carnivore Diet

Julia Slavin

W. W. NORTON & COMPANY

NEW YORK   LONDON

Copyright © 2005 by Julia Slavin

All rights reserved
Printed in the United States of America
First Edition

For information about permission to reproduce selections from this book, write to
Permissions, W. W. Norton & Company, Inc., 500 Fifth Avenue, New York, NY 10110

Manufacturing by Courier Westford
Book design by Lovedog Studio
Production manager: Anna Oler

Library of Congress Cataloging-in-Publication Data

Slavin, Julia.
Carnivore diet / Julia Slavin.—1st ed.
p. cm.
ISBN 0-393-05998-7
1. Politician's spouses—Fiction. 2. Prisoners' families—Fiction.
3. Washington (D.C.)—Fiction. 4. Mothers and sons—Fiction.
5. Child actors—Fiction. 6. Monsters—Fiction. I. Title.
PS3569.L296C37 2005
813'.54—dc22   2005011967

W. W. Norton & Company, Inc.
500 Fifth Avenue, New York, N.Y. 10110
www.wwnorton.com

W. W. Norton & Company Ltd.
Castle House, 75/76 Wells Street, London W1T 3QT

1 2 3 4 5 6 7 8 9 0

for my parents

Acknowledgments

I would like to express my thanks to Jill Bialosky, Evan Carver, The Corporation of Yaddo, Raul Correa, Amy Hempel, The Rona Jaffe Foundation, Jan Linley, Fiona J. Mackintosh, Pearson Marx, Beth Millemann, Rick Moody, Esther Newberg, Claudia Plepler, Paul Slavin, John Arnholz, and Andy Sewer.

Carnivore Diet

A man swallowed a pearl that hung from the neck of a slain dragon because he believed it would give him power and physical strength. For a period of time, it did. His military and political might gripped the east and much of the west. But soon a disastrous campaign in the north and an ultimate defeat in the south as the man grew weak and distracted. From the pearl had hatched Chagwanadon, a beast so huge it could not fit the screen of the man's imagination. Springing into the deepest cell of the man's sleep, it showed itself in pieces, a claw, a cavern of a mouth, the fork in a furless tail. It drove the man mad not to know what lived inside him. He demanded the beast show itself in its entirety at once. The beast would not. The more the man insisted, the more the beast pulled up into the man's head, giving him pounding headaches. And still the beast grew. He roared and shattered the man's eardrum. He studied the movements of his prey at night and the man became blind. Soon the man could not contain the enormity of the beast, so he took an axe and split his own head in two. The beast spilled out and ate the man. Only then could the man sleep tight.

Book I: Dylan

MY YEARS WERE THE cartoon's best, and I'm not bragging. The action figures and the lunch boxes, the videos and the web site, the books and the clothing line: my reign. There was talk of a *Harlan* cologne. If there's money changing hands, aren't you bound to get some? Not if you had the job every kid in America wanted, would have paid to have. Not if your father had given term limits a whole new meaning by getting sentenced to three to five at Ainsville in the middle of his fourth year in Congress and you wanted to stay the hell out of the papers by not suing. And not if your vocal cords were sitting on a fault. The fault is in control, not you. You wouldn't buy a house on the edge of a known mudslide.

"You should feel fortunate." Well-wishers consoled me in an

odd way. "You've held out a lot longer than the other Harlans." It was true. At fourteen, I had three seasons as the voice of the postapocalyptic rodent of questionable phylum. Was he rat? The animators were not permitted to say. Gold Street Productions said most definitely not. A rat is a pest. Rats bring plague. But look at the ears, the snout with buckteeth for gnawing, the way he chattered his incisors when he was glad. Marsupial, Gold Street said when pressed. But mostly Harlan was a boy. And this was what my contract enjoined: stay a boy.

"Don't you think we should take our finger out of the dike?" My mother brought a thicker towel to drape over my head while I inhaled chamomile and steam, a home remedy I got from a former Harlan who said he bought himself six more episodes with the prescription. Sweat from my forehead dripped back into the pot. *Dike* gave me an unwanted hard-on.

She ducked her head under the towel. "Can you breath?"

"A little."

"We don't need the money." According to her. On my mother's government salary we barely paid rent. My golden pipes were settling Dad's legal bills, maintaining our home back in Canton, where there was a rambler—bought to establish residency—and a garage with a rusting hoop, "just waiting for us to come and die," she said. I'd never been to Canton, but that didn't keep me from calling it home. My mother had never been there either before the campaign. She even refused to pronounce the name. She called it can-TON, as though it were a province of China. Still, I tried to convince her to pay off the mortgage. We needed a place where no one would know us.

I came out from under the towel and went in the bathroom

to scrub Phisoderm into zits. Looking in the mirror was a disturbing thing to do, but Mom stepped up behind me.

"Women are going to love you when you're older." Girls thought I was queer. "Wanna go for a walk?"

"I sort of do and I sort of don't." My voice spanned three octaves.

"We could go to a four o'clock movie after."

"We could go see Dad." I couldn't have meant the suggestion. I never visited Ainsville. She hated it too.

"Wanna help paint the dining room?"

"I'm painting Andre's dining room."

"I made some ice tea." The bathroom was tight, covered top to bottom in wallpaper with a pattern that gave the illusion of a palm forest growing in around you, my father's remodeling before going into Ainsville. He wanted Morocco. I saw the trees fall in around me, the vines from the ceiling lower, knotting into rope collars.

"You'll go straight to Andre's?" She followed me to the door. "There was another attack. In the woods. Behind Carter Baron."

"That was a gang war."

"You'll be home for dinner?"

I headed down the walk. "Probably eat there."

"It's more fun at Andre's."

I zipped my windbreaker, foraging the lint and wrappers in my pockets for gum. I walked with my head down, navigating by the tar and cracks in the asphalt. Andre and I stopped being friends in the fall when, inexplicably, he became good-looking. By the middle of the year, he told me I couldn't sit anywhere near him in hockey carpool, even if the only available seat happened to be next to him. So I contorted myself into the back-

back of the Toyota wagon with my equipment and ill-fitting pads sticking out the neck of my jersey, while Andre whipped his head around, thinking I was going to try to touch him. I wasn't going to Andre's. I was heading downtown to the War Memorial, for some peace in the exhibit in the crypt, to nod hello to my friends who worked the MIA/POW booths and never remembered me, to run for ice tea and egg rolls while they sold patches and YOU ARE NOT FORGOTTEN stickers in the rain, decades after the war had ended.

The Mall was empty because of the Tree Murders. I shuffled across the grass to the white path and came to the directory of the dead and missing. I looked up anybody, then walked down into the exhibit to weep with the other weepers, pretending my father was among the thousands of dead. I scanned over the names until I got to the one I picked. Then I reached up my hand. I always came apart at that moment. This was a place for grief and I had plenty. I was ugly. I'd lose my job. My family was a disgrace. The girls I loved were always lost to me, hidden behind the providence of athletically promising boys. Everything cried out of me. I knew nothing about these souls who stepped on mines or bailed out of planes during secret bombing raids. And I rarely thought of them. Almost always, someone stepped up to help. Once, a guy in a Hell's Angels jacket put me on his shoulders so I could touch a name. Someone else offered to make a rubbing, no charge. A woman gave me Kleenex. Everybody said God bless you. Hardly ever did anyone ask questions. Though I did tell some kids on a field trip from Tennessee that a name was my father, my voice wobbling and cracking. But it didn't matter because that's what a voice is supposed to do at the Wall. Today, a guy with no legs rolled over. He held my hand as I wept and pointed up toward the name Private Princeton Dagman. "All that crying's gonna make you blind, boy," the guy said. I rubbed my sore eyes. But I started up again and cried so hard I thought my eyes would wash right out of me onto the guy's lap, two eggs sunny-side up.

Mom was in front of the TV when I got home, leaning forward instead of turning it up. Some bow hunters had quite a shock as they crept through the woods near Fort De Russey and found two house painters dangling from the trees. Their torsos were gone, connected to their lower and upper bodies by nothing but backbone, ice-pick punctures covering what was left of them. Their eyes bulged in an expression of terror, how they must have looked as they died. A preliminary autopsy revealed massive infection throughout the remains, bacteria sweating through the skin, gangrene setting in immediately. Nearly wound for wound, the killings mimicked the other attacks in the Palisades. Police pulled over every gray van in the city. My mother wouldn't leave the TV. She watched the story she already knew again and again. All the usuals were rounded up: the homeless park dwellers, the veterans with restraining orders, the gun show enthusiasts, the parole violators. All sorts of leads were followed. But the police remained clueless in pinpointing a killer.

"I don't want you to see this, Dylan." Mom held up her hand to cover my eyes. Too late.

FOUR O'CLOCK Monday morning I was up gargling with Cepacol, leaning over steam, doing verbal acrobatics, "La la la la la," forcing tones high above my normal register. At five, the car picked me up and drove me out to the Gold Street Studios in Broomsville. Usually I sat up front with Billy, the driver. I'd done that from the beginning, at Dad's suggestion, just to show I was no better than he. Billy was a former Harlan, from the seventies, for one season before his voice changed. Then management gave him a few bit parts, the evil crossing guard, the guy who takes tickets at the fair, one of the Rough Rats. But he went through a windshield, had some head trauma, gambling trouble, joined the Army, got an honorable discharge with bad numbers and started to drink. Since then, they kept him around as a driver and a courier because "Gold Street takes care of its people." Billy tried to get on a *Where Are They Now* show, but no one remembered him. Lately, I'd been sitting in the back, to show my displeasure about his racist jokes.

"Just tell him you find that kind of humor offensive," Mom told me.

No, thank you. We had to drive over three bridges and he liked to pretend the car was out of control. But then some days I felt sorry for him and I'd sit up front and listen to his stories about the dog races in Fort Lauderdale. "It's not that I liked going to the dogs that much, but the dates loved it." Or I'd ask about a Gold Street secretary I knew that he liked.

"Angry buttons on the blouse today," he said. "*Angry* buttons." I looked at his messed-up face. No one gets adequately put back together after going through a windshield. They have a Frankensteinian mix 'n' match about them. I imagined the moment of impact, the crown of his head parting the glass, the Chevy Corsica giving birth to Billy on Route 1, only the asphalt there to catch him. But the green sign still loomed over the highway like a death warrant: BAY BRIDGE, 1 MILE. My stomach lurched. If we survived the 197-foot fall he'd humiliate me in front of the girls at the cartoon for gakking in the Seville.

"Hey, Billy," I tried to distract him. "NBA draft should be pretty exciting this year with all those high school players coming out."

"Yeah," he said. "But what about Rahim Wilson?"

Rahim Wilson. My most favorite player of all time. He took Our Lady of the Highways to the state championship three times. "What about Rahim Wilson?"

"I don't think he's going to get drafted." Rahim was an All-American, on the cover of *Sports Illustrated*. Lord of the No-Look. He led the league in assists. "Here's a guy, five-nine—"

"Six feet," I said. "Don't forget Spud Webb. He was even shorter. And Mugsie Bogues."

"Rahim don't shoot like a Bogie."

"Mugsie. Rahim's got a great shot."

"Everybody in the NBA's got a shot." I wanted to shoot Billy, but we'd just sped through the SmartPass booth at the toll. The shadow of the central span of the bridge clipped the front seat. My breathing became short.

"So . . . Billy . . . who do you think will get drafted? Sean Cummings? Vinnie LaTrel? Who's your number-one pick, Billy? Billy?"

"Whoa."

"What? What's the matter?"

"I don't know." Billy looked down at his feet. "Something feels out of whack." We were over the water, heading upward toward the first tower of the suspension bridge. "I'm sure it's nothing . . . *Whoa!* Did you hear that?"

"Hear what, Billy? I didn't hear anything."

"That knocking sound. I was supposed to get that twenty-thousand-mile tuneup thing." We were just before the highest point of the bridge, twenty stories above the water. Yachts and schooners were bathtub toys, the whitecaps miserly lines of cocaine. I held on to the strap above the window with two hands, as though that would save me when we plunged. "Whoa! Whooooaaa! I can't control her! We're going over!"

"Stop it! Stop it!" I squealed. Then it happened. My silvery voice dropped into the deepest part of the ocean. "**I SAID STOP.**"

Billy straightened the wheel, saying nothing until we got over the bridge onto quieter streets. Then he looked at me in the rearview.

"Do I have a man in this car?"

I wiped the sweat off my face with my shirt. "No."

"That sounded very grown-up. Like one of those big-nutted Austrians named Jorg."

"It's just me."

"They know at Gold Street? That they got a man playing the rat boy?"

I didn't say a word. I looked at his face again in the mirror, all the cracks and scars and fault lines turning upward in cartographic syncopation, alongside his horrible smile.

FIVE MILES after the Bay Bridge, you started seeing tremendous cutout characters from *Harlan* pointing the direction to Gold Street. At the entrance, a twenty-foot iron Harlan split in half down the middle when the guard waved you in. Over the years, Harlan looked more and more like me. Back in the early seventies, he was quite ratlike, but now he was rounded out, more human. He was me now, with rat ears and a snout. "Unless it was *you* who changed to look like *him*." Billy laughed and laughed, letting me off in front of the studio, making certain to skid on the gravel as he peeled off to park the Seville.

Walking the halls of Gold Street was like navigating through an endless Strait of Dardanelles: one ex-Harlan after another, cropping up like jagged rocks, offering morning greetings as they went about their now-menial rounds.

"Morning, Dylan." Pat from copier repair. Harlan #11.

"Hey, buddy, put it there." Sam, the production assistant. Harlan #18.

"Wizards! Creamed by Chicago!" Connor, from the mailroom. Four years in jail for possession and robbery, two years in rehab. Harlan #8.

"Dyl-ster!" Charlie, the security guard. Harlan #10. One year at the top, then overthrown by early puberty, poor guy. I signed in on his clipboard.

Alex from the tape morgue just nodded. I took over from him. They tried to keep us apart.

Paco, Harlan #29.

Nat, Harlan #31.

Anton, Harlan #32.

And then there was Billy. Hanging out by the Snapple machine, watching my every move. "Appreciate it while it lasts, kid. 'Cause it ain't gonna."

I headed for the green room, passing Marty Helpern's show. He had a guest from the Brookings Institution. They discussed whether gas was underpriced. Always the wrong topic. Someone was stalking the nation's capital, ripping men to pieces and decorating the trees with what remained, and Marty talked about prices at the pump. When the Lufthansa planes were hijacked at Dulles Airport, his show was dedicated to the Oscars and actors who had criminally never been nominated.

I went in the bathroom, waited until it cleared out, then practiced keeping my voice steady. "Mi mi mi mi mi." I thought of the great castratis, nutless men who were the idols of their times. "Glorrrrrrrrria." The littlest angel. "You're the greatest," I told my larynx. "Don't leave me." Andy, the head writer, came in and handed me my pages. Andy was one of the first Harlans. He stayed on after his voice changed, working his way up. He liked putting stories from my life into the show. When my dog ran away, Andy wrote that Harlan's angelfish, Penny, same name as my dog, dies of old age and his little sister, Lizzie, hosts an open-casket funeral. Or the time Dad took me to New York City because the prison family outreach counselor suggested we do something special together before he went into Ainsville. We stayed at the Plaza. We shopped for hockey gear at Paragon's. We saw *The Beverly Hillbillies* on Broadway. I was so nervous about being alone with him that I spent most of the weekend in the bathroom with colitis. Andy wrote that Harlan's dad takes him to the Baseball Hall of Fame and they have a blast. On the bus to Cooperstown they meet a cartoon Yogi Berra rodent who gives them a private tour.

"I used what you told me about the prison musical," Andy said. But then his mood changed. "Look, Dylan. I managed to make it Lizzie's show, she and Dad in the school production of *Bye Bye Birdie*. Dad's Conrad and turns out he's tone-deaf, whoop-de-doo. But I couldn't get around your embarrassment scene and I don't think I'm going to be able to get you much more. You've had a good run, Dylan. No, a great run." He looked down at the black and white beehive tile. "You were the best Harlan I ever had. And, you know, if it were up to me . . ."

"I'm canned?"

"Not yet."

"What do you mean, not yet?"

"I mean, Paul's got a hard-on about the age discrimination suits so he's not paying attention to the show. Neither is the Fifth Floor. But I've been through a lot of Harlans and I know how things go."

"How do things go?"

"Dylan . . ."

"I've got plenty of shows left. I had a slip last week. I'm in control."

"The steam?" Andy said. "The inhalants? You think I didn't do the same? Snake oil. None of it works. The cords get thicker, they spread out to make way for the new register, there's no stopping it. Get out before it becomes humiliating. The time comes sooner or later. And there's something I think you should know." He inhaled a few times, whistling through a deviated septum. "They want to replace you with a woman." I felt like I'd been slugged. "It was inevitable. Come on. All the flux. The viewers getting used to a new voice every other year, the cast adjusting, finding the right chemistry. They want something built to last. It's the end of an era, Dylan." He leaned back next to a urinal from the 1940s. "I suppose I understand where the Fifth Floor is coming from. Though you have to admit, a woman's voice just doesn't have the same pure white quality."

"I got time," I said.

"Okay. I respect your decision. Good luck today."

✦ ✦ ✦ ✦

"SPEED," GLENN, the tech director, signaled us from the control room. Bert, Harlan's dad, cleared his throat and horked in an ashtray before he read his line. Everybody groaned because it was disgusting. I thought of poor Doug Mullins, the night custodian, Harlan #13, who had to clean up after him.

"Son, you're not excited about seein' your old dad in the musical?"

I sat up as straight as I could, straining my neck toward the ceiling, imagining I could stretch my vocal cords into the thinnest elastic.

"No, Dad, it's just that I neVER . . ." My voice split in two. Up to a squeak, down into hell, a radio station you couldn't tune.

"Let's take that back," Paul's voice boomed over the executive producer's intercom. I tightened my stomach and chest muscles.

Bert horked in the ashtray.

"You know you can tell me anything, son."

Turning down my mouth, I strung out the tendons of my neck into the shape of a webbed foot. *Steady, now. Don't fail me.* "I know that, Daaaaaaad . . ." A cat being strangled.

"Keep going, Dylan, we're still at speed," Paul said.

"It's just that I ne . . ." Glass shattering. "I ne . . . ne . . . ne . . ." Paul and Andy leaned over the console, gesturing for me to spit it out. I clasped my neck with my hands.

"Fuck it." Paul threw a pencil. "Pull up a *never* from the server," he called over to one of the production assistants.

"There's a *never* on the Thanksgiving show," Andy offered.

"There's no *never* on the Thanksgiving show." Klemmer,

Paul's assistant, Harlan #28, had every word of every show memorized. "There's a *never* on the February third show."

"Oh, Christ, forget it. Andy, write me another word for *never.*"

"What? There isn't any other word for *never.*"

"You're a writer, goddammit, you can't come up with another word for *never*?"

"Um . . . *ne're.* Dylan, try 'I *ne're* really liked musical theater.' "

"What's this, the Elizabethan Hour?" Paul said.

"My choices are kind of limited."

"How 'bout *at no time*?" Glenn offered. "At no time have I enjoyed musical theater."

"I got the *never,*" the production assistant shouted.

Paul flung his cigarette into Andy's coffee.

"*Ne're.* Jesus. Bert, pick it up."

"Son, you're not by any chance embarrassed by your old dad, are you?"

"Me?" I said. "EmbarrAAAAAAssed?" For a few endless moments there was silence. Then the voice of Paul.

"What was that?"

Viveca, the voice of Mom, rushed over to my chair and hugged me. "My little boy is becoming a man!" I wanted to throw up and die.

"Sit down, Viveca," Paul said.

Andy slapped his script on the console. "Dammit, Paul. Why the hell can't we write puberty into the show?" This was the worst moment of my life.

"Because the rat is nine, that's why."

"He's been nine for four decades. I've had it. It's time he grew up."

"Harlan stays nine." Paul pounded his fist.

"What about early puberty?"

"Early what?"

"It's public TV, for chrissakes."

"It's not *that* public, for chrissakes." This led to the same old fault-finding-in-the-other-guy free-for-all that included the time Andy wanted to write in a socialist mayor. And how Paul climbed a ladder to interview the Lufthansa hijackers and now he was doing this crap, but this time it was at my expense. I looked up and saw the night custodian emptying Bert's phlegm-filled ashtray into a black trash bag.

"You're here early, Doug," I said. Doug tried to say something, but he couldn't form the words. He moved his jaw up and down, not making a sound. "What's the matter, Doug?" The guy was in his forties but his face was wrinkled up like he was eighty. Then I started seeing all the old Harlans coming out from places in the voice-over room. Victor squeezing out from the water cooler. Charlie slipping under the studio door. Alex chewing right through the soundproof padding on the wall. And Billy, lurking behind Andy and Paul in the control room, his face lit from below.

I couldn't face anybody. I found the back exit that led down into the tunnels below Gold Street. It was a dark and small passageway. The cinder-block walls were covered over in fuzzy brine, stalactites of mold hanging from the ceiling just inches above my head. I passed the boiler room where Brunston, Harlan #1, stoked the fires.

"I wondered when you'd come."

Brunston's eyes had no irises, just two pupils staring out from caked soot. I left him in a coughing fit and moved on, passing the janitors' closet, sealed with a padlock, a GONE FISHIN sticker diagonally across the door. Up ahead, a room glowed from a Coke machine. Inside, four former Harlans, Victor, Charlie, Connor and Pat, sat around a table drinking Cokes. They wore gray shirts with oval name patches.

"Hey, Dylan. Join us." I stopped at the door. "C'mon, Dylan. I'll treat you to a Coke." Charlie dropped quarters into the machine.

"We're talking about the draft, Dylan."

"What do you think, Dylan? All five high schoolers going to jump?"

"Excuse me." Alex was behind me, trying to get into the room. I moved aside. He took a seat at the table and glared at me. The name patch on his shirt read HARLAN.

"Speak up, Dylan. We can't hear you."

I heard the thud of a Coke landing in the hole of the machine. Charlie bent to take it out.

"C'mon, Dylan." He held out the can. "How about the high schoolers?"

"High school's too young for the draft," Alex snapped.

"Not anymore," Pat said.

"Who's your number one pick, Dylan?" Victor asked.

How could they not know? It was so obvious. "Rahim Wilson."

The guys looked at each other, baffled.

"Rahim Wilson?" Charlie moved toward me. "Dylan. Rahim Wilson isn't going to get drafted. Ever. The St. Joe game. Smashed his knee to smithereens."

I became nauseated. "But... he was a... an All-American." I thought a sip of Coke could help the nausea, but I'd gotten a defective can. It didn't have a flip-top. I turned it over and over, looking for an opening. Charlie took the can from me, opened it and handed it back. The Coke had a metallic taste. I spit back into the can.

"You look tired, Dylan." Charlie put his hand on my shoulder.

"Sit down, Dylan." Connor pulled out a chair and patted the seat.

"You heard what the man said, Dylan. Sit down," Alex growled.

"Don't yell at him," Charlie said.

"I wasn't yelling."

"You were being harsh. It's okay, Dylan."

"I was just talking," Alex said.

"Sit down, Dylan."

"Sit the fuck down."

I turned and sprinted. The tunnel stretched out before me and every corridor I turned down became longer and narrower. A hand grabbed my wrist. I swung around, nearly slipping on the greasy floor.

"Where you going to so fast, Dylan?" It was Doug, the night janitor.

"Let me go." I ran as fast as I could. Just ahead, I saw light around the cracks of a small door. I bounded up three steps and fell out into the parking lot.

"More steam. Make it hotter," I yelled from under the towel, inhaling and exhaling over the measly bowl of chamomile.

"I can't make it any hotter." Mom scurried helplessly around the kitchen.

They wouldn't dump me right away, would they? I'd get the elderly rat who sets up pins in the bowling alley or the hall monitor who says, "Get to class, rodents, get to class." They'd offer the dignified street sweeper who's seen it all, the cranky boss, the newscaster who's always a step behind, the sadistic crossing guard with the heart of gold, or, maybe, eventually, somebody's dad.

I whipped off the towel and stomped over to the stove. I turned the kettle back on and when it started to whistle, I grabbed up the towel, draped it over my head and put my face above the burner. Steam shot into my mouth.

"Stop." She gripped my collar. "Stop it. Please." I tried to push her away. I felt my lips bubble into blisters, my nostrils begin to burn. The corner of the towel touched the stove and lit. Let it happen. Scorch the cords. Burn them away. But a gallon of freezing water put an end to it all. I lifted my drenched head and saw my mother in the center of the kitchen with the empty pitcher in her hands. "Enough," she said. "No more."

I remembered the way Andy looked at me the first time he heard my voice. He was slumped in a swivel chair, collating pages, muttering at the changes the Fifth Floor made in his script. Auditions had gone on for days. No boy was right. And then I spoke into the camera that the animators use to sync up the voices. He lowered his papers and gazed up at me through thick frameless glasses, as though I'd come down the stairs in a strapless number for the prom.

BILLY AND I drove along without saying much, my arm hung over the box of stuff from my Gold Street locker. In my new basso profundo, I asked Billy for a joke. He looked at me warily in the rearview and said he was fresh out. I asked him for a cigarette. He said he didn't smoke and neither did I. He brought the car to a halt at the edge of my subdevelopment. "Know why I quit betting on the dogs?" he asked.

"Because they get eaten when they're over the hill." I looked at the blur of the evergreen forest that backed into the development, a pine gas cloud.

I got out. He called to me through the window. "I guess I won't be driving you no more, because, you know, I only drive the Harlans. That's in my contract and everything." He took off up Connecticut Avenue. I imagined the new kid pleading for his life over the Bay Bridge.

I slouched down the middle of Hemlock, kicking a rock, saying *Canton* the way Mom said it, the stress on the second syllable. We'd move there. So what? People live everywhere, even ugly places. Then they run out of reasons for living there. Then they get stuck. We lived in Ruth Bay now for the same nonreason. I'd improve my nonexistent game at the rusted hoop, all day, shot after shot. It's like taking photos. Snap a hundred times, you're bound to get a nice one for the wallet.

On Ironwood, I walked toward the hazy image of my mother. She sat on the front stoop in a blue dress, talking on the phone. A colander sat next to her, and a bowl. Was it possible she was cooking? I sat beside her. The bowl was an ashtray. Holding the phone to her ear with her shoulder, she opened mail, notes and contributions from the last smattering of partisans. She scooped out the money and floated the bills into the colander. She smiled at me, lowering the phone.

"Do you want some ice tea?" I shook my head. "Do you want to talk to me?"

"No." But I didn't mean it. I wanted to tell her *Harlan* was the only thing I'd ever find vaguely satisfying, that I was afraid of bridges and most everything else, that I had to believe Dad was dead in order to miss him. But I didn't tell her anything and never, never would. She put her hand on the back of my neck and pulled my head down into her lap, combing my hair over my ear without a thought. This time I let her, though, believe me, it was the last. I could hear a man's voice on the phone. The voice said, "Wendy, Wendy."

She said, "How lovely, how lovely."

Then the five o'clock whistle: all the TVs in the neighborhood tuning in to *Harlan.*

"You know you can tell me anything, son."

"I know that, Dad. It's just that I never really liked musicals. They hurt my ears."

"You're not embarrassed of your old dad, are you, son?"

"Me? Embarrassed? Of you? Not a chance, Dad." Thanks to the magic of digital editing, the track was seamless, crystal-clear, without a crack. *"Aw, Dad, seeing you up on that stage'll make me the proudest kid in all of Sunnydale."*

"My boy."

I crammed a finger in my ear, pressing the other ear against her stomach, hearing her laugh and yak on the inside. She rested her arm across my back like it was nothing. She had no idea she'd never touch me again. I pushed my finger as far into my ear as I could. And that's when I saw it. The chagwa. I learned about the chagwa at Lowry Friends School, but that was only in

Intro to Ancient Art. There were crude paintings of him on the walls at Lascaux, descending from the sky above a herd of mammoths, attacking a bull, his eyes on one side of his face, four mysterious black dots on the bull's stomach. Later, he was depicted over the doors in the tomb of Ibikhamen as a hunter and companion to the queen. But he was shown as female, gentle and sensitive, bowing to the pharaoh. And then again, as the only symbolic representation in Mayan temple decorative tile. But not since Byzantium, where he was put forth as a ravenous beast with wings that tore his victims in two, flinging their top halves to hell, their legs remaining on earth, condemned to walking bodiless forever, had he been documented in art.

Here is the place my mother's story and mine part ways. She said there was no chagwa that day, that I was delusional from grief. She said it was days before the first special report, that a secretive animal like a chagwa would never have come out in the open like that, and besides, wouldn't she have seen it too? And, if there had been a chagwa and it had put its mouth around my hand, didn't it occur to me I wouldn't have a hand anymore? I lay with my head in her lap, hearing the track from *Harlan* move through her body, despising the sound of my digitally improved voice. Then, over the top of the azaleas in the Messingers' yard, an enormous head appeared. Whatever I was seeing made no sense. Black eyes the size of softballs, the two sides of his face not even vaguely similar, gashes of stripes on one side, bludgeons of spots on the other, a nose triangular on one side, smashed in on the other. One ear hairless, the other with tufts. After a few seconds, the head decoded into that of a chagwa. He stood motionless, surveying the scene. I didn't move. He stepped out and, with measured strides, walked across the street, up our front path and stood before us. He was bigger and more horrible than I could have imagined, a five-hundred-pound knife with paws. I didn't dare look him in the eye. I was certain he would kill us. My mother yammered away on the phone. I reached out my hand, to let him smell, as you're supposed to do with a dog you don't know. He took my hand in his jaw. I waited for him to bite, to take my hand, but he made a judgment and let the wrist go, covering it first in brown saliva. Next time. Then he bounded across the street, ran up into the yard and disappeared behind the Messingers' house.

This happened. But it was not in a jungle. It was right here in Ruth Bay.

Book II: Wendy

THEY FOUND SOMETHING WRONG with Solisan. In high doses it raised liver enzymes in rats. I drove to Our Lady of Incumbency.

At the nurses' table, I reached for a paper cup of Desenserol, twice as addictive, but spared you the detox. "Did you fill out the form?" A nurse cuffed my wrist with her fingers. "And then you gotta get in line." I looked back at the drug line that stretched twice around the parking lot. Since the chagwa sightings, everybody needed Solisan.

"Where do I get the form?"

She pointed to the form line, which also wrapped twice around the lot but heading in the opposite direction. The lines were enough to make anyone want to sue, but the class-action line swirled around the lot in enough concentric circles to make a sinkhole.

"Wendy!" a lawyer called. I recognized him from the Eliminall and Gondutricette days. "Are you ever the one for us!"

But I'd had enough sitting on display for one lifetime, even if it meant skipping the lines. I pushed through the crowd to my car. People refused to step aside, thinking I'd have the gall to take their space. The man in the epicenter was the most frantic of all.

"I'm the end of the line! I'm the end of the line!" he shouted, hanging on for dear life to what little he had, the very last of everything.

NEWS GOT in the house like mice. There was no protecting Dylan from it. The print media criticized the electronic media for not checking sources. After falsely reporting that a five-month-old baby girl had been ripped from her mother's arms and shaken by the neck in the Sunny Mellow Projects in Anacostia, the anchor from *Eyewitness*, who'd been on the air eleven straight hours, whipped around in his seat and yelled at his production staff, "Could somebody please nail this *motherfucker* down?"

On the Scene reported that the chagwa walked through traffic into a development. He bit through a child's plastic pool. He ate a Scotty. He held a mail carrier hostage until a sanitation truck barreled through, which scared the beast, causing it to bound into the woods behind the elementary school.

Channel 4 dragged in Ben Sotterburg, The Expert, for no reason other than he attracted women viewers during sweeps.

"Unfortunately, the history of the chagwa has been studied along the sights of a rifle. If we could know the animal, understand what drives him, respect him, then we could remove the terror within ourselves." He said the same thing during the Lufthansa hijackings, word for word.

I wrote to Matt:

Better you're not here. Everyone is scared, waiting for the next strike. Everyone addicted to tranquilizers, law enforcement power-less, everyone blaming everyone, but how can you kill what you can't see? All we have to go on is illusion, the creature's best defense. There's talk of defoliating the parks where he's believed to hide, cra-zier talk than that, digging ditches around upscale neighborhoods, walling the city! Matt. I try to think of what you would do. I'm glad the decision isn't yours. Dylan and I miss you miserably. I can't believe there was ever a time when lying beside you was ordinary.

All my love, W

The facility sent the letter back:

Dear Mrs. Dunleavy,

Bad news hurts the morale of our residents. To better serve you and your family, we have included a sample letter, which you should have received in your When a Loved One Is Incarcerated *infor-mation packet:*

Dear Bradley,

Little Bradley is doing swimmingly in school! He gets his hard work ethic from you! Never afraid of a challenge! While we miss you, we are getting along fine! Please stay on good behavior, darling, so we may be reunited soon!

Kisses, your loving wife May.

I sent the form letter to Matt.

Downtown, T-shirts sold that read: I SAW THE BEAST. A bumper sticker: THE CHAGWA IS GETTING HUNGRY, written in a space between a chagwa's jaws. The caption under a cartoon in the *Washington Post* of the Senate majority leader riding a chagwa through the Senate chambers read: "I dare not dismount." Another rumor circulated that the animal attacked a twelve-year-old boy, but the boy turned up later stoned on inhalants—antibacterial Lysol—by the reservoir, where he'd skipped school with some girls. In fact, it was never confirmed that the chagwa had indeed bitten through the pool or eaten the Scotty. *Newsroom* decided to chuck the rumors and open with a special report: "Inhalants, Breathing Death." A mistake. Dead last in the ratings. The news director was fired. All anyone cared about was the chagwa, the chagwa, the chagwa, so we turned to Channel 7, where minute-by-minute reports were issued of new sightings on opposite sides of the city, in ten places at once. Every lead, which had to be checked by an exhausted police force and Animal Control, came to nothing.

"The chagwa is a solitary animal." The conservationist Dr. Rohatyn Jovanavich appeared in a live two-way, speaking from the deck of his house on his big game animal preserve in Honolulu. A boisterous party could be seen taking place behind him. "So it is unlikely that he'll step out in the open. But of course he could come out for a kill."

"Dr. Jovanavich," the anchor asked, "are we all in danger?"

The doctor looked thoughtful. "The chagwa is a predatory creature. Meat is the only substance he can digest. Finding prey in the streets of greater Washington can be difficult."

"Will the chagwa attack people on the street, Doctor?"

"Chagwa kill animals, madam. But if resources are limited, then yes, as we have seen, sometimes chagwa kill people. Now, if you'll excuse me, I need to attend to the predatory needs of my guests." Two nymphs in halter dresses took him around the waist.

Parents walked with their children to school. The homeless shelters filled up despite the warm weather. The parks closed. The 5K for Carcinoma was postponed.

We were unable to go to the market without sedatives, unable to sleep without meds. Even on the maximum dose of Solisan we couldn't chase him out of our dreams. In our peripheral vision we saw him and the smallest sounds made us jump, the metal door closing on a truck, the school bus backfiring on the highway. We developed facial tics and worry lines. We got our priorities straight. We fixed up our homes, renewed old connections, then remembered why we'd broken those connections and ended them again. But the threat of a beast hovering made everyone wittier, enlivened. Ruth Bay was the center of the universe.

The Suskinds' annual Memorial Day barbecue. Everybody had a drink. Portobello mushrooms in pastry and lime shrimp were passed by grad students with expansive ideas in tight tuxedo pants and kinte cloth cummerbunds, too much clothing for such a warm afternoon. Dan Suskind was about to give up making margaritas in the blender and start pouring them on the rocks. Some of the orange men from the gas company drove by on a tractor. On the back sat a man with a bandaged hand. A dangerous job on those gas mains. I assumed by the way he bled through the gauze they were taking him to the emergency room for stitches, but they parked by the Grafmans' Sable. Sherry Suskind carried out a tray of punch and blondies. The workmen joked about her being stingy with the beer and margaritas. She said, Help yourself, there's plenty and the guests cried, Yes, come! Join us! No thanks, no thanks, not on the job.

There was Toby Lapinsky, The Greeter, welcoming guests as though this were his own party. "Hello! Gorgeous dress! Zippy tie! Look at you! Grab a drink! Several! Everyone else has!" But his social skills stopped at the threshold.

For heaven's sake, look at Martha Johnson, pregnant again. In this jittery day and age, the only woman in the first world with six kids. A space cleared on the grass. Here came her happy husband. Charlie Johnson, The Inseminator. Out for blood. He already had three kids from a previous marriage. And Lord knows how many more. Women stepped out of his way, wanting no part, convinced it happened just by brushing against him. He was searching. He needed to breed. Don't look over here, no, no.

Chatting away in a group of similarly dressed women was Stephanie Panetti, who brought fashion to this enclave of Ruth Bay, that standard of self-mutilation: the bag dress. She owned and operated Wear Art Thou, an entire store of these dresses made of rayon or linen in fish pattern, floral or little pigs smoking cigars. During the last days of Matt's trial, when all we could hope for was to bargain for minimum security, I would go into her store, walking the gauntlet of jumpers and chunky knits. I went right up to Stephanie, because she catered to the women who no longer wanted to associate with me, and said, "Do you have anything that's . . . fitted?"

I was alone. I was avoided. My presence made people uneasy, especially those who hadn't contributed to my husband's defense fund. But I was content sitting up on the hill watching the party, leaving the chore of conversation to others. People talked about the gas mains, speculating whether the work would ever be done. There were jokes about the chagwa. "When you buy a new house you ask about whether the streets are safe and the schools are good, not if there's a chagwa in the neighborhood!" The men looked at the women, but not for sex, more as a point of comparison. Who had recovered from child-birth, who was exercising. There was nothing strange about the evening. We'd taken the last of our Solisan. Mixed with Dan's margaritas, a fine downward rush was forthcoming. I felt good in what I was wearing.

The hill where I sat sloped down from the swing sets to the street, where Dylan sat cross-legged on the asphalt watching the other boys shoot off rockets. The rockets went up fast when Kevin Allingham and Bryson Pfeiffer slammed their feet on the plastic valve, and spiraled down to the street when the canopies of parachutes opened. Kevin tied some of his old Power Rangers to the parachutes and they were landing in funny ways. The boys scattered to either side of the road each time a rocket went up. But Dylan didn't flinch. He sat leaning his elbows into his knees, resting his head on his index fingers. At least he was joining in somewhat, just by virtue of being here, instead of sit-ting at home watching video scramble, eating Little Debbies and weeping.

I'd been coming up with words for him, despite my insis-tence he say and write his own. Last week he came to me with a piece of wrinkled construction paper, announcing he had to write a newspaper article on the Civil War, due the very next day. "What should I say?" He looked lost standing before me at the kitchen center island. The essay wouldn't get done. What was the point of letting him fail? I wrote the paper, making it all up, facts included, putting Grant and Lee in the same little inn in Sharpsburg, inventing a gang of scouts called the Antietam Five and a daily paper called *Bugle!* We got an A-minus, the minus for misspelling *emancipation.*

Dahlia Bowen crouched next to me on the Suskinds' lawn. We watched Dylan, his fingers sliding up his cheeks, pushing the flesh over his eyes.

"Some of his behaviors appear autistic." Dahlia had recently gone back to work as a psychologist in the public school system. I watched a grease spot from a wild mushroom in pastry spread out on her American flag napkin.

"Thanks, Dahlia, but I don't think he's developed autism." Dylan was staring at his fingers. Dahlia then noticed Lillian Robertson and headed off down the hill. Dylan glanced over at me. I waved. He looked away. He blamed me for the state of affairs, I knew. I didn't do enough to keep Matt out of trouble. I didn't do enough to keep his voice from changing. I didn't make him handsome enough or tall enough or funny enough or smart enough.

"Let's be careful sending up those rockets around the girls, now, Mr. Pfeiffer," Peter Allingham called over to Bryson, who kept sliding his launch pad closer to Hunter Suskind, who was showing off a gold purse on the hood of the Grafmans' Sable. The Pfeiffer boys were disreputable and unsupervised and it was up to the community to keep an eye on them. Otherwise, it would have been unacceptable to scold someone else's child. Peter Allingham joined the few smokers left in the community, who were mostly older, and huddled by the boxwoods in an area called the Den of Inequity. "Are you all right?" He mouthed the words to me. I pretended not to understand, holding up my hands, looking puzzled. He then noticed his wife Adrianne, hobbling around on displaced hips, a condition for which German shepherds are euthanized. She took the Saran Wrap off a plate of conga bars at the dessert table.

Zach Grafman stood on the grass by the Sable with the Grafmans' dog, Spunky, showing off some new tricks. He held up his arm and rubbed his thumb and index finger. The dog stood on her hind legs and twirled. She was a little Samoyed, a white fluffball that darted yard to yard and certainly lived up to the name Spunky. I thought perhaps Dylan could get interested in the dog. Then maybe we could get a new dog and that would really cheer him up. He was so downhearted these days. A dog might be just the thing. I'd suggest it tonight. Spunky ran diagonally across the street to our yard, relieved herself in our pachysandra and ran off into the woods. Zach called after her, then turned his attention to Hunter Suskind and her new gold purse. Soon Tom Sutherland and Elissa Knapp, who had spent a lot of time talking, joined me. They needed a third party to break it up. Tom slipped on the grass and fell on his knee, staining his khakis. We all laughed.

"You look too comfortable." Tom brushed off his pants.

"We've come to disturb your sleep." Elissa pushed her bangs out of her eyes.

"You're holding up great." Tom lay back on the grass, his fingers laced behind his neck.

"You've shown such courage." Elissa leaned on one arm, curling her legs to one side, a beaded cardigan around her shoulders. "I'd break under such circumstances." And almost immediately the two got back into it with each other. They'd reached the stage where he was slapping a mosquito off her forearm and she was pulling a grass blade from his hair and he was commenting that one of her eyes was two colors. I didn't mind. Nothing would come of it. I knew Tom Sutherland. An *affaire du coeur*, at the most, that would end when one or the other snapped out of it. Infidelity was for the older, boozy set.

I was the first to see him. Just a glimpse of orange through the beeches. At first I thought it was one of the gas men who had stepped into the woods to urinate, or sunlight and shadow from the trees. But he stepped onto the road to test the air. Then he turned and strutted back. I jolted up. "Th-th-the chagwa." I slid down the hill with my arm outstretched, my finger pointing. "In the woods. In the woods."

Dutch Waring, successful enough at the litigation firm of Gainy & Diamond to keep a ponytail last year and a shaved head this year, drive a Harley to work and collect antique guns, was talking about all the car break-ins lately. Thieves had jimmied his Montero and stolen a case of beer. He said he was going to inject poison in the beer, wrap concertina wire around his property, then sit in the bushes and wait. Dutch saw the chagwa next and then everyone saw it, stalking left to right at the woods' edge. Something was in his jaw. There was blood around his muzzle. He stepped out onto the road, looked at the party and dropped from his mouth the head and shoulders of Spunky. Everyone gasped. Brendan and Kevin stepped backward, joining kids on the roof and hood of the Sable. Dylan stood alone in the street. I moved toward him.

Peter stopped me. "Stay still."

The chagwa paced and growled, then roared. The air filled with the scent of buttered popcorn. There was utter quiet as we listened to him push air through his bloody mouth and watched, his fur like burned leaves, his wet, flared nostrils, red eyes, yellow teeth, bits of white fur between them. What was the evolutionary advantage of a beast so ugly, that smashed-in nose and crooked mouth, one eye higher than the other? A stripe of brown hair ran down his back, a forked tail of two bare cords, tufts of bleached fur at the ends. And his testicles. You couldn't *not* notice. They were huge. Dark and swollen, banging against his legs with every step.

"Dylan," I called in a whisper. "Don't move." The chagwa stared at him. Dutch bent down and took a pistol from his ostrich boot, a 9mm Russian Makarov, a gun meant for people, not for chagwa. He stood and aimed. I saw his hand shake. He leaned over to Dan.

"Here, Suskind." His speech was slurred from the margaritas and Solisan. "You've been to Africa. You do it."

"That was a conference on securitization." Dan sweated through every inch of clothing, even his belt. "I never left the hotel."

"Don't kill him." Dutch's daughter, Pearl, stepped up next to him.

"It's not a pet, honey."

"Let me handle this, Waring." Peter Allingham took the gun from Dutch. "I'm licensed."

"Shit, Allingham. It's a chagwa, not a security guard."

Peter was on suspension with pay for his SWAT team's response to the Bank One Savings robbery.

"Cease and depart, Waring. One of my responsibilities with the department is animal containment."

"You've distinguished yourself in that theater too." Dutch

passed the gun to Peter. Peter took aim. The chagwa sat back on his haunches, daring Peter to shoot. "If you're gonna do it, Allingham, do it. Just don't shoot any innocent bystanders."

"I'm calling Animal Control." Sherry Suskind leapt up the steps to her kitchen.

I moved closer to Dylan.

"Wendy. Stop." Peter lowered the gun. Now I was in the street alone with my son and a killer who could slay us with a single downward rake of his four-inch claws. He turned his head up toward me, his mask of razor stripes and black holes, as if to say, Your move. He was bigger and more terrifying than I could ever have imagined. But still I moved toward him, pushing air through the tip of my tongue on the roof of my mouth, making a purring sound. He turned his head to the other side just slightly and I thought, *I've won*. But then his right eye slid over next to his left, rolling across like a bocci ball, glaring at me, two eyes on one side of his face. He stepped closer and the eye shot back over to the right. Someone screamed. Debbie Grafman headed for her kids on the Sable. Dylan stumbled backward. A tangle of people formed around me. I saw the gun up in the air, the men batting it about like a rejected wedding bouquet. The mothers bellowed their kids' names. Hurdling bikes and big plastic toys, they stormed the Grafmans' car, grabbed their kids up in death grips and lay them on the grass, covering them with their bodies. The chagwa seized Dylan around the middle. Dylan convulsed into the shape of a prawn.

"Please, God, no." The party chased the animal with my son in his mouth up the street, Dylan's legs dangling to one side, his arms waving for help.

Dutch yelled commands. "Call 911. Allingham, come with me." The two men doubled back to Dutch's house.

"Animal Control is on the way." Sherry Suskind waved an indigo cell phone. The chagwa ran into our yard and around the house. I charged after. On a branch among the forsythia, one of Dylan's shoelaces had caught. And then the Adida itself by the supercan. *I'll find his head, a last breath coming up from his mouth.* I rounded the corner of the house. *If he's taken him into the woods, he's gone forever.* I looked in vain through the beeches and poplars. They had disappeared without a trace.

"Wendy." Elissa faced the back of the house. The door was open. I walked up the steps of the deck, stopping dead at the threshold.

"Dylan?" I whispered. "Sweetheart? Are you hurt?" The chagwa had heaved Dylan on top of the refrigerator. He moved across the linoleum in an S pattern, filling the entire space of the kitchen, never taking his eyes off my son. He stretched his body against the fridge, trying to rear up to Dylan's level. But he could gain no grip on the stainless façade of the KitchenAid. He fell back. A lethal catcher's mitt of a paw caught on the ice-maker, ripping a claw. Bleeding and braying like he'd cut an artery, he paced back and forth in his own plasma. The KitchenAid shot round after round of crescent-shaped ice.

"No." Dylan's face was white. "I'm not hurt."

"We're going to get you down." The neighbors crept up next to me. The chagwa roared. I jumped back, then made the same purring sound I had made in the street. It seemed to calm them both. The animal then backed up against the center island and urinated, giving off the same scent of buttered popcorn. Out of the spots on his face emerged new eyes, one focused on each of us. One eye followed Debbie Grafman as she fell to the ground unconscious.

Peter and Dutch entered the back yard with an assortment of antique rifles and shotguns I recognized from visiting the gun shows Matt had worked so hard to shut down: an early Remington, a .220 Swift and a Winchester Model '73. "The Gun That Won the West," Dutch assured me. "In a moment you'll have dead chagwa to wipe up."

"I think it's jammed, Dutch." Peter turned the Winchester around in his hands.

"I just cleaned that one, Allingham. I don't own anything that jams."

"I'm not getting any movement."

"Give me the Winchester. Take the Remington. If we can't kill a chagwa in a barrel, we ain't fit to neuter a sloth."

"This Winchester is jammed, too, Dutch."

"Take the fucking Swift."

"Let's move before this godforsaken animal kills us all."

Elissa and Sherry Suskind led me over to the azaleas.

"It will soon be over." Sherry stroked my back.

"Dylan will be fine," Elissa said.

"Thank heaven for the Neighborhood Watch," Sherry said.

Dutch and Peter stepped up to the back door, one foot on the threshold. We braced ourselves for gunshots. Bringing their rifles to their shoulders, they pressed the triggers. Peter's gave under the pressure. Dutch's made a click. They pulled their weapons away and stared at them.

"They're not loaded, are they?" Peter said.

Dutch sadly shook his head. "I got a Kentucky half-stock at home. You should see the barrel."

I heard sirens and the static from police car radios. Officers came around the house from every direction. Animal Control rushed in with tranquilizer guns. A helicopter was in the air.

"Move away from the house." A cop ordered us to the street.

"My son is on the refrigerator."

"Move to the street, ma'am."

A storm of gunfire rang out in the kitchen. Our eyes and noses began to burn. Something set fire to our lungs.

"Mace," Peter cried.

"Get down!" A cop dropped to the grass and covered his head just as the firing stopped and the men came out. An Animal Control officer had been shot in the hand. He stumbled out the door. I ran up the back steps to the kitchen, swatting the poisoned air, looking for Dylan through my tears. He lay curled on the top of the fridge with his fingers crammed in his ears and his eyes squeezed shut. My kitchen was peppered with bullets, the Corian shattered to bits, the glass door of the microwave shot out, holes in the ceiling, through the counters and the linoleum on the floor. And there was the chagwa, pacing out from the dining room, unshaken, very much alive.

"May I ask a question?" I turned to the men on the grass, who were coughing and moaning, pouring canteens of water in their eyes, helping each other with various wounds. "In what manner are you shooting at this animal that you are unable to make him die?" Again, the men looked down, ashamed. "Are you all right, Dylan?" He was smiling now, looking at me so sweetly. He closed his eyes and went to sleep.

"He took a hit from the tranq gun, ma'am," the injured Animal Control officer informed.

I shook my head at the level of incompetence.

"How long can we expect him to be out?"

The Animal Control men looked to one another for an answer.

"The tranqs are meant for big game, ma'am, not kids." One Animal Control officer said, and shrugged. "I'd say, two days?"

"Two days," another agreed. "At the most. He'll be groggy and disoriented. Probably a little hungry, too." The helicopter hovered over, dropping a couple more tear gas canisters just to be sure.

THE POLICE kept the crowds back from the house. I moved aside Matt's birdhouses, lining them up in what used to be the garden, now some straggling tomato vines and dead marigolds, and sat with the neighbors at our picnic table. Sherry Suskind brought over a tray of cinnamon coffee and some cool washcloths scented with lavender.

"I'm glad Dylan's asleep," I said. Elissa Knapp put her cardigan around my shoulders. Tom Sutherland and the other men turned the garden hose on their faces to flush out their eyes.

Elissa handed me Sherry's cell phone. "Wendy. It's Dr. Jovanavich. I've got him up to date."

"I understand you're in a spot," Dr. Jovanavich said. I could hear a party in the background, laughing girls, clinking ice.

"No one seems to be able to kill this animal," I said.

"It takes a strong individual to pull back the bolt of a gun, Mrs. Dunleavy. As soon as your eyes lock on to the creature, every reserve of strength leaves you in a volt. I wasn't always a preservationist. I was once a hunter myself."

"He's treed my son on the refrigerator."

"He hasn't even begun."

"Tell us how to kill him."

"Madam, I doubt even with *loaded* rifles these men, or any men, or the strongest man alive could kill this particular animal."

"What do you mean this *particular* animal?"

"Does his left eyebrow look like a sitting bull?"

I squinted into the kitchen. "I believe so."

"And the right eyebrow, does the shape resemble Nova Scotia?"

"Absolutely."

"And is he missing an upper bicuspid?"

"How did you know?"

"Did you happen to notice the testicular region?"

"Yes."

"How 'bout those things! I hunted the very same animal at Dabidhura. And again in Muktsar. He moves around in various ways. He probably allowed himself to be captured illegally and shipped, on his way to a rich man's farm or, worse, on his way to becoming pelt or ground into powder for medicine. Why else has no one stepped forward to claim him? I know the beast you're referring to. And no. Your men will not be able to kill him."

"Then he will kill my son."

"Relax with your coffee, Mrs. Dunleavy. If he wanted to kill your son he'd be dead already. Perhaps he's saving him for later, for winter when the food supply dries up. More likely for mutually assured destruction. Consider it détente in the kitchen. No harm will come to the chagwa because the boy is just above, no harm to the boy because the chagwa is just below."

"I don't accept the treaty."

"We have to learn to trust."

"He has eight eyes."

"Many more."

"They move."

"Hence the saying, 'If I only had eyes on the back of my head.'"

"I want him to leave."

"Eventually he will."

"What do I do in the meantime?"

"Surrender." I could hear a woman laugh, then begin to moan as Dr. Jovanavich let the phone drop to the floor.

Peter and Dutch gathered up the guns and headed home. Debbie Grafman sat rigid on one of the Adirondacks, traumatized by what happened to her little dog. "What kind of animal is this that won't die?" Again, she began to cry. I held her hand.

"What if we offered him something else?" Elissa asked. "A dog from the pound or a duck."

"I think if he wanted any of those he'd go get them." Tom Sutherland poured hazelnut creamer into his coffee. "There's certainly no shortage of dogs and ducks."

Dan Suskind agreed. "He wants Dylan."

"It's true." Bob Grafman stood up from the bench. "And he won't leave us alone until he gets him."

"He'll eat all the dogs," Debbie cried. "He'll come for our children. Give him Dylan, Wendy, or we're all done for. You saw what he did to Spunky."

"He'll do the same to us if we don't give him what he wants," Bob said.

"We can't give him Dylan," Elissa said. "He's her only child."

Charlie Johnson, The Inseminator, rounded the corner of the house. He asked if we needed anything. He wanted to help.

The women looked down, avoiding eye contact. The men assured him we were fine, held up fists in Neighborhood Watch solidarity and sent him on his way.

"Wendy's been through enough," Tom said.

"What about another boy?" Elissa proposed. "What about one of the Pfeiffers? They have so many boys, they won't notice if one is missing." The suggestion seemed reasonable, so one of the dimmer Pfeiffer boys, the one with the harmonica, was brought to the house and placed at the threshold of the kitchen. But the chagwa turned up his nose. The boy skipped off with his harmonica between his teeth, inhaling and exhaling through the reeds.

"What about a girl?" Elissa asked.

Tom Sutherland had already grown tired of her. "The chagwa wants Dylan."

"Give me a gun," Bob Grafman demanded.

"Bob, we've shot at the chagwa," Tom said. "The chagwa won't die."

"Then I'm going to shoot Dylan," Bob yelled. "We've offered him other children. If we shoot Dylan, the chagwa will leave us alone." The neighbors looked around at one another. Then they set their eyes on me. It became clear I was in this trouble alone. They finished their cinnamon coffee and went home.

I needed to get to Dylan. I'd give myself to the animal if need be. I went around the house and tiptoed through the front, the police too busy with a crowd of animal rights activists to notice. The chagwa smelled my presence and roared. I shrieked. But I needed to stay calm. I crept upstairs for a shot of Dimetapp. I could hear him pacing in the kitchen, his nails tapping on the linoleum, the sound of urine spraying the drawers.

I then remembered that in the basement freezer I had several gift boxes of Omaha steaks, left over from the days when people gave us presents, fellow statesmen and constituents wanting to curry favor. I scurried down two flights to the deep freeze and with a rusted chef's knife I cut through the shrink-wrap of a ten-pound box. Then I carried the meat around the house to the back and threw it into the yard.

"Here, chagwa. Here are some steaks."

On seeing the flying filets, the chagwa turned on his feet and leapt through the door. After licking the ice crystals, he ate the steaks all up. Then he went over the fence and vanished into the woods. I took Dylan down from the fridge and carried him up to his room.

"THE POOR animal's a refugee. He's disoriented. Imagine if they partitioned *this* neighborhood." Weekend furlough. Matt stood on a teak side table screwing in a motion sensor on the alarm system. He put three screws between his lips and with his spare hand snapped his fingers and pointed for his battery-operated screwdriver. The metal rod spun into the ceiling. A thick breath of plaster fell in his hair. "Speaking of refugees, the Price-Brundages want to sponsor the Nowhere to Go Ball and Charity Auction."

I swallowed hard. I'd seen Nancy Price-Brundage's name on the visitors' log at Ainsville. I knew she had visited more than once.

"The Price-Brundages?" I tried to keep my voice steady. "What have they done? We've got more sponsors than invitees."

"I say *hot dog!* that they want to put up the capital. Nancy raised a hundred and eighty grand for lymphoma." I should have asked if anything had ever happened with Nancy. But I couldn't bear the answer. "The facility is going to let us have the ball there."

"At a prison?"

"I think it's a neat idea. Most of the world knows I'm a scape-goat. Let them see how well I'm faring."

"I don't want to bring one speck of attention to that facility." The thought of being in the same room with Nancy Price-Brundage and Matt made me sick. I'd blend in with the cinder blocks while she soaked up every ray of fluorescent. She'd look exquisite in Givenchy. Or worse, she'd play on the prison theme, a Versace update of the black and white stripe that would get her in the next morning's "Reliable Source."

"Nancy's come up with a fabulous theme. Parking. We auc-tion off desirable parking spaces around the world. Parking by the Capitol steps, parking at the Vatican, the Taj Mahal. Think of the places you don't go because there's no parking. We get landmarks to donate a space, no cost to them, money for refugees. How neat? That Nanny Price. What a fine auction-item solicitor she is. And best of all? We dress up like valets!"

"You don't think that's sending the wrong message?" I asked. "You're the one who encouraged your constituents to use pub-lic transportation."

"The people spending twenty grand on a parking space within Buckingham Palace are not exactly the folks I was speaking to about the bus."

"How hypocritical."

"If I can pull down a couple of hundred grand to stop dysen-tery in one refugee camp, if I can get some food in the mouths of a couple of starving kids, some shoes on their feet, a book in their hands, I don't give a good goddamn where the money comes from."

"Clearly not."

"After all this time you still don't believe me?" Matt jumped down from the table. "You knew Mascotti was after me on the gun bills. The Republicans have held a grudge since the tax rebellion." I was relieved he was locked up. Being in Ainsville meant he couldn't be with *her*. "I made it clear when we went after slot gambling that I would pay dearly. You're the one who told me to go forward." But there was the problem of desire. If he couldn't have her, he'd want her more. They'd gaze into one another's eyes across the table in the visitors' arena.

"It was all right there on the videotape," I muttered, picking stripped screws off the rug.

"Did I hear you?" Muscles tightened in his face.

Better or worse in Ainsville? Venue is important in affairs, a bathroom, a stairwell, never the master bedroom. At home they could switch locations, keep it going, a rented room, the back of a rental car.

" 'I have a good place for this'?" I quoted him from the FBI tape that showed him patting a briefcase filled with newly minted hundred-dollar bills.

"The money was for the camp. You know I was set up. When did yachts, planes and hotel suites ever mean a good goddamn to me, Wendy?"

In jail was better. The employees' lounge would get stale. "You should have given the committee what they wanted and resigned," I said. "You'd be home today."

"I'd rather be dead than give in to Ren Mascotti."

"You didn't give a thought to what it would do to us."

"I thought of nothing but you and Dylan."

And Nancy. Matt dropped the screwdriver. We collapsed on either end of the ripped chenille-covered couch, turning our backs to each other. Why I chose such an off-green I'll never know.

"It's not lost on me, Wendy. The price you've had to pay. I think about that every day. But understand what I've had to pay. I get a trickle of barely lukewarm water as a shower. A thin gray towel has to last me seven days. The food. Yankee Pot Roast, Amish Chicken, names used to cover up bad smells and over-cooked meat from mysterious animals and starch. I've lost my friends. Being away from you. Missing Dylan grow up. I took a gamble..."

"Stakes we never put up."

He picked up a stack of checkers on the coffee table and with one hand split them in two. After graduating from Michigan I had an internship at the *Harbor*. I wrote small pieces, hundred-year anniversaries, a tour of local fruit stands, working my way up to education reporter. One day I walked into the Forum on Literacy and Equal Education Partnerships in New Orleans and there was Matt—as always, a crowd forming around him. I knew of Matthew Dunleavy. He was the young lawyer who spent two years with no pay traveling around the country convincing residents in areas with poor schools to join a tax rebellion. When the states filed suits to collect back taxes, Matt got the people to stand firm. A junior congressman named Renny Mascotti called Matt "Un-American" and vowed to crush the movement as the tax revolt spread from town to town. Matt waved off a question from a reporter, saying Mascotti was inconsequential. But I noticed in his other hand he rifled two even stacks of Mardi Gras coins, expertly combining them into one. After that I never left his side. Until the day the U.S. marshal came to take him to Ainsville.

"I never wanted Washington," I said.

"You knew if we wanted to change anything we had to be where the changes are made. The Organic Hybrid Bill was your idea."

"I was mumbling over a bad salad. Washington is finished for us."

We looked over and saw Dylan tiptoeing out of the house.

"Where ya off to?" Matt asked.

"Uh, the canned foods drive. At school. I did tell you about it, didn't I?"

"Great tradition, these community drives," Matt cheered. "One of the earliest forms of altruism."

"Lowry does a superb drive," I said.

"As a Friends school would."

"I'll get you some cans." I brushed past Dylan to the kitchen and opened up the bullet-riddled cabinets. I pulled out a grocery bag to fill, but the cabinets were nearly empty. There was moth-infested flour and cornmeal and some old chocolate chips that had turned gray. I took out a dented can of chestnuts in water and a can of white asparagus from when we bought the house to establish residency before Matt lost his bid for state's attorney.

I handed the bag to Dylan and watched him plod up the street from the window.

"Our son is lost to us," I said to Matt. "Soon we'll walk past him on the street. We won't know we were once related." It hit me that he wasn't wearing his chagwa headgear. I raced out.

Since chagwa rarely attack from the front, we bought face masks at Kent Variety to wear on the back of our heads. The pickings were slim. By the time we got to the store there was only Ralph Nader and Wheezie from *The Jeffersons*, Reagan and Schwarzkopf selling out the first hour.

"Dylan! Your headgear!" He categorically refused. "At least rub yourself down with the urine cloth?" But he kept going.

In our bathroom, Matt brushed his teeth with toothpaste I'd gotten as a sample in the mail. He washed his face with a motel-sized bar of Dial.

"Winston Maple's new book on Alexander Hamilton?" He called to me in the bedroom. "Pure gossip and entertainment. I felt guilty reading it."

"I was thinking of asking the city for a third supercan," I said. "It's not like they keep track. The Suskinds have a third super-can and it's not like anyone is calling the cops."

We traded places, stepping around each other in the door so I could get in the tub to shave my legs. I thought of the Daisy shaver as a steam shovel, smoothing out the hills to make high-ways to the big cities.

"I've been missing Penny," I said through the wall between us.

"I don't want another dog." Matt changed into a Yale T-shirt and fresh boxers.

"I said I missed Penny, nothing about another dog." I rinsed the razor under a stream of cool water.

"It's a family decision. Not something you go out and *do* and then introduce me to the dog you *got*."

"I thought I saw her in the TV room. It was a stack of videos."

"Did I tell you we're getting a complete set of the Russians in the library? On tape. At my insistence. Not that anyone's going to listen. They just want to study the law." He folded the clothes he wore that day into perfect squares.

"Another time I thought a Hefty Cinch Sak was Penny."

"They should have studied the law before getting in trouble. Some of these men, Wendy. Especially the young ones. They are in such trouble. One could almost end up thinking like Renny Mascotti and the One-Strike-You're-Out Bill. Bite it off before it grows. In my quiet moments I wonder if our gun bills were shortsighted."

"You're not serious. Your gun bills are who you are, Matthew Dunleavy. I married you for your gun bills."

"I thought it was the tax rebellion."

I pulled the drain stopper, got out of the tub and dried my legs.

"I'm thinking of refinancing," I said, walking into the room.

"I'll handle it." Matt took the bolster pillows off the bed, piling them neatly on a chair.

I ravaged my drawer for something to sleep in. "You don't think I can handle it?" I asked.

"Did I say that?"

"It was implied," I said. "Anyway, it's easier on this end."

"Oh, because I'm *inside*?"

"Because I'm here. Because I have the time to stay on hold for forty-five minutes."

"We have phones at the facility. And time to stay on hold. I have nothing but time."

I could hear the humiliation in his voice as he pulled down the spread.

"You've become quite the tennis player," I said. "Marshall tells me."

"Not really. Though. Well. I beat Super E."

"The rap star? He used to play the circuit!"

"That was long ago. We're old men now."

"You've always had natural athletic ability," I said. "There's nothing you couldn't master." I found my oversized Michigan T-shirt. "Marshall goes on and on. I'm still searching for something you're not great at."

"Are you finished with that towel?"

I picked it up off the floor. "You got the tennis balls I sent?" I asked.

"Didn't I mention them?"

"I don't need to be thanked, I just wanted to be sure you got them."

"They were appreciated by everyone," Matt said. "Especially Super E."

"Super E used the balls I sent? Really?"

"He's a fan of yours. Watched you on *Newsroom* during the trial. He says you're, quote, easy on the eyes."

"Well . . . you know, TV adds, TV takes off. That looked nothing like me." I crawled across the mattress and rubbed his back.

"I'm bereft." He hung his head over his chest. "We should have had more children."

"We were busy," I said. "You didn't mention the topaz earrings." I pinched the stones on my ears, his wedding present to me. I'd put them on for his homecoming.

He glanced at me only briefly. "We need to do more charitable works."

"You've done so much," I said.

"Couldn't have done any of it without you."

"You said that at the Kittering Community Center ground-breaking."

"No, I said you were the star around which I orbited."

"You said *that* at the Firemen's Picnic."

"Someday we'll tour the Pinehurst Projects," Matt said. "And the LaMont Boyers School. I'll get a printout of literacy statistics in Greer County. I'll show you school lunches and hot breakfasts. I'll feed you heirloom tomatoes that taste like tomatoes, thanks to your idea for an Organic Hybrid Act. I'll show you how much you have helped."

We hadn't kissed since before he went into Ainsville and we hadn't had sex since . . . I didn't even know. His body was different now, grown over in a shell of muscle. I missed his old physique. I'd taken comfort in his fat. He took off my shirt. I became rigid. Something felt wrong. I yanked back the covers.

"I have those lists from the printer you asked for, Matt." Nancy Price-Brundage sat up in our bed, pen poised, clipboard in arm, in a tea rose Chanel suit and two-tone pumps, looking fantastic, I might add. "And great news. L'arc de Triomphe has pledged a space!"

I jumped up from the bed.

"We're just trying to do some good work, Wendy," Matt said.

"Is this a bad time?" Nancy asked.

I ran to the bathroom and slammed the door. I could hear them talking in hidden tones. I turned on the faucet so I wouldn't have to hear. But then I wondered what they were saying, so I turned it off. Then I didn't want to know. Then I did.

". . . leave her . . ."

"... put together a mailing list for the Heat the Homeless auction ..."

"You're the woman for me, Nancy."

"Just hor d'oeuvres."

"... can't do that to Dylan ..."

What about Dylan?

"Dial in to a national directory of sponsors ..." Oh, *dial in*, not Dylan.

I crept back into the room. It was eight o'clock and we were going to bed. Matt was already asleep, hugging a cylindrical neck pillow.

FROM THE window I saw Toby Lapinsky, The Greeter, waving to boys riding bikes. He welcomes the mail lady. He signs for a package and shakes the UPS man's hand. He ribs the gas main workers about the work never getting done. He calls out, "Someday they'll be pushing you!" to the mothers pushing strollers. "Lookin' good!" to the joggers. "Welcome to summer!" to the nannies. He waves at the meter man and the truck that sucks up the leaves and the trash collectors and the house painters and the gutter cleaners and the Guatemalans with the blowers and the paperboy who is really a man. But never a tip at Christmas.

I STOOD outside in my Michigan T-shirt with Matt, waiting for Marshall.

"You're not going to chase the car this time, are you?"

"Oh, please," I said. We looked up and down the quiet street.

"I gave you the new birdhouse?" He asked.

"I put it with the others. It's really your best work, Matt. I like the earth tones."

"Not too subtle?"

"It's the subtlety I like."

"You didn't like my Florida period?"

"I loved the Florida work. I love the early work, the later work. It will be interesting to see where you go next."

"Probably my last birdhouse," he said, hurt.

We looked down the street for Marshall. I was ready for this furlough to be over.

"You'll say good-bye to Dylan for me?" he asked. "I looked in on him. Sleeping with one foot out of the covers." We smiled. "His whole life, one foot in, one foot out and always the left."

Again, I should have kept quiet. "Mmmm, no, it's the right foot."

"No, it's the left," he insisted. "I'm certain."

"We can run up and see."

"Marshall—"

"He'll wait. For you, he waits," I said.

We sneaked inside and up the stairs. Matt was crestfallen when he looked in Dylan's room.

"How could I have gotten that so wrong?"

"He's turned around," I said. "It's an easy mistake. Half the time I don't know if I'm coming or going."

We headed back down to the street to wait for Marshall.

"I should know his feet."

"Why are you beating yourself up? Over this?" I said.

"Do you have to say *this* that way?"

"I didn't."

"You said *this*."

"I didn't say that." I wanted him to leave.

Marshall rounded the corner.

"You're my light, Wendy. My daybreak and afterglow."

"You said that at the cholera fundraiser."

"No, I said I way overachieved in marriage."

"You said that at the Amnesty Ball."

Marshall and I said good morning and some words about the barometer, which I knew he enjoyed watching closely. Matt kissed me and got in front. They shook hands and began chatting. I waved good-bye. The Caprice rolled down the street and turned on Hemlock. As soon as they disappeared I couldn't bear the weightlessness of his being gone. I chased them down the street and around the corner. Marshall stopped and let Matt out. I ran into his arms. "Don't leave."

"Wendy."

I sobbed. He held me, then got back in the car. Marshall drove off. Again, I chased the car all the way to Brookmont Road before Marshall stopped. Matt came around the car.

"Marshall says to get in. We'll give you a lift home."

"There was a chagwa sighting at the canal, Wendy," Marshall called out the window. "Get in."

"No, I'll walk back." I said I'd visit on Tuesday. He held me again. After a few moments I truly wanted him to go. He got in the car and they drove off. I chased after, the car stopped, started, backed up, rides were offered, wrenching refusals, pulling forward, lurching, breaking, until Marshall threatened to put me in chagwa headgear, a mask of Leona Helmsley. I got in the car.

✦ ✦ ✦ ✦

I SOLD the topaz earrings for groceries. Pulling the bags out of the back of the Range Rover, its bumper attached by duct tape, I noticed that something had been in our trash. Garbage was everywhere. Coffee grounds covered the asphalt. A milk carton, a tin of old lasagna, soiled napkins, fruit peelings, peas and wrappers. A tuna can had been licked across the driveway. Mr. Flanagan pulled down a slat in his blind and watched me tiptoe through the garbage, daintily picking up wet paper towels by the edge, their centers eaten out, a rancid package of sliced turkey covering a drain. Inside an orange juice can, maggots created settlements. I finished loading the supercan and went back to the car for the groceries, hooking the flimsy bags onto my wrists and carrying them up the path, aware of their precious weight. I searched my purse for the keys, unlocked the door and took the bags inside. In the kitchen, a broken jar of Newman's Own cut through the plastic bag and crashed to the floor. A trail of marinara had followed me to the kitchen from outside. I grabbed paper towels. The roll flung off the holder and landed in the sauce. I picked up the broken glass and tried to wipe spaghetti sauce off the linoleum and cabinets with a saturated sponge. Sauce had splattered everywhere. I'd stepped in it. My sandals made sucking noises and prints all over the kitchen and dining room. The more I tried to clean, the more sauce I tracked through the house. Finally I kicked off my shoes into the sink. Red stains seeped up between my toes. I opened the basement door for a mop. A paw shot out of the darkness, its nail catching me at the base of my neck, ripping through my breastbone, cutting me in half.

"Shhhh. It's me." Peter Allingham.

"Jesus, you scared me." I looked down. I was intact. "This no-knock policy has to stop."

"You've got holes in your security. There was a sighting in Mount Pleasant." He fiddled with a window lock.

"This part of our friendship is over, Peter."

He looked at the mess.

"I'll help you clean up the Newman." He leaned against the sink, crossing his arms over his green shirt, eyeing every part of me. "How's Matt?" I wouldn't answer. In three swipes of a paper towel, he soaked up the sauce. Then he unscrewed the head of the faucet and replaced the old washer with one he had in his pocket. He tested the pilot lights on the stove and picked at some crud on the stainless with his thumbnail. Then he put his face in his hands. I touched his back. He smelled like moss.

"Let's do something about it," he said.

"What do you propose?" I asked.

"Leave Matt. No, don't. Never mind. I can't ask you to do that." He faced me. "I loused up again."

"Dutch Waring loused up."

"Animal containment is part of my job."

"But you're on suspension."

"Thanks for reminding me." His SWAT team had gone to the wrong bank. They shot a guard.

"Sorry."

"Don't be. I'm a wretch." The recent shortcomings had been hard on his self-esteem. He had nothing to do but attend men's meetings on weekends. He put his hands on my waist. I wanted him to touch me, but I couldn't sacrifice myself to his postcoital remorse.

"You'd better go." He headed for the basement. "Use the front." I led him through the dining room.

"I'm glad we decided against the sponge pattern. You wouldn't have liked living with it. I like the paint we chose. A touch of black in the green."

"Sea Mist."

"Who would have known from the paint sample?" He saw the place in the ceiling from where the plaster had fallen in Matt's hair. "It would cost you nothing to put a motion sensor on that alarm system. I can do that work for you." He glanced into the library. "A twenty-five-cent elbow joint would keep that bookcase from leaning."

I went down in the basement and searched around the washbasin for the elbow joint. Sex with Peter always started with something handy. I found the joint and some screws and Matt's battery-operated screwdriver. Then I opened the dryer for a fresh pair of underwear.

"Ah, the congressman's *tool.*" Peter examined the screwdriver.

"I never say anything bad about Adrianne."

"You once called her 'that cloying midget.' "

"I did. I apologize."

He got to work on the elbow joint and before long the bookshelf was attached to the wall.

"What color did you say the paint was? I don't recall." He stepped in front of me. I put my hands behind his neck. He lifted me up and pushed me into the Sea Mist.

"OH, MAN. Now I really loused up." Peter buckled his belt in front of the mirror. I snapped the front of my jean skirt. "I can't keep doing this to Adrianne. The time between feeling good and feeling guilty has become so minute, it's not even fair to you anymore. Matt is a friend of mine. I admire him. He's a great man. What he's done for policemen's benevolence, no one can take away. Poor sweet Adrianne, hobbling around. I have to go. We're taking Kevin to Chuck E. Cheese's. I came to tell you something and I'm afraid to say it. Our application was accepted to Colonial World."

I was dumbstruck.

"I thought you wanted Frontier Town."

"Frontier had over ten thousand applicants. Colonial's fine. Adrianne still gets to churn her own butter."

"But . . . I just don't see you working the land, Peter. You write haiku and paint morning glories."

"I'm also a cop who can bench-press his weight."

"It's your haiku that I love."

"I never imagined we'd get accepted. I have to do this for Adrianne. And Kevin. There's no safety to be had anymore. It was all an illusion. We're one thread from complete chaos at all times. The chagwa proves that. Colonial is ordered and guarded and balanced. What the Founding Fathers intended." He removed a square of sandpaper from his back pocket and began rubbing it between his hands. "We were told to callus ourselves. Of all things to come up. Colonial World. Sowing the fields, sleeping on straw. And we just got a new bed. Did I tell you about it? Adrianne cajoled me into getting a two-thousand-dollar mattress. But the good part is the excellent frame and sheets. It's much better than the old rank king-size on two twins that we had before."

"How nice."

"It's improved sleep." We used to share insomnia stories, counting backward by sevens from a thousand.

"So this is really the end." I leaned against his Toyota wagon.
"Again."

He packed his shovels and wrenches. "You knew the vultures were circling."

"Will you be coming home for the holidays?"

"I could use some support."

TIME FOR a purge. It had been a while. There would be a lot. But I knew where everything was and got right down to work. I bolted the door and marched upstairs, marinara footprints fading behind me. Popping my very last Solisan, I crept into the crawl space off the study. I moved aside some Peruvian throws and *National Geographic*s, found the box and dragged it out. Some pictures of Peter from the Metro section of the *Post* when he left Wobley & Fowell for law enforcement. His first SWAT photo. A coaster from Reason & Rhyme Bookstore Café the first time we admitted that love might be involved. *The Faber Book of Love Poems. The Meridian Handbook of Mythology.* A dried violet from the Vermont trip where we went for his counterterrorist training. A hotel receipt from Louisiana where we went for hostage rescue training. An empty carton of Protein Blast from our jujitsu class. What about the letters? Not yet. The haiku? Maybe a separate trash run for those. A staple gun. Six paint stirrers. Two elbow joints. Some washers. A wheel of paint samples from when we tried to find the right yellow. Lingerie: A pink slip. A black slip. A leopard slip. A red slip. A white slip. I put it all in a Hefty, poured in the morning's bowl of soggy Grape-Nuts to keep me from changing my mind and lugged the sack to the supercan. Sayonara. Then I turned my face toward the sun. But later on that day I worried I might need that book on mythology, since I could never keep straight who Daedalus was or which of the nymphs Zeus chased. I scared some squirrels, stretched a hole in the bag, put my hand through the wet cereal and pulled it out. And again, I turned my face toward the sun.

The next night Sheila Moore called to ask if I had any Solisan or knew where she could get it. No luck, I told her. Try Carolyn Giles, she's a stockpiler. Then she said she wanted to write something nice on a card to her husband for his fiftieth and did I have any ideas, maybe some Tennyson or someone like that. I said, yes, Sheila, as a matter of fact I do, I have just the thing and I went back to the supercan for the Faber. I was able to locate just the right Tennyson, the bit about love *coming up with the sun from the sea*, and she really appreciated it. And then Sue Moyers walked by wanting some yellow ideas for her new family room and as I was digging out, Carolyn Giles ran by and said she was feeling out of sorts from Solisan withdrawal and did I know a protein supplement and what is the point of throwing out elbow joints? Paint stirrers are useful for many things and one should have a staple gun on hand and these photos and clippings might be amusing someday and these slips are practical under dresses for work. As for the muck, anything can be wiped clean.

A CALL FROM school said I'd better come pick up Dylan from lab. The frog he'd been assigned for dissection woke during the autopsy. I drove over to Lowry.

"Did you make it right with the frog?" I growled at the receptionist.

"He went quickly once we realized what was happening."

"And at a Quaker school, no less." I pulled Dylan out by the wrist. The head of the school and the science teacher waved from the steps of the school and promised they'd discuss it in meeting. Dylan laid his head against the window.

"Do you want to talk about the frog?" I asked. He wouldn't speak. He still refused to say anything about the chagwa, claiming to have not remembered. I passed him a Little Debbie and some juice and asked if he wanted to go to the National Gallery of Art. After two stoplights he said they should have named the Smithsonian the Museum of Boring Things.

We ducked into the Freer to get out of the rain. A security guard took away Dylan's popcorn and scanned our bodies for sharp objects. His repulsed look said, *You don't seem the gallery types*, but he couldn't find any reason to arrest us. The museum was empty, no tours today. I was glad. Dylan shuffled along behind me. His shirt was drenched, painted onto his tiny ribs and concave stomach. Matt and I were tall. Dylan came out small.

We came to a gold scroll with horses painted across. Some of the horses were in the water, some on land. Their expressions were human. But there were no humans in the painting to put them into service. They were wild horses but painted as though they were tame. Some smiled. Some were thick in conversation. Some were serious and resented the others' light attitude. One stopped in the water to drink, the horse behind annoyed that he wasn't keeping up.

"I've always loved Japanese art," I said.

"Too bad it's Chinese."

"Is it?" I looked at the characters at the top. They read side to side. "You're right," I said. "What do you think? Do you like the painting?"

He hesitated.

"I don't like the expressions on the horses' faces. They look more like human expressions. I don't like the anthropomorphizing of animals. If you ask me, horses should look like horses."

We walked on. Dylan's shoes squeaked on the shiny floor, which attracted a guard, who told him to stop. The guards had worked there a long time. The art was theirs now and they didn't want to share. I led him to a small exhibit on the influence of esoteric Buddhist iconography on the development of animal painting in Japan. I felt reasonably sure we would find a chagwa among the tigers and oxen. I wanted to jog Dylan's memory so he could begin to talk and heal. My suspicions were right. To the left side of a bronze Buddha was a small watercolor and ink on paper from the Choju Giga animal character scrolls, a loosely painted horned man riding a chagwa backward. The title of the piece was *Detail from the Third Corner of Hell*. The stripes on the animal looked as though they could twist and gnarl in movement. The spots swirled as though they could suck you inside. Everywhere you moved, six eyes never left you. And the testicles. The artist had mastered the depiction. I took a breath and settled myself.

"What do you think of this, Dylan?"

He was looking at a six-armed Kwannon in the center of the room. He stepped over and examined the painting for a while, not a glimmer of recognition on his face. He shrugged.

"If you ask me, I'd say that guy should turn around, watch where he's going."

Dylan began to cry. I put my arms around him. Too much had happened for a boy his age.

"In Canton we could be camouflaged," he said. The echo made his voice bounce all over the room in surround sound.

"Oh, Dylan. If I'd known you wanted it I wouldn't have sold it . . . it . . . it . . ."

"You sold it . . . it . . . it . . .? But I kept asking you to pay off the mortgage . . . gage . . . gage . . . Ruth Bay is finished for me . . . e . . . e . . ."

"I'm so sorry . . . y . . . y . . ."

"You were invisible during Harlan. You wouldn't lift a finger to help . . . elp . . . elp . . ."

"I couldn't stop it from happening . . . appening . . . appening . . ."

He put his head into my chest and sobbed. I stroked his head.

"He was inches from me," he whispered so the walls wouldn't hear. "I could feel his breath. His eyes, he looked straight at me. When he opened his mouth I thought I would die!"

"I should have killed him myself," I said. "I should never have let such danger come into our lives. If the chagwa comes near us again I'll rip him apart with my hands, I swear I will."

He shook his head, trying to get a word out.

"Not the chagwa." He gasped for breath. "The frog! . . . og! . . . og! . . . og! . . ." His cries reverberated everywhere, spilling out the gilded walls, overflowing the urns. Kwannon crumbled, Buddha wept.

A PRIEST SAW the chagwa running down the steps of the shrine. Then he was seen tearing across the helipad at Holy Redeemer just as medevac was landing. I couldn't sleep. I called Peter on his cell phone, the one reserved for police emergencies.

"Sightings in Brookland," I said.

"Nothing confirmed."

"The mattress. I was wondering what kind. Maybe it would help me too."

"It's a Sealy."

"Do you know where you got it?"

"The Mattress Store."

"When do you go into Colonial World?"

"Tomorrow. I thought you were the precinct. Adrianne's right upstairs."

"I'm devastated."

"So am I. I have to do this experiment. I have to see where it leads me. I still love you."

"How can I reach you in Colonial World?"

"You can't. Phones haven't been invented."

"Will you call tomorrow?"

I sobbed into a pillow, then dug myself out of bed for some warm milk. I was surprised to find Dylan on the stairs, looking out the back through the window box.

"He'll be coming from the woods," he said.

"What are you doing?" I asked.

"He's watching us. The chagwa." He remembered

"I don't see him," I said.

"He sees us. He's sizing us up. That's all he does."

"He does other things. He has to eat. He has to sleep."

"He's not sleeping."

"He's in Northeast. He's not going to hurt you."

"How do you know?"

"I won't let him."

"Yeah. You can control him." He stared at the woods. "Can you open the jar?" He asked.

"What jar?"

"I'm stuck in the jar."

I then realized that Dylan was sleepwalking. In the morning he'd have no memory of this conversation having taken place. I walked him back to bed.

I LAY ON my back listening to AM radio escape the windows of the Fieldings' Toyota Avalon, where Ashley Fielding sat smoking and kissing Bryson Pfeiffer, disobeying the curfew that had been put into effect after the first reports of the chagwa. I thought of calling Marcia Fielding as part of my Neighborhood Watch responsibility, then remembered my own late-night car escapades at fifteen. At two A.M., Ashley and Brendan left the car. Wearing chagwa headgear, Rocky the Squirrel and Nixon, they ran home in different directions, two cicadas pulled apart while mating. I closed my eyes. I kept seeing the chagwa. Materializing out of fire, landing weightlessly before me. Something struck me. At the Ready Set Go picnic I'd worn an ill-fitting pair of yellow chintz Capri. I remembered I'd slid one Solisan into the change pocket. I hopped into the closet, praying I hadn't wastefully sent pants I'd never wear again off to the dry cleaner's. Sure enough, it was there. I nearly cried from joy as I swallowed the last Solisan in the city.

After a half hour I felt the first dip of comfort. Then the famous Solisan downward fandango. *I am going to feel this way for the rest of my life.*

At four, I jerked awake. I heard something in the supercan. I went to my window but saw nothing. Like a cornered gunfighter, I walked room to room in the upstairs, looking out. I went down to the dining room and searched out the back to the yard. The chagwa was there. I ducked below the window. After I caught my breath, I peaked out from behind the curtain. I saw him sharpen his claws on the biga tree, jumping down, pacing, then disappearing into the shadows, reappearing in the light. *Calm yourself. He won't get in. Just watch. He'll leave.* The Solisan made my heart thump heavier. My skin expanded with every beat. He was something to behold, all right. Five hundred pounds not making a sound, the perfect thief, jumping up, his forepaws landing on the window box, dirt and dried geraniums spilling out like milk. I pulled the phone down from the dining table and called Dr. Jovanavich.

"Whatever you do, don't feed him."

"Too late."

"Build a stockade fence twenty feet high."

"I'd need a Parks Commission permit."

"Eventually he'll find greener pastures."

The chagwa circled the perimeter of the yard. I moved along, watching.

"Why don't you take him for your park?"

"Assuming I could get him, which I can't. No one can, I told you. I wouldn't want him. I have enough big game. There's only so much okapi to go around. My game understands that there's a limited supply. This beast of yours doesn't respect that system, Mrs. Dunleavy. He wouldn't fit in here."

"I think he's gone."

"There, now. I told you he'd go. Feel better?"

"I do."

There was a bang against the house.

"I think he's trying to get in." He banged again. I screamed.

"Do you have an interior room? Mrs. Dunleavy, do you hear me? I said, do you have an interior room?"

"Stop! Get away! He's trying to get in. Yes, there's a crawl space off the study."

He smashed against the back door.

"Get to the crawl space. Hang up the phone. I'll call your police. Lock yourselves in."

"We can't live this way. Help me."

"We have to learn to exist together, Mrs. Dunleavy."

"I want you to come to Ruth Bay," I shouted, heading for the stairs.

"I'm out of the business of man-killers, Mrs. Dunleavy. I want to enjoy my life."

"Don't make me beg." The call was disconnected. When I got to Dylan's room the banging stopped. I looked out the back through the study, and then from the window on the first landing on the stairs. The chagwa was gone. I met the police halfway down the path so the bell wouldn't wake Dylan. They wanted a description.

A HEAVY KNOCK. Did I sleep through work? No, it's Personal Integrity Day. A holiday. Thank goodness, because there was talk of outsourcing, of closing down the department. I couldn't risk such a mistake. We were broke. Again, the wolf-head knocker. How I hated that thing. Why do people use it when we have a perfectly fine bell that plays the first six notes of a Bach prelude? More banging. All right, all right. I stumbled downstairs and looked through the concave glass that allows you to spy on your tormentor. A big eye looked right back at me. I jerked away and opened the door. A large man in a safari jacket and gray slacks stood on the stoop.

"Morning. Medley Bigelow, Hunters for the Homeless." He handed me his card. "I think we can help each other."

"You do?"

"I understand you have the chagwa problem. I'd like permission to sit on your roof so I can take him down." Even barely conscious, I didn't trust this man. He smiled with only half his face. And his one open eye appeared to wander. "I'm a pretty-looking guy, aren't I?"

He caught me staring.

"I wasn't, I didn't—"

"Ma'am, a chagwa that size will give us two hundred meals."

"Two hundred meals?"

"Two slices of bread, one slice of chagwa."

"Won't they know they're eating chagwa?"

"If you're hungry, ma'am, you don't care if it's chagwa or elk or lynx or okapi. You are just hungry." Ignoring his face, there was still something suspicious about him. "No, ma'am. It's the face."

"I wasn't . . . And what about the skin? Who gets that?"

"I get the skin. The Chinese pay for the bones. You and I split the proceeds unless you want to donate them to one of the area kitchens."

"Look me in the eye and tell me the reason you do this is for the homeless and not for the skin and bones," I said.

He covered the bad eye with his hand.

"I do it for the skin and bones. And while I'm at it, I feed the homeless. There. Was I looking in your eye the whole time?"

"You certainly were."

"Do I have your permission?"

"Other men have tried."

"If I shoot him he dies instantly."

"Well, then. You're the man for me, Mr. Bigelow. What's first?"

"Throw some meat. I'll set up on the roof."

"I have some Omaha rib eye."

"Shame to waste it." He went for his ladder.

"Would you like some ice tea?"

MY DENTIST said no more Extacette until I came for new X-rays. I left Medley Bigelow on the roof and went to see my prescription-friendly gynecologist, Dave. Dave's was an excellent practice. Many of the congressional wives saw Dave. The nurses dressed in pastel overalls and Keds and they never made you get weighed. There was always fresh coffee in a silver service and home-baked cookies in the waiting room, though you never had to wait. Dave waited for you. He didn't believe in stirrups. He didn't make you lie down. I came in flustered from traffic, the parking garage, capricious elevators, and there was Dave sitting calmly in the examining room. I asked how he'd been. He said he'd spent the day trying to gather support for a bill that would require free pelvic examinations for the working poor. He looked away as I changed into a soft Lanz nightgown. Nurse Vickie asked if I wanted cocoa or mint tea. Dave turned back when I was finished dressing and produced a petition asking if I'd be willing to stop buying Chinese products. Then he talked about his wife, Ashanni. She worked in a clinic in Anacostia.

"She's the real doctor in the family," he said, palpating my breasts.

He went on to talk about Ashanni's frustrations with the city, how Medicaid was willing to pay $4,000 for a broken hip but unwilling to dish out $20 for the installation of a shower support bar. He then knelt at my feet and reached up between my legs with the speculum. "How's Matt?" Matt had invited him to join a committee to enlist doctors in volunteering their time to families with no health insurance. Dave had given significant money to Matt's campaign and legal defense fund.

"He's well. You should see him. He's lost weight. He's in great shape."

"I thought he was fit to kill when he was fat," Nurse Vickie said.

Dave took a gentle pap smear and asked if I'd be willing to take some literature about slavery among women in Afghanistan. I said certainly, and by the way, while I'm here, could I get a prescription of Dozazine? Dave wiped the harvested cells on a slide and handed it off to Vickie. She left us alone. He looked at me closely, then turned to wash his hands in an old-fashioned pitcher and basin.

"They found something wrong with it. Cancer in rats, the usual. There's a class-action, but you wouldn't want to get involved. Too many forms."

"What's the replacement?"

"Sombulin." He dried his hands on a pink fluffy towel. "But I don't want to prescribe sleep meds. They're habit-forming. And memory loss." Dave got stingy every time he was slapped with a new malpractice suit.

"What do I need a memory for?" I asked.

"Who knows? You may want to remember some things."

"How about some Palliadan for headaches and mouth pain?" I tried.

"Have you seen a neurologist about the headaches? Did you talk to the dentist about the tooth?"

"My back has this wrenching, my rotator cuff is on fire. And no, ibuprofen isn't enough. Maybe some Numburall combined with Calmator. That will relax the spasm."

"Seen an orthopedist for your back?" We stared each other down. He began filling out my chart. I pulled on my pants.

Then something struck Dave.

"Are you aware of the Violence Against Women Act?" He asked. I nodded. "Did you know the Republicans are holding up passage? Once again Brent Falk is playing politics with women's lives. My group will be holding a sit-in outside Rayburn. Can I count on you to be there? It would mean a lot if you were to be with me on the front line." I agreed, wholeheartedly, I'd be out in all my glory, assuming my back didn't keep me in bed that day. "And another favor. Would you be willing to donate yourself to the College Scholarship Auction? Just have lunch with someone at West 31, talk about what it's like having your husband in prison, its effect on your son. We pulled in three thousand last year for Ruth Ginsburg's pancakes. You'd be worth at least that much."

"I'm your girl."

He wrote me a prescription for Tylenol with codeine, the trash fish of painkillers.

◆　◆　◆　◆

THE POLICE had set up barricades at the end of my street. Microwave trucks set up their cameras. I left the car and grabbed a police officer.

"My son is in there."

"No one in, no one out, ma'am."

"Was there an attack?"

"Ma'am, move your vehicle from the fire lane."

"Listen to me!" I screamed.

"Wendy!" Tom Sutherland called from the other side of the barricade. "Dylan's fine. He's in the house. The chagwa's in your yard. Bryson Pfeiffer is missing."

I tore down the street, ripping my arms away from a cop who tried to stop me, darting through a couple of dozen human shields that had lain down in the street.

Medley was in the front yard, looking through the grass with the nose of his rifle.

"The chagwa's in the back," he said.

"Where's my son?"

"In the house."

"Why haven't you shot the chagwa?"

"Before I kill a chagwa I must first kill a snake."

"You said you'd take down the chagwa. Now go up on the roof and kill him."

"I have a system."

I ran into the house. The chagwa banged against the back door, demanding food. I screamed for Dylan.

"I'm up here." I found him in the crawl space in the study, sweating and white. I grabbed him up in my arms. "I think he's hungry."

"I would say so."

"We have only peanut butter."

"I'll get him some food. And something for us too, don't worry." The chagwa smashed against the house again. Plaster snowed down from the study ceiling.

"He's coming in."

"He can't get in."

I had to work fast. I threw the last of the Omaha steaks out the study window. They barely served as an hors d'oeuvre but it bought me some time to flip through the yellow pages and order a new deep freeze and a six-hundred-pound steer. In less than an hour it came in several large pieces with the freezer just minutes behind. A deliveryman tossed a frozen leg by the hoof into the yard to keep the animal occupied while they brought in the steer. He licked the ice crystals, then became annoyed that the meat was hard. He lifted the leg in his mouth and with a jerk of his head flung it right back at us.

"How long is that cow going to last?" Dylan asked from the top of the basement steps, munching a slice of pizza.

"I'm not sure." I set up a workspace on Dylan's old train table.

"When's the National Guard coming?"

"Let's just get through the hour, Dylan."

I found some rubber gloves and knives that needed sharpening. Then I lugged a twenty-pound slab over and set about scraping the meat away from the bone and cutting it into chunks. Was I supposed to trim the fat? I heard a thump upstairs.

"I think you need to work faster." Dylan tripped down the basement steps and stood by my side at the train table. I filled a pan and carried it up to the back porch, opening the door a few inches and sliding it out with my foot. We stood by the window and watched. He went through the meat in ten seconds. I ran down to cut up more. Again I filled the pan and again he sucked up what I'd given him. I slammed the knife into the steer. My knives were so dull I had to rip the meat from the bone with my hands. But the chagwa went right through what I'd cut, flipping the pan in the air when he was done.

"Mom! Mom!" Dylan cried. "He wants more."

He was going to eat the whole cow in a day. If I didn't cut more he'd start attacking the human shields. "Did you find your damn snake yet?" I yelled to Medley out the window.

"Not yet."

"Dylan, try 911 again."

"It's still busy."

I switched on a paint-splattered radio. There was coverage on Bryson. Poor child. What his parents must be going through. But I needed to concentrate on my own problems.

I cut all night, blood up and down my arms, dripping into my rubber gloves, blood in my fingernails that would not scrub out, my hands permanently stained. I bent into the freezer and by two ropes that had been coiled around it I pulled out a twenty-one-pound loin end, smashing it down on the train table. My back hurt. I took three of Dave's Tylenol with codeine. They did little for the pain.

"Did you get through to the police?" I asked Dylan.

"They're getting calls from all over the city. Everybody's calling in sightings. There's an infestation."

Then we are done for, I thought. I sharpened my knives on a steel, cutting flesh and connective tissue into butt steaks and roasts. The maggots that strolled along the ribbons of fat didn't faze me, neither did the iridescent spots of cancer on the large slabs. I fed him the bugs. I fed him the cancer. Just feed him. Faster. Dylan fell asleep on the broken beach chair near the table. As I covered him up with some towels, the chagwa crashed his paw through the basement window.

"Dylan! Get back to the crawl space now." He woke, disoriented, stumbling over his feet to the stairs.

I hit the paw with a hockey stick.

"Back. Back. Get out!"

He pulled away. Then he stuck his face in the smashed-out window. I hit him on the forehead with a bone-in rib eye. He backed off. Meat was all that worked. He swallowed the rib eye and stuck his head back in for more. More more more.

At some point in the evening he allowed me a break. He sat down, his forepaws stretched out, forked tail wagging, staring at me through the broken window. I rested my arms and examined him. His pug nose, mottled brown whiskers, bloodstained teeth, three inches long.

"You are very ugly," I said.

He closed his eyes, proud to be vile. Then he lunged at the window and roared. Back to work.

By dawn the chagwa was sated. He would spend the day lying in the sun. Some performance artists had the idea to sing lullabies over loudspeakers set up through the city to keep the chagwa at bay. The songs sounded like Gregorian chants. Up on the roof, Medley sang a different song, a rising and falling wail that was supposed to bring out a snake. In the dining room, I turned a chair toward the window and watched the chagwa sharpen his nails on the biga tree. I felt tired but satisfied that I'd done all I could. I watched him play with a raccoon. It was sort of sweet. The raccoon jumped, the chagwa jumped. The raccoon rose slightly on his hind legs, the chagwa did the same.

"Do you know how rare it is to even see a chagwa?" Dr. Jovanavich asked on the phone. "Most chagwa photographers have never gotten a shot off. And now with the population nearly gone. Realize what you are experiencing is a symbol: the loss of the goodness of life. When he dies he'll leave a disarrayed ecosystem. The sun will burn our flesh, the wind will blow like a firestorm."

"So I should be grateful," I said.

"Look at his power, his grace, his tension."

"There's talk of an infestation."

"People are seeing things. He's the last. Believe me. And he's all yours, Mrs. Dunleavy." Dr. Dave's codeine began to make me feel drowsy. A sensation I could no longer achieve on my own.

"I want you to arrange to get me strychnine," I said.

"For the animal?"

"It's used on bear traps, you're a hunter, you know that. If food is all he'll come out for, then I'm going to poison him."

"Do you believe no one has tried? The chagwa digestive system absorbs nothing but meat and excretes the rest. Feed him an ounce of strychnine, you'll poison the entire water supply."

"I get the idea that you are trying to protect this beast, Doctor. That saving my family is in fact the last thing on your mind."

Dr. Jonvanavich laughed. "My dear. You are delightful. What do you look like?"

"Me? I don't know. Pasty, permanent scowl."

"Breasts?"

"Yes. What?"

"I have some down time."

I hung up.

The chagwa batted the raccoon. The raccoon rolled, crouched on its haunches and pounced. The chagwa did the same. But then the raccoon tripped over itself and skidded on its side. The chagwa killed it. Then he ate it. It's still a chagwa. Don't forget. Slip once. You're dead.

RUMORS ABOUNDED in the office about the government outsourcing. I'd missed three days because of the chagwa. If I didn't do the hard push, I'd be out of a job. The chagwa was gone, leapt into the shadows, but Matt was coming home for the weekend. It was our anniversary. I would have to shop for dinner before Dr. Dave's auction lunch and I'd have to be quick about it. Then the sit-in tonight at Rayburn.

At noon, I raced out of the building for a gourmet shop on M Street. It was hot on the sidewalk, another scorching summer on the way, but I rarely got out during lunch so it felt good to be in the sun. Many people came out to enjoy the fine day, including the Tongan prime minister, kicking along, escaping the stifling air of the economic summit. He walked a quick pace, stretching his arms, breathing deeply, surrounded by his security staff, who would have preferred he stay in the cafeteria. An armored limo drove alongside. On the corner of 37th Street, a petite old woman stepped up to the mailbox where she dropped in a small package. Two of his staff shoved the prime minister into the car. The car sped off. The other agents produced metal cutters, separated the legs from the cement and ran up M Street with the mailbox. We waited for an explosion. It never came. Order restored.

Women cried on the street, I noticed. They dried their tears on lace handkerchiefs, sobbing into silk scarves. Something bad had happened. I didn't have to look long or think hard. Strolling up M Street in the opposite direction was Ben Sotterburg. He took the hands of an exquisitely dressed woman I recognized, certainly one of Washington's most beautiful women at one time who was now gaunt with a bad eye job. He kissed her knuckles and said something to soothe her. She ran her fingers through a silver lock that fell over his forehead, then, wiping her eyes on a tissue, stepped into a chauffeur-driven stretch Prius. I stood at the corner of 38th Street waiting for the light, a weeping woman on either side of me. "Are you all right?" I asked the one on my left. She was too overcome. I turned to the one on my right. "Tell me, is this all for him?" I gestured toward Ben. She nodded. "He's done this to all these women? You don't despise him for it?"

She was incredulous.

"No!" The light changed. She ran up ahead to greet him.

"Audrey, how nice to see you," Ben held out his arms.

"I miss you, Ben," she cried. "Will we be spending Thanksgiving together?"

"Of course, darling. Just like last year. Why, Marnie, how are you, dear?" Another woman had practically crumpled on the curb.

"My life has gone to hell since you. No one else can hold my interest."

"I'm so terribly sorry."

"No, no, it was worth it. I'm drinking lots of water. Thanksgiving?"

"I'm looking forward. Best to Angus. Sophie, love."

"I'm living for the day you'll come back to me."

Secret Service agents cleared a space on the sidewalk as a black armored car pulled up. An agent, tears streaming from under her Foster Grants, opened the back door for the Secretary of State. A few weeping members of the press moved toward the car in front of Bistro Le Que. "Madam Secretary, Madam Secretary, to what do you attribute the breakdown of talks with the Iraqis?" A reporter who had slammed Matt on several occasions tried to squeeze in a question, but the Secretary of State noticed Ben.

The woman who couldn't spare an inch of the West Bank or Gaza was now giving up tears like acres at a foreclosure.

"You'll call, won't you?"

"Of course."

The door to Bistro Le Que closed behind her. I ducked through the crowd, briefly making eye contact with Ben, pretending not to know him.

Ben Sotterburg. Desegregationist. Civil rights lawyer under four presidents. War hero. Philanthropist. Best-selling author. Real estate mogul. Painter. Counterterrorist expert. Single father. Filmmaker. Gourmet cook. Hostage negotiator. He made tremendous contributions to Matt's causes and gave the most of any individual to his defense, never asking for anything in return. It shouldn't have been any surprise that he was pursuing me now, chasing me up M Street calling my name as a pack of women trailed him. I quickened my pace.

"Mrs. Dunleavy. Mrs. Dunleavy. Oh, hello, Prudence, how are the children? Stand up, darling, please, you must release my leg."

I slipped into Vidam & Chandler, the gourmet shop. It was the wrong store to go into, I knew immediately. A lot of women Ben knew shopped there. There was weeping on a mass scale, cries for Ben, who entered just seconds behind me.

I moved as far from him as I could. I'd done all the longing and purging I was ever going to do.

"Mrs. Dunleavy." He squeezed out from between two women who began ripping his clothes. "I'm Ben Sotterburg."

"I know who you are, Mr. Sotterburg. I seem to be the last woman on the planet who hasn't made your acquaintance."

"We did meet. Briefly. I was auctioned off at the Nowhere to Go Ball."

"Yes, you raised an impressive amount for refugees. My husband and I appreciated your help."

"Twelve grand. Just for drinks at the Mayflower. A magical night. The bidding kept going up up up. And we met once again at the illiteracy fundraiser."

"Not precisely what I meant about making your acquaintance, but yes, we did meet at those events, very nice to see you again, good-bye." I sidestepped my way through the crowd to the case of prepared foods. I could get the twice-baked potatoes with some of the vegetable confetti. But I'd wanted pasta and that wouldn't go with potatoes. I was about to give my order for the confetti when the man behind the counter noticed Ben.

"Mr. Sotterburg. Your calamari recipe was a hit. It was so successful, in fact, we've been sanctioned for overfishing the squid stock." I moved over to cheese and ripped off a number.

"Oh, I understand now." Ben stayed on my heels. "You're referring to the *Washingtonian* article?"

"I don't read *Washingtonian*."

"*L.A. Times?* Oh, *Whisper!*, no doubt. None of it's true. You know how the press works, Mrs. Dunleavy. They decide what to write before picking up a phone. I ran a news organization in the seventies. We did the same sorts of shoddy—"

"I don't read magazines or newspapers, Mr. Sotterburg. I'm talking about two friends of mine."

"Who?"

"Vanessa Duane, Kelsey Reisenfeld."

"How are they? You're friends with Vanessa? Did she manage to get her son into Yale? And Kelsey. She's a kick, a real tonic. What a mind. What news do you have?"

I put back a can of miniature corncobs.

"Let's see. Vanessa's son did get into Yale but not because of anything Vanessa did. She's far too busy checking in and out of the hospital for dehydration. Kelsey, well, let's just say she lives in the moment, no memory whatsoever."

"That's not fair. I had nothing to do with those women's difficulties. Their sorrow predated me. I was clear with them. With each we parted as friends."

"Vanessa Duane was the highest-ranking woman at the Postal Service. A devoted mother. A scratch golfer. An avid reader—"

"Yes, Vanessa's a pistol. One of the brightest people I've ever known. Cerebrally sexy."

"She's developed a pathological fear of her own children."

"Georgie and Christopher? I'll drop her a note immediately." I could do a cheese plate. Three cheeses with some grapes. "But

Mrs. Dunleavy. What has any of this to do with me? Let's have tea. They have a nice café here. You'll see I'm not such a monster."

"I don't have time. Thank you anyway. My husband is coming home. It's our wedding anniversary."

"I know what you are going through. These short furloughs are difficult. The range of emotions played out in thirty-two hours. Such little time to prove yourself. Nothing is ever quite right. Let me put together a dinner."

The cheese man called my number.

"I'll have an inch of the aged cheddar and an inch of the smoked cheddar and an inch or so of the mild cheddar." He rolled out several wheels. Ben leaned into my ear.

"Instead of a cheese plate, or, in your case, a cheddar plate, why not some hot appetizers? I can show you how to make a delicious wild mushroom in puff pastry. It's easy. And you'd still have time for a roast and a confetti of fresh vegetables." I canceled the cheese order and moved on. My basket was empty. I stopped at caviar. Matt's favorite. But I didn't have enough cash. I'd spent it on meat for the chagwa.

"Keep moving," Ben whispered. "Overpriced. A sturgeon shortage in the Caspian. I wouldn't trust what you're getting. But if you really want it, I'll buy it for you. It would make me happy to contribute to the dinner in some way." I headed back to the prepared foods. "I wouldn't," Ben warned. "When a person comes from having eaten institutional food he appreciates anything cooked at home, no matter how little effort went into its preparation." I moved around the cases, trying to lose him. I stopped at pastry. A nice cake could compensate for a lousy dinner of spaghetti or eggs. "How about a selection of homemade sorbets?" Ben suggested. "It's easier than you think. And refreshing for summer. With some lace cookies served along-side? Do you have an ice-cream maker?"

I had to get away from him. I looked for an exit. A crowd of women started to close in around us.

"Ben, it was the happiest time of my life . . ."

"The happiest eight weeks of my life . . ."

"Water . . ."

"I'll always love you, Ben."

"Ben."

"Ben."

They engulfed my pursuer. I dropped my basket in a pile of imported soda crackers and made my escape, up a flight of metal steps to a narrow catwalk where cookbooks and copper saucepots were stored. The emergency door was open. Some men brought in boxes of meat. I scurried across the catwalk and was almost to the door when I heard Ben scream.

"WEEEEEENDYYYYYY." The store became quiet. The men sealed the exit from outside, locking me in. Down below the women cleared a space. He walked the aisle they'd created, looking up.

"What?" I'd had it with him and anyone or thing that would put my family or me in danger. This man stank of it. "What the hell do you want?" I gripped the bar on the catwalk.

"I want what you have."

"What do I have?"

"The chagwa."

"I don't have him."

"He'll be back."

"What could you possibly want with him?"

"I want to go in the ring as though I'm never coming out. And I can't get anywhere near him without you."

"Why don't you go home and play with your cat?"

"I'm not interested in domesticated animals, Mrs. Dunleavy. It's the wild spirit of the chagwa that captivates me. You don't realize how blessed you are with his presence. In your own yard. I'd give anything—"

"I'll seat you now." The maître d' took us from the back of the line. Ben had won me in the Scholarship Auction, breaking all human auction bid records since Jason Priestley. Codeine ate away at my gut. I collapsed in a chair and drank an entire glass of water.

Ben smiled as I drank.

"You were good to auction yourself off like this, Mrs. Dunleavy. Such a worthy cause, these youngsters that would otherwise have no means—"

"I only agreed to come here as a favor to Dr. Dave. And I'm inexplicably thirsty." A busboy filled my glass. I downed it like the first.

"Drink up. We don't even need to talk." He picked a red crayon from a shot glass on the table and began scribbling on the paper tablecloth.

"What are you doing?"

"Oh, just an idea I had for a medical thriller. A woman has a secret which is a threat to national security, so she has her brain transplanted into the body of a dying man. What do you think?"

"Not much."

"You're right. I'm a disaster."

"Matt loved *Fourth Down, Time to Punt*. He says it's the best book on college ball ever written."

"He's generous. I was nineteen when I wrote it. It embarrasses me now."

"Ben." A puffy-eyed waitress came to the table.

"Charlotte."

The maître d' hurried over and shoved her out of the room.

"I'm stunned," Ben said. "She used be the Pacific Rim expert at Brookings . . . Anyway, tell me. What is it like having the beast in your midst?"

"Terrifying. Expensive."

"Exhilarating? You know, not long after I helped liberate Qasmarra—"

A waiter came for our order.

"Ice tea."

"Please," Ben said. "Order something more. They have a nice chicken Caesar."

"I'll have the millet and cauliflower croquettes." Clearly not the restaurant's specialty, based on the waiter's scowl.

"I'll have the usual, Kenneth. Steak Jennifer. Full-blooded."

"Red or purple, sir?"

"Purple today."

"Very good, sir." He took away our menus.

"I'll come straight to the point, Mrs. Dunleavy. I've been researching animal training and behavior, Skinner, Pavlov, Karl von Frisch, even Siegfried & Roy. If you would allow me to set up in your home, to get involved in his upkeep . . . and yours . . . I know the financial strain you've been under since your husband's trial. The whole business has been a nightmare, for you, for your family, for the country. I still believe Matthew Dunleavy will be vindicated."

"Matt appreciated your op-ed piece in the *Times*," I muttered.

"The man was a scapegoat, preyed upon by a certain speaker of the house. I should have done more. Now, of course, my coming to you is in my own self-interest, but I believe we can help each other."

The waiter served the table next to us. Two orders of lobster sashimi. The claws still clattered on the plate. The customers clapped their hands in awe.

"Would you like that?" Ben asked. "It's elegant as hell. They do it quite well here."

"They're still alive."

"Not for long."

"I think it's horrible." I tasted bile. "Horrible."

"It's just retribution for bad times, a transfer of power. Once we were under the mallet of the lobster, before we crawled out from the sea. It's a celebratory dish like the croissant."

"Is that right?" I glanced at my watch, wondering when my croquettes would arrive. The customers stabbed their forks into the raw seafood.

"Someday the bib will be on the other neck, if you will, so I think we should just try to enjoy ourselves while we can. Don't you?"

Another round of sashimi came for the table behind, claws tapping like fingernails in a typing pool.

Our meals arrived. The croquettes looked tragic. I had no appetite.

"Excuse me." A woman behind Ben left her clattering plate and stepped up to our table. "I'm Wanda Peterson from Comma Publishing."

"I thought you looked familiar," Ben said.

"How much would your tablecloth cost me?" She touched the paper where Ben had been scribbling.

"This? It's nothing." Ben tried to cover the words with his hands.

"I'm willing to offer you this much for your tablecloth." She wrote a dollar amount on a card.

A man in paisley tie and foulard stepped up to Ben's left. "I'm willing to offer you this much for your tablecloth." He handed Ben one of his cards.

"I was making some notes," Ben insisted. "I beg you, let me be."

The publishers pulled back and forth on the tablecloth. "You only wanted it because you knew I'd want it!"

I saw my escape. "Thank you for lunch, Mr. Sotterburg."

"Mrs. Dunleavy. Wait. Please."

"And thank you for your generous contribution to the Scholarship Auction." I waved.

I raced out onto the sidewalk. But when I got to 39th, I saw him behind me. "Do you need a new challenge?" I asked. "Why don't you run for president?"

"Because I would win."

"You've certainly got the women's vote."

"This is difficult. For me to ask for anything. Don't humiliate me."

"Train something else, Mr. Sotterburg. Yaks. Or buffalo. A pig. Work your way up. Pay your dues. Everything comes easy to you."

"It's true. It's horrible."

Women pressed against the insides of store windows, gazing out, devastated. I lifted my skirt to step through the river of tears.

"Look at them. You should be ashamed."

"I cry too."

"What in the world could make you cry?" I pushed open the door to my building. Ben was stopped by security. I squirmed into the elevator with a pack of lawyers from Wobley & Fowell.

"You, Wendy Dunleavy," Ben called after me from the front desk. "You could make me cry."

The doors to the elevator closed. I was among men. No sniveling, no one making a spectacle, just men commanding situations with their nondescript nature. A relief.

"That was Ben Sotterburg," a young lawyer said.

"The billiards champ?"

"Hell of a cellist."

"Negotiated the Moske treaty."

The doors opened on seven. They stepped out into their handsome firm, where a large party was being set. The doors closed. Immediately the elevator became rickety. In twice the time it took to get to seven, the elevator let me out on nine. I went to my office, collapsed in my swivel chair and swallowed three Tylenol with codeine with some cold cappuccino. The secretary had left three pink message slips on my desk. "Dr. Dave called to say pad thai and remind you of today's sudden procedure." Pad thai. Pad. *Pap*. Pap fine. My pap smear is fine. My sudden procedure? Ah, the *sit-in* procedures. "Hole in one. On the green. Fun for all, nine A.M." Hole in one? I don't even like golf. Hole. Green. *Holman Greenly*, the twenty-term senator.

Fun for all? *Funeral.* Holman Greenly died finally? Not possible. "Sun: Chondrul in house." A knock came at the door. Ben Sotterburg had slipped past security.

"I would think twice before accepting a job in an office without a window." He played with the mini-ball-bearing set on my desk.

"It's temporary." I became aware of every speck of dust. "They keep moving my office."

"I would think twice about that too."

"The department is going through changes."

"What exactly do you do?" He asked.

"I design forms."

"A graphic designer."

"No," I explained. "The graphics are outsourced. I figure out what needs to be said on the form and where on the form to put it."

"Really? That's something I never thought about."

"Passports? Lose your birth certificate? Apply for a visa?"

"You mean when I get in the wrong line at the DMV and stand like a fool for two hours, then get to the front at last and an angry person on a personal call looks up and asks if I filled out the form and I say no, I didn't know I had to fill out a form, and I get sent to the end of another long line . . . that's you? You design those forms?"

"Of course not. Those are outsourced. I design the forms that the various departments have to fill out in order to obtain the forms you are referring to."

He was uncharacteristically silent for a moment.

"You design forms for forms." He burst into laughter. "Sorry. It just seems funny."

I didn't see anything funny about it at all. I had work to do and preparations to make for Matt's furlough. And the sit-in. I promised Dr. Dave. I had galloped through his paltry bottle of Tylenol.

"I'll walk you to the elevator," I said.

"We still haven't solved your dinner problem."

"We?"

"Come downstairs with me."

"Where are we going?"

"Shopping." He pulled my wrist into the elevator and pressed seven.

"Wobley & Fowell?" The only firm with four ampersands.

The doors opened to a party, Wobley & Fowell & Coolidge & Shank & Worburn's annual client bash. I leaned over and tried to push nine. He dragged me from the elevator.

"I'm a client," he whispered. At the front table he found his name on a sticker. We walked through crowds of men in suits, through reams of chitchat:

"... It's not the shark you gotta outswim, it's the guy in the water next to you ..."

"... I told him sixty grand more, he'd be our new ambassador to Nigeria ..."

"... You have a greater likelihood of winning a Section 42 dispute with the IRS than coming in contact with the chagwa ..."

"... Just run it through the income statement. Nobody'll be able to reverse it ..."

I had never seen so much food. Stations of delicacies were placed throughout the sprawl of bleached oak, Roy Liechtensteins, a four-square Warhol of Stanley Wobley and Harvey Fowell and open ceilings with exposed pipes. There was a blini bar. An enchilada bar. A raw bar. A savory waffle station. The inevitable roast beef and turkey carving station. A pasta bar, seven types: farfalle, pappardelle, linguini, orzo, gnocchi, penne, rigatoni, with your choice of nine sauces. An entire dessert room. And no one eating a thing, though drinking plenty of scotch. And over by the spiral staircase, a caviar station. Golden Osetra, jet-black beluga, lustrous gray Sevruga, bowls of chopped purple onion and brown toast squares. In the center of the table was an ice sculpture of Mt. Rushmore with the faces of the five named partners.

"Open your purse," Ben whispered, attempting to drop in a can of beluga.

"That's stealing."

"It'll just go to waste, believe me."

"I'm sure they have an arrangement with a soup kitchen."

"Yes, Koreen's Kitchen gets whatever the office manager doesn't pilfer." He stuffed a fistful of cheese pastries into my bag. "They need only be reheated." Then three salmon fillets wrapped in a napkin. "Put them in an inch and a half of clam broth to keep them from drying out. Rice or pasta?" he asked himself. "Roasted potatoes." We looked around. Somehow there were no roasted potatoes, an oversight by the party planner, whose desk would be out in the hall tomorrow. "Scratch the potatoes. When in doubt, go to the risotto. Just stir in some Parmesan, a scant amount of olive oil and some broth to keep it from sticking to the bottom of the pan." He filled a crystal water glass with risotto and peas. "But you must keep stirring. Stop for a second and it will burn. That's the drawback of risotto, but it's worth the trouble."

"Benjamin."

"Wonderful to see you, Harvey." Ben introduced me to Harvey Fowell.

"My wife keeps jawing on about Thanksgiving. What have you done to her?"

"I'd love for you and Matilda to come."

"Have lunch with me at the Metropolitan. In the meantime, eat, drink and be wary."

"Open your bag," Ben whispered in my ear.

"I can't," I said.

"See the bovine man over by the Francis Bacon? He's the office manager. Ten to one he's stockpiled a dozen of these tins in his supply closet. Koreen's Kitchen will not see a single egg whether we take it or not." He dropped the tin in my bag along with a wheel of Brie, several handfuls of vegetable confetti and a caramel torte. After we were quite laden down with food, I scurried to the elevator, Ben waving at partners with a baguette and a bottle of Pinot Grigot that he lifted from the bar. "We forgot to do a salad," he called.

"I can handle salad." The doors closed.

"FOUR LEGS GOOD! TWO LEGS BAD! FOUR LEGS GOOD! TWO LEGS BAD!"

"Excuse me. Is this the Violence Against Women demonstration?" I asked a girl in a hooded sweatshirt.

"What? I can't hear you."

"Join arms!" a man cried through a bullhorn. "Human chain!" The girl in the hooded sweatshirt linked her elbow through mine. I turned to a young man on my right with two braids.

"Is this the Violence Against Women demonstration?"

"What? FOUR LEGS GOOD! TWO LEGS BAD!"

Four legs, two legs. I'd come to the wrong rally. "Are you with PETA?" I asked the man with the braids.

"PETA?"

I had misheard. They weren't chanting "FOUR LEGS GOOD! TWO LEGS BAD," it was "NO ONE IN! NO ONE OUT!" We were blocking the doors to the WTO. A reporter stood by helplessly trying to get into the building.

"I'm on your side," he insisted. "Let me get in to write my story. It will help your cause."

"NO ONE IN! NO ONE OUT!"

"Can you let go of my arm?" I asked the man with the braids. "I'm at the wrong rally."

"What?"

"I'm supposed to be at Violence Against Women."

"Violence?" The man yelled. "There's going to be violence?" The police moved in and started to push against the crowd.

"Sit down! Sit down!" The man with the bullhorn shouted. "Passive resistance! Passive resistance!" The line lowered to the sidewalk. I was pulled down with the rest. The girl in the hooded sweatshirt was lifted by her wrists and ankles and carried into the back of a truck. The police dragged the man on my right by the braids.

"I'm at the wrong demonstration," I told the police officer. "Don't lift me, please, I can walk." I stepped up into the wagon. "I came to the wrong rally," I yelled to the young woman sitting to my right. But she was singing "The International" along with everyone else in the back of the loud, jerking truck.

"I went to the wrong rally," I told the guard getting out.

"The Rome rally? That was at Thirty-fourth and Mass."

The light in Block B was harsh. There were no places left to sit. It smelled like—what else?—urine. Girls skipping class surrounded me. They sang "May the Circle Be Unbroken," but then rumors started to fly and the mood changed. In preparation for the economic summit there had been a tightening of procedures handling arrests at demonstrations. We would have to spend the night. We would be thrown in with the general population. And then the most dreaded words that we knew: strip search. Panic broke out. Girls piled up at the door. I stood on a bench. "There aren't going to be any strip searches, girls. That would be unconstitutional. I'm sure you all wore clean underwear just in case." The mood lightened up. We sang "Suzanne" and swore to always keep in touch. In the midst of "Both Sides Now," I began codeine withdrawal. The steel wedge planted in the cranium, the maul coming down, splitting my head in two. There were too many people in the room. I moved over to a wall and picked a spot on the cinder block to stare at. I began to suffocate. I had to get home to Dylan. A girl with black hair and blond roots sidled up next to me. "Ever go to Fidge Ellers?"

"Where?" I gasped for air.

"Fidge. Fidge Ellers. His wife's a nurse. He can get you whatever you need." She tried to kiss me. It was time for my phone call. I couldn't call Dylan from jail, not a chance. Peter was lost to me, gone for good into Colonial World. I looked up at the soundproof paneling on the ceiling, scanning my mental address book, pages flying off in the wind. All my friends disappeared after Matt's conviction. Sure, I got the obligatory earnest handhold and the "But how are you really?" when I cornered someone at the grocery story, but no one ever reached out. Standing there in that piss-reeking dormitory it hit me: there was no one to call. I had no choice.

"The judge is a friend from civil rights days. You won't get a summons or a desk ticket." Ben Sotterburg and I crossed the lot to his Jeep Cherokee. "I didn't realize you had strong feelings about the WTO."

"I went to the wrong protest. I was supposed to be at Violence Against Women. You'd think I could find the steps of Rayburn." He opened the door for me. I belted myself in. I was cold despite the hot weather. I stank. He put his jacket over me, tucking it under my chin.

"I was at Rayburn. We could have used you. A lot of these proposed amendments don't belong in the court, but Violence Against Women is just too crucial not to be." We drove out the lot to freedom.

"I don't have strong feelings about that particular issue either, Mr. Sotterburg. I owed a favor to Dr. Dave. I'm not political."

"Considering all you've been through, I understand. But there's still good work to be done."

"I know this town, Mr. Sotterburg. When we were born the drinking fountains were segregated. All us white heroes who marched arm in arm alongside MLK, for instance, did we ever fight the Jim Crow laws? There's a memorial to every living thing that ever breathed but no statue of Martin Luther King, Jr." On the median strip of North Capitol, I saw Medley, searching through crab grass for a snake. "What I'm trying to say, Mr. Sotterburg, is that everybody has an atrocity in his back pocket, but somehow it seemed worthwhile to lock up my husband because of 'the good work.' Forgive me, but when you say those words you sound naïve. This town is a cold place. No one much cares about anyone else because no one has to, because no one is here to stay."

Ben pulled up in front of my house and turned off the car.

"I did, for the record."

"You did what?"

"Fight the Jim Crow laws. And I'm on the committee for the MLK memorial. And I am here to stay."

"Well, then, you're excused. Thank you for picking me up from jail. Good night."

"Won't you let me come in?" he asked. "Just so I can see where he was? One pugmark? One scratch on the door?"

"I have a tremendous day before my husband comes home. And I have to attend a funeral in the morning."

"Sorry to hear that."

"No, it's a good one. Senator Greenly finally died."

"Holman Greenly? It's not possible. I hadn't heard. I knew he'd had a leg off. He died finally? I'm stunned. Especially that you are attending his funeral. With all due respect. He wasn't exactly a friend of your family's."

"A technicality. They forgot to take my name off the bunting committee."

"Old Holman. I thought he'd go on forever, if for no other reason than to keep his ex-wife from running for his seat." Ben put his hand around my forearm.

"If you want to help me, Mr. Sotterburg, arrange the delivery of a ten-pound box of strychnine. I know you know people."

"This is not what you want to do, Mrs. Dunleavy."

"What do you really want with him?"

"Back him off with a chair? Put my head in his mouth?"

"So he can bite it off?"

"One footprint?"

"All right. There are some prints by the biga tree and scratch marks on the doors." We walked up the front path. "My son is home. He's having a rough time these days."

"My son was a teenager once," he said. "About a hundred years ago."

"I apologize in advance for the condition of the house."

"You should see mine."

The smell of chagwa urine wafted through the door.

"It reeks. It doesn't wash out. You never get used to it."

Ben inhaled deeply. "To smell such a thing!"

I opened the door. Something was wrong, I knew immediately.

"Mom?"

"Dylan?" He was on the refrigerator again. The chagwa stalked the kitchen, back and forth, around the center island, protecting his catch.

"My God, he's beautiful," Ben gasped.

"How did he get in?" I cried.

"Through the back," Dylan said.

"Were you wearing your headgear?"

"In the house?"

"Try to think of something cheerful. I'll get him his food."

"Is he going to eat me?"

"No, Dylan. Think of . . . the nice time we had at the beach."

We got sand lice and sun poisoning.

The chagwa stepped to the edge of the kitchen. Ben backed up against the front door, tripping over the umbrella stand.

"If you act scared, he will kill you," I said. "Don't turn around."

"I never imagined anything so glorious."

The chagwa moved toward us.

"Keep your eyes locked on his," I said. "Walk in reverse. No sudden moves." We backed out onto the front steps, running around the side of the house. The door to the basement was locked. "We'll have to break a window."

"Let me." Ben kicked in the glass. I reached around and unlocked the door. It was painted shut. Ben forced it with his shoulder. I rushed to the freezer, hauling out a roast. "This meat is frozen solid. I'll never get a knife through it."

"I can." He crashed the roast down on the train table. "What a creature. Exquisite, but not in the way you'd expect. What testicles! Have you noticed?"

"Please hurry."

"Better yet, throw him this. It'll keep him occupied."

I grabbed the roast and ran up the steps to the basement door. "Look! See what I have for you!" I flung the meat Popsicle into the yard. The chagwa leapt out the kitchen. Ben and I tore upstairs to Dylan, slamming the door to the outside.

"Are you all right, darling? Did he hurt you? Let me see your side." Dylan climbed down from the fridge. "I'll make you some dinner." I brushed flour and dust from his shirt.

"I ate at Andre's."

"I thought Andre was coming here."

"None of my friends want to come over because of the chagwa."

"Say hello to Mr. Sotterburg, Dylan."

"Hello, young man."

Dylan marched upstairs to his room without shaking hands.

"Dad's coming home tomorrow," I called after. "Try to get some sleep. No video scramble." He slammed his door. I needed to get to work. The morsel I'd thrown wouldn't last five minutes.

Ben was already down in the basement moving furniture.

"I never knew that light was there." I began to cry. He put his arms around me.

"Wendy. You've endured so much. When I feel my problems bear down I need only think of your family. I wish I could take some of your pain."

I moved away from him. "That's a kind offer. I don't know . . ."

He sharpened the knives on the steel. He cut deep behind the shoulder blade and a large chuck from the top. "Do you want the lower leg for soup?" I shook my head. "Can we warm this somehow? Cold meat causes intestinal problems in chagwa."

"Let him have intestinal problems. What do I care?" I cut a flank steak from the muscle flap on the belly. Then I put a new liner in the trash can and tossed in some scraps.

"All of what you're throwing away can be used for hamburger," Ben said. "And what a shame to give up that brisket. I love a good brisket. My mother used to make it with Coca-Cola. Oh, I miss her."

Together, we cut more than three times as much as when I was alone. But he was more efficient, less wasteful, cutting right down to the bone and trimming all but the slightest rim of fat. He made neat piles. He lifted the large slabs from the freezer with ease.

I felt I was in his way, so I sat on the broken beach lounger and smoked.

"Have one of those for me?"

"They're Dylan's." I lit him a cigarette from mine and placed it in his mouth. "They're all over the house. I never smoked before my son did."

"Same thing happened to me with my kids." He stacked the chunks into a pyramid.

"You're good at this."

"I went undercover at St. Ives Packing a few months in the eighties."

"You organized the meatpackers?"

"Well, not all the meatpackers," he said modestly. He seemed happy in his work. "This is good meat. You're feeding him well."

"It's riddled with cancer," I said.

"You just cut around it. See here?" He pointed to a purplish lesion with the tip of his knife. "The rest is fine."

"Feed him the cancer," I said.

He tossed the diseased chunk in the trash can, cutting what was left into identically sized cubes. "It must be hard to keep up with him and all this meat. You don't supplement with Carnivore Diet?"

"With what?" I asked sleepily.

"Carnivore Diet." I sat up on the beach lounger. "It's an entire ground cow with some vitamins thrown in. It would cut down your costs too. Of course, you would still want the meat chunks along with it."

"How was I supposed to know about Carnivore Diet?" I became upset.

"Call the zoo? Call a trainer?"

"I'm on my own here. I've done pretty well considering." I slammed back in the chair.

"Hey, hey." He patted the air with the knife. "I'm only trying to help. There's no reason you should know about Carnivore Diet. You've done a fabulous job caring for him. What do I know? Nothing." He lifted a backbone from the deep freeze.

"How do I get this . . . Carnivore Diet?" I asked.

"Let me make a call. I worked with a zoologist while I was drafting the Cruelty Toward Animals Act."

"What about the strychnine?" I asked. "You seem to be able to get your hands on anything."

"Something like that could cause more harm to you than him, Wendy. We have no idea what the effect of strychnine would be on a chagwa."

"I'm willing to take the chance."

He examined a tenderloin. "Would you mind if I cut a couple of steaks?" he asked. "I could make us a supper. A cool center with a sauce Veronique? If you have some greens, a nice salad?" He saw the disgust on my face and went back to work, glancing over every time I took a sip of my water.

"Why do you look at me when I drink?"

He smiled. "I like imagining it . . . going through you."

"Anatomy."

"Spilling over your throat, flowing by your larynx." He stopped cutting meat, staring dreamily into a naked bulb. "Down your esophagus, splashing into your stomach, your kidneys, your infundibula, your tubuli, Wendy—"

"Stop." I pushed back in the beach lounger. "We're not going to get involved. I'm not going to end up like those women."

"But you wouldn't—"

"I said stop."

"I was only looking."

He went back to the meat. I felt a flush of loneliness. After the inevitable silence following a botched advance, I got the nerve to ask.

"Did you ever date Nancy Price-Brundage?"

"Nan? Nanny Price! Yes, of course, years ago. Lovely gal. Nan! Nanny! Extremely dedicated."

I slumped in my lounger. I'd flattered myself into believing that Matt and I were the only ones who could see her beauty.

Before long there was enough meat cut for three feedings. Ben washed the knives in the basin and wiped down the cutting area. He packed the scraps in the trash bag and tied up the ends.

"May I feed him?" Ben asked.

"You did the cooking." We went upstairs.

Stupidity was perfume to the chagwa. To feed him, you opened the door only enough for the meat tray to be slid out onto the deck. But Ben walked right out into his lair.

"Have you lost your mind? Get inside! Don't turn around! He attacks from the back!"

The chagwa smelled Ben's clumsiness coming from the basement. Meat delivering meat. He leapt up from the ground. Airborne, he stretched out ten feet. Ben was down before the chagwa had a chance to do it himself. A nail caught on the neck of his cashmere sweater. His hand disappeared into the chagwa's mouth. I picked up a broom, hurried down the steps and tried to bring it down hard on the beast's head. I missed and hit Ben. He yelled out in pain.

"Oh, I'm sorry," I cried.

"He's not letting go of my hand." I wedged the broomstick into the mouth of the chagwa. It was the closest I'd ever been to a wild animal. I could feel his breath. I could smell him. As though trying to jack up a car, I began pumping the stick. The chagwa nodded his head up and down. Ben pulled his hand free, rolled over and scurried into the house on all fours. Still pumping, I shoved my foot out and kicked the meat tray into the yard. The chagwa jumped after the meat.

Ben lay on the kitchen floor against the oven. I was furious. He could have gotten us both killed.

"I wanted him to like me." He was delirious.

"Your main concern should be to stay alive."

"My hand was in his mouth."

"You're lucky he didn't bite it off. Let me see. Are you bleeding? Infection will set in immediately. You need antibiotics." I squeezed a paper towel soaked in peroxide into the holes in his neck. He moved to one of the dining chairs, looking out back at the chagwa, who was happily chomping.

"I'm all right." He was exalted, a faraway look in his eyes.

"He's not a puppy or a kitten. He's not tamable."

The chagwa finished his food, moved across the yard, mouth-breathing, blood smeared across his face, and dug his nails into the tree.

"Why do you think he came to you?" Ben held a square of gauze on his neck as I wrapped his other hand.

I shook my head. "He's all over the city. We're nothing special. I just made the catastrophic mistake of feeding him."

"That tree," Ben said. "He likes it. It's a biga, right? It has medicinal properties. I've never seen one in this part of the world. How did you come by it?"

"Matt brought it back from Tamauritius. When the government reinstated the prince. One of those boondoggle peace missions."

"It has an astringent. A red gum that works as a disinfectant." He deposited the stained gauze on the table. Then he reached his hand over and put it on the back of my neck, pulling his fingers through my hair. My breathing became unsteady.

"He likes to sleep under it," I said. "And he likes to run around it."

"Maybe he'll turn to butter."

"Don't tell me. You were on the committee to get that book banned."

"Not banned, just changed, updated." He pulled my head down to kiss me. I stepped back. His fingers got stuck in a tangle. He had to reach the bitten hand in to try and pull a finger out of a small rat's nest of hair.

"I'm terribly sorry," he said. I handed him the surgical scissors from the first-aid shoebox. "You're sure?" he asked.

"You shouldn't be in there, anyway. Ouch!"

"Voilà." He presented the little fur ball. I felt embarrassed about my hygiene. "Can I take you to breakfast, at least?"

"No."

"Allow me to cook something for Matt?" He went into the kitchen and pulled out whatever was in the fridge, some potatoes with eyes, a soft onion, a carrot you could tie into a clove hitch, and made potato soup. "Just heat it and sprinkle some chives in each bowl." He washed the dishes, apologized for being inappropriate and left.

I turned on the TV. Bryson Pfeiffer was found stoned on Easy-Off at Fort Reno. He was being held at juvenile corrections because no one would come to claim him.

I looked out at the chagwa, who paced the back yard and scratched his nails into the tree. He appeared to be walking differently. He'd lost weight, I noticed. Then I looked at his hind legs. I had to look and look again and get the flashlight and continue to look for his testicles. It wasn't a he at all.

"Sucked into his body," Dr. Jovanavich explained on the phone. "He's changing sexes."

"I thought only mollusks could do that."

"Chagwa are the original hermaphrodites. Legend has it they went both ways between the pharaohs and their wives. He needs to breed, to preserve the tribe. He couldn't find a mate, so he's going to go it as a female. Fascinating. I've never seen hermaphromorphism in progress. Poor girl doesn't realize she's the last. She'll have no better luck getting a date. It's hard not to feel pity."

"It's a predator, Doctor. He or she. I want you to come to Ruth Bay. Your whole life you've studied this animal. Now it's here. Tell me what you want. I'll give it to you."

"I'm not well, Mrs. Dunleavy. I become weaker every day."

"I'll take care of you."

"You can barely take care of what you have."

"What a selfish bastard you are."

"Good night, Mrs. Dunleavy. Sleep well."

"Ha, ha."

I heard a low rumble becoming louder every second. The night lit up like day. The chagwa leapt over the fence and vanished into the woods. I went to the front door, peaking out. Tanks rolled down the streets. The National Guard. Neighbors rushed out in their bathrobes, bringing coffee and muffins and peaches, throwing their arms around soldiers' necks as though the Allies had come to liberate France. But all I could see was fresh meat, trimmed and dressed in jungle camouflage.

"Dad's home!" Dylan cried. I sat up in bed and looked out the window for the first glimpse of Matt. *"What are you doing here, Dad?"*

"Things are slow at the shop, son. Thought you and I could practice throwing the old horsehide." Harlan. Dylan watched the morning edition in bed. I slumped back down, trying to find sleep. *"Why such gloomy skies?"*

"I'm just not any good at baseball, Dad." You could already hear the crack in his voice, the new register banging down the door of Dylan's childhood. Gold Street should never have kept him on so long.

"What's important is gettin' out there, tryin' like heck and havin' fun."

I struggled out of bed and went in to say good morning. "Wanna go to a funeral?"

"No." He had the covers pulled up to his neck.

"We could get some breakfast at Johnny Rocket's after."

Harlan threw an eighty-mile-per-hour fastball into Dad's mitt. *"Hot dog!"*

"What will you do today?" I asked.

"Go to Andre's."

"I've asked one of the guardsmen to look in on you. Dad will be home by six—"

He turned up the volume.

I had one hour to shower and get to Holman Greenly's funeral. I wasn't going to miss it. The looks on the faces of the other bunting committee members when I grabbed up a staple gun and a yard of black rayon. I called Dr. Dave at home. He didn't believe in answering services. His wife, Ashanni, answered. I'd woken her.

"Not a problem! Here's Dave!" I could hear the sweet chaos of children coming into their parents' bedroom. Their day was just beginning. My yesterday never ended.

"We missed you, Wendy," Dave said.

"I went to the wrong demonstration. The WTO."

"Did you get arrested?"

"I did."

"WTO opposition is a good cause. Though we really could have used you at the VAW."

"I woke up with a toothache."

"Did you call the dentist?"

"It's related to the headaches."

"Did you see the neurologist?"

"I could use something to get through."

"Have you tried Aleve?"

"Bastard!"

"Pardon?"

"Nothing, I'm watching a flak for the energy companies on C-SPAN. Some Soporifan could get me over the hump, Dave."

"I can't prescribe Soporifan, Wendy."

"How about Nirvanidan?"

"Nirvanidan is as addictive as heroin. Twice as hard to detox."

"Son-of-a-bitch. You make me feel filthy."

"What do you mean, Wendy?"

"Not you, Dave. The flak. I mean, of course he doesn't want caps on rates."

"Yeah, the energy companies pilfer *before* they kill—"

"Oblivan?" I asked.

"No narcotics, Wendy, I'll give you ten Tylenol 3—"

"Oh, God . . ." I started to cry.

"It's all the pain reliever you need."

"It makes me constipated."

"Take it with prune juice. I'll prescribe a stool softener."

"Ten Tylenol 3 will get me to dinner on this headache. An extremely early dinner."

"Ten will last you a good several days, and by then the neurologist will have come up with the preventative plan. Wendy? Wendy? Answer me. Hello? Are you there? I know you're there, Wendy. Answer me or I'll call 911. Hang up so I can call 911. Answer. I'll call 911 on my cell phone if you don't hang up. There are cells now by the mailbox and I will use them. I'm calling now. Wendy? All right, I'll give you thirty. Thirty will take you into the week after next. But understand that I don't expect you to take them all, or any, for that matter." *Thirty!*

"And there's something I'd like to ask you. A favor."

"Anything, Dave." I meant it.

"We're going to sit on the Russian Mission and we're going to get arrested. Are you aware of what health care is like for women in the Steppes?"

"Will you be calling in that prescription now?"

I WAS THE only member of the bunting committee to show up at Senator Greenly's funeral. Still, there would be plenty of satisfaction in seeing Holman Greenly in a casket. A bin of wrinkled, dusty black bunting was left for me at the VIP table, barely enough for the front row of the bleachers. A security guard searched my purse and confiscated my staple gun.

"But I need it for the bunting."

A friendly Secret Service agent stepped up and explained that there would be no bunting today. The staple guns posed a security risk.

I was shocked at how few people showed. True, Holman Greenly was a nasty piece of work. There was always talk of questionable campaign finance and favoring the big energy companies and the mysterious deaths of those who stood in his way over plant closings. He wouldn't budge on tobacco. He once introduced legislation to split a district in two to get his way. But he'd been in the Senate over sixty years, had handed over the presidency to three men. He'd done little for his home state, one of the poorest in the nation, but that never mattered. His constituents just liked that he was still alive. Hate him or not, you'd think at least a handful of his colleagues would come out for his funeral, just out of respect. No remarks from the President, or the Senate whip or the Vice President or any of his Supreme Court judges. Lined up Pennsylvania Avenue were just a scattering of tourists who looked like paid extras. The folding chairs and bleachers were skeletal without the bunting. There was a time when I would have been on the front lines stapling. I looked around for someone I recognized. I considered leaving, but I heard bagpipes. And then drummers playing a dull cadence getting closer. I stayed put in the bleachers. The casket rolled down the avenue on a horse-drawn caisson, a flag covered coffin, and oh!, the nerve. The Greenly family had tried to recreate President Kennedy's funeral procession right down to the horse following, which the stable man prodded to rear up and refuse and behave as skittishly as Black Jack. As though we'd lost our memory. Just like Holman, to make the sacred profane. Unable to stir up any grief, he'd stolen our saddest moment. I'm surprised he didn't sell ad space on the back of the caisson. The procession passed. The mourners looked to one another, shrugged and went about their day. I bought an egg roll and coffee from a vender and hightailed it into work.

MATT'S VISIT was disastrous. He drank. He wouldn't eat the potato soup Ben made, too fattening. He would only eat Chicken L'orange Lean Cuisine in front of the TV. I saw Nancy Price-Brundage all over the house. She rose up with the water in the tub as I bathed, suggesting liposuction. She wore a hundred different outfits, her breasts growing or shrinking depending on the neckline. She placed my head on the mantel after showing it to my detached body. She feather-dusted dressed as a French maid. Dylan wouldn't touch the soup either.

"Potatoes are empty," Matt encouraged Dylan. "Wish I'd had the heads-up when I was your age." He patted his stomach.

"I'll have a Lean Cuisine too, I guess," Dylan said. Nancy whisked away the soup dishes.

"Something wrong with your legs?" Matt asked Dylan.

"It's all right," I said. "I'll get it."

"Stop waiting on him, Wendy. It'll affect his relationships with women."

"I need more juice," Dylan called to me in the kitchen.

"What about the magic word?" Matt asked. "A few things have slipped in my absence."

Nancy whirled into the room with apple juice and a cherry in a martini glass.

I gave Dylan a juice box.

"Why do you let him have so much juice?" Matt asked. "You'll give him diarrhea."

"I don't like water or milk," Dylan said.

"You don't need to like everything that goes into the body, Dylan. Wendy, Marshall is going to bring over a Have-a-Heart big game trap." The chagwa had taken the meat from every Have-a-Heart trap in the city. Matt was behind on everything, living three months in the past. "Orioles have come on, eh, Dylan?" After the first four weeks of the season, they'd dropped to last place and stayed there. "How about summer plans, Dylan? Super E's kids do Outward Bound. Turned their lives around."

"He doesn't need any more fear, Matt," I said.

"Bravery is learned in the face of fear. The way you baby this boy, Wendy. He'll be thirty-five still living at home. I just took a fresh crop of men through the chemical house at Ainsville." Matt was part of the new boot camp approach to incarceration.

"Under the protection of Ainsville. We have a five-hundred-pound beast living in the back yard. Under the protection of nothing."

"You fed him, Wendy."

"How dare you."

"Don't Outward Bound me," Dylan said. "Please."

"When did you get so hard-hearted?" I asked Matt.

"You don't know where I've been, Wendy."

"Wherever it is, you put yourself there."

"I see Renny Mascotti's been by."

Grabbing a stack of Little Debbies, Dylan prepared to leave for Andre's despite my insistence he visit with his father. "Oh, let him go." Matt sopped up a film of sweet sauce in the Lean Cuisine tin with his finger. "I'll have Marshall drive us downtown to look at my name on the Wall. Am I missing in action or just plain dead?" Dylan fled without his chagwa headgear. I ran after him. A National Guardsman offered him a ride.

Matt ate pears from a can in front of the TV.

"This new *Newlywed Game*. You'd think the prizes would be bigger and better. But in fact, they are smaller and less valuable."

I picked twenty-dollar bills out of letters of support from constituents, carefully saving the return addresses on the envelopes for thank-you notes.

"Joan Creech got laid off at the agency," I said. "She was excess, but still. It shows we're all vulnerable."

Matt looked down at himself on the couch. "The food at Ainsville is so starchy. I'm growing a new gut."

"If I ran an agency I'd be trimming the fat too," I said. "In this day and age. But then, I don't run an agency, and probably for good reason."

"Great news," Matt said. "My request for transfer to the north wing went through. No more basketball dribbling while I'm trying to read."

"Not a single bulb came up this spring. Well, maybe one or two. The squirrels could have gotten into them, but one hundred bulbs? That's a lot of squirrel."

Matt tried to get me up to date on one of the evening soaps and I tried, but I found the show incomprehensible, confusing the various teen stars, the boys short and cute, the girls busty and mad. We went upstairs.

Matt flossed.

"All those Zen-and-the-art-of books," he called to me from the sink. "There's now one called *Zen and the Art of Forgery*. Even Zen gone over to the bad side. I should have this tooth looked at. Though a half hour in the medical wing is more torture than I can bear."

"Was it ever good?" I asked from the bed.

"You and me?" He dried his face on a worn hand towel. "There was the time I came in from raking the leaves. And the entrance I made at the Inaugural Ball, remember? We arrived in separate cars?"

"My heart skipped a beat. Literally."

"Even though you had a mild angina, I knew you loved me."

"Mmm."

"And when I left for the arms factory inspection in Samoa."

"I felt certain the plane would go down."

"For me it's been constant, Wendy." He sat beside me. "Ever since I climbed up your hair in that tower where your mother had you locked up." He rubbed the skin around his ankle bracelet.

"Is it uncomfortable?" I asked. "Why is it necessary? Where would you go?"

He pulled off his loafers. "Why were the cuffs necessary at the arrest?" he asked.

"Twenty million viewers," I answered.

He held my hands. "Shall we go to bed?"

"I need my milk," I said.

"Would you like me to get it?"

"You're dear. I'll get it. What can I get for you?"

"Just you."

I went down to the kitchen for a cup of hot milk. In the cabinet over the fridge I found a package of stale Cheddar Goldfish. I leaned against the counter eating them, one by one.

"What's wrong?" Nancy Price-Brundage appeared by the sink. She wore a cream knit dress over tan skin. The dress fell over one shoulder. Bubbles rose up from a lime in her glass.

"I just can't tonight."

She put her arm around me. I rested my head against her chest.

"But it's your anniversary."

"I'm not up for it. Do it for me? He won't know in the dark."

Nancy laughed. "You have to do it. Take yourself by the hand and all that."

"He's had a couple of gimlets. He won't figure it out."

"Well . . . all right."

"He might already be asleep. Just climb in."

She started to leave the kitchen. "What does he like?"

"The usual."

I stopped at the dining room window. The chagwa hung her head, leaning against the chicken wire of the fence waiting for the weekend to be over.

I SAT ON the front stoop watching Ben Sotterburg walk up the path with a bouquet of flowers and a bottle of springwater. "Where did you find such beautiful lilies, Mr. Sotterburg? Don't tell me you were on the commission that liberated tiger lilies from July."

"You look like you might be happy to see me for a change, Mrs. Dunleavy."

"The Carnivore Diet arrived," I said. "It's a miracle."

"I'm glad. Of course, you'll still need to give her meat, but the workload has been cut seventy-five percent. And as for the cost, I'd like to contribute."

"I can't accept. And I'd like it if you would stop looking at me that way."

"I can't help it, Wendy."

"I told you. I'm married. I can't end up like those women. I don't have room."

"I'm not asking you for anything. Just that you accept my feelings as real."

It was a rare beautiful day, dreamy in the sun. We went inside and moved to the back of the house to see the chagwa. The grass had become long and yellow. Her disruptive camouflage made her momentarily difficult to spot. She'd retired to a shady patch of lawn to wait out the hottest part of the day. Feeling that she'd been well fed and would sleep until night, Ben and I came together and kissed.

"Where's your son?"

"A friend's house for the night. Still, here's not right."

"My place?"

I shook my head. "Home team advantage."

In Crystal City there were five Marriots: the Gateway Marriott, the Crystal City Marriott, the River Marriott, the Marriott Key and the Key Marriott Gateway at Crystal City. Ours was the River. The lilies lay on the table, a basket of star fruit nearby and several bottles of Perrier. Ben was good, technically perfect. He said, "Before now I could only dream of a body such as yours," but I got the idea he was more interested in his legacy than me. I couldn't get excited. I like miscues and misfires, the potential for lethal mistakes. And why should he be the only one around here with a legacy? Why couldn't I be the best *he'd* ever had? I turned it around. It didn't work, it couldn't, the two of us chasing the same title. We tossed on the bed and floor fighting for legacy control. But in our sparring came a wonderful clumsiness that had been lacking before. His tongue went inside my nostril. I kneed him in the balls repeatedly. His rhythm thrown off, he rolled away. We lay with our backs to each other.

"I'm willing to lay down the record books if you will," he said. I turned to face his back. Below his left shoulder blade he had a mole with hair sprouting. If he dumped me, I could remember this mole, that he was nothing but an extension of it, that his arms and legs and head grew out from this black spot. The image could get me through any breakup, I was sure.

"I'm willing."

He turned over but I saw he'd gone limp. I too was deflated and dry. He touched one of my breasts. It didn't feel good. He dropped his hand.

"I think I'm impotent," I said.

"I think *I'm* impotent," he said. He opened his arms. I moved onto his chest.

"We could watch hotel porn," I suggested.

"The olestra of the sex industry. It makes it worse for me, in fact."

"A rousing game of Senator/Intern?"

"Too close to home," he said.

"Explore our fantasies?"

"Go first."

"It's strange."

"I can handle it."

"I have a desire to cook for you," I said. "And I don't cook. If it doesn't come from a jar, it doesn't get made. But here I am basting and braising, patting tuna fillets with cracked pepper, serving them alongside roasted potato *moutarde*. I'm poaching pears in brandy, using a melon baller in rum raisin ice cream, homemade, decanting cabernet."

"That's nice."

"I've never said the word *moutarde* in my life."

"Maybe you should give into to it. Make me dinner. Though you might want to serve a chilled grappa alongside that poached pear, or even a calvados. And I wouldn't do the cabernet with the fish. A woody chardonnay. But for the most part, the menu is celestial though the *moutarde* and cracked pepper may clash. Act on it. It would remove the taboo and you'd probably never want to do it again. It might improve things . . . here." He looked down at our useless sex organs.

"I feel ashamed."

"You shouldn't. That sort of musing is natural. I'm sure."

"And what about you, Mr. Sotterburg? What's yours?" He became erect. "Must be something good." He handed me a bottle of Perrier. "You want me to drink? Ah, the water cycle you spoke of when we were cutting meat." He looked shy. "Oh. That. You want me to . . . complete the cycle. On you." He rolled on top of me. I urinated on a boy in college once but we were drunk and it was an accident. There were certainly stranger activities. I knew about a man who could only ejaculate if a woman was bent over on a bathroom scale watching the numbers spin by saying, "I've got to drop five," as he entered her from behind. Seeing Ben so aroused, the world records set aside as he thrust about clumsily on top, holding my hips too tightly, contorting his face, excited me too.

"All right, then." I sat up and drank the Perrier. He watched. We waited. "Shall I turn on hotel porn while we wait for this to kick in?"

He shook his head.

"Maybe there's a cooking show."

He tossed me the remote and brought me a can of Cranapple. Just the act of bringing me water and juice, walking back and forth to the minibar, watching me drink, was causing his eyelids to tick. I flipped around the channels and found a cooking show. Two women cooked squab in a sizzling pot of garlic and ginger. They were overly made up, breasts spilling out the top of jewel-tone spandex. Giggling, they ignored the squab, pretending to pop each other's breasts with large forks. Then they put their tongues together. The camera panned down to the squab, their little legs dancing in broth. I'd inadvertently clicked on the porn channel.

"I apologize," I said. "It will show up on the bill."

"If it makes you happy, it makes me happy." He handed me a diet Coke. "Still you don't need to go?" He nodded toward the bathroom.

"I'm afraid I can drive across Ohio without looking for a gas station."

An hour went by. I depleted the minibar.

"Still nothing?" He brought tap water. We watched the news. The screen was so cut up with stock quotes, weather maps, movie previews and video from a traffic helicopter that I couldn't find the anchor. Ben zeroed in and located him amid a cluster of regional crop reports.

"Does it just build up till the dam breaks?" He handed me another glass of water.

"Thinking about it makes it worse," I said.

Another hour passed. He tried distracting me with stories of his life as I drank and drank and drank.

". . . If President Carter had accepted our plan, the hostages would have been home that night . . . I carved the canoe from a single downed poplar, those being the tallest and straightest of the trees . . . The tricky part was getting the rice *to* the Ethiopian people . . ."

"I think it's time."

"Are you . . . what? Oh. That."

I led him into the bathroom and pulled back the shower curtain. He knelt in the tub. I placed one foot on the side and stood over him. He looked up at me in the dearest worship. I put my fingers in his hair. *Here goes.* But alas, I couldn't. I adjusted my stance. He rearranged himself to take the pressure off his ankles. *Go. Go, go, go, go.* But still, I couldn't. I pictured the first runoff from a mountain, a melting ice cap, water escaping, a pool in a hollowed rock, rings and ripples, rain dripping from roof tiles, spattering the wet, wet ground.

"Do it, Wendy. Please."

"Yes, I want to." The storm was coming. I lowered my hips over him. He rose up to meet me. "Could you wait here for one moment?"

"Certainly."

I got out and turned on the sink. Just a trickle, rain bouncing on a leaf. That always helped when I was at a party and there were people just outside the door. I stepped back into the shower. Nothing happened.

"I'm so excited, Wendy." Water running off soil, soil so dry it can't accept the gift of rain.

"Me too, Ben." Runoff. Water. Irrigation. Get water to the desert and anything will grow. But you've got to have water. The crop report. Calling for rain. Birds fluttering their wings in grandma's birdbath, *don't bring Grandma into this*, worms unearthed, washed out from the ground and into the streets.

"Wendy, darling." Again, he rose up on his knees. Brimming wine glasses. A champagne fountain. New Year's Eve, 1989. A party with all our friends. Matt stacked the glasses into a pyramid. Then he poured Moët & Chandon into the top glass, which overflowed to the three glasses beneath, which overflowed to the five beneath that, which overflowed to the seven, to the nine, to the eleven. I wore a black cashmere shift with specks of silver in the wool. I never put on shoes. Matt kept his hand on my lower back. I remember the smell of his Tenex. What happened to those friends?

I looked down at my stomach, puffed out from my engorged bladder.

"It's not working, is it?" Ben leaned back on his heels. "You're grimacing."

"I have to go so badly."

"Do it. On me."

"I can't."

He stood next to me in the shower, stroking my hair. "Do you need more to drink?"

"Maybe something other than water or juice," I said.

"I'll call room service immediately." He went to the phone. I leaned against the doorframe of the bathroom, my hand on my stomach, panting. Ben placed the order. ". . . And it's a bit of an emergency. I'm happy to pay extra to have it here right away. Yes, Sotterburg . . . No, no, Massad did that, we just got the hostages off the plane. Thank you, and what was your name?"

He handled everything so well. That was the type of phone call I had to work out in my mind for twenty minutes, then write the script on hotel stationery before I could pick up the receiver.

"Good God, Wendy." Ben saw me bent over by the door. "We can call this off." He put his hands under my arms and straightened me up.

"Oh, no. I can do this. Anything left in the minibar?"

"Just salted nuts."

"I think I'm ready." We resumed our positions in the shower, though now I was stooped from a stabbing sensation in my gut. One drop came from my urethra.

"There we go," I said proudly. But it was merely condensation.

"Look," he said finally. "I think you should, you know, go the conventional way and I'll get the hell out of the bathroom."

What a failure I was. He left the room. I switched on the fan, limped to the toilet and sat. Nothing. Now I was in trouble. The pain was excruciating. Ben knocked on the door. I slid off the seat onto the floor. I crawled to the door and opened it. "You're not all right." He bent and tried to lift me. There was a knock. "One moment," he called. He grabbed two terry robes, wrapping them around us as he went to greet room service. I looked down at the rose-colored tile that appeared to spin. I felt my forehead. I was sweating. The wheels of the service cart screamed into the room, the presence of another person filling all the spaces like a poison vapor that turned Ben and me back into strangers. I glanced up from the floor and saw a man I recognized, the gas company worker on the back of the tractor that day at the Suskinds' barbecue when the chagwa grabbed Dylan, stealing what little peace and safety we had left, the man with the cut hand. He'd gotten a new job as a hotel waiter. His hand was wrapped in gauze, a drop of blood seeping through. We made eye contact. Ben signed the bill. The waiter thanked him for his generosity and left. I must have been a sight, covered in sweat, mascara down to my jaw, mouth open in pain.

"Coffee?" Ben offered.

WE TOOK the park. "It happens to the best of us."

I curled my legs up to my chest in the passenger seat, staring out the window at the trees.

"I'd like another chance," I said.

"Of course. There will be many other times like this." He patted my thigh. I forced a smile. He turned onto Beech Drive and got stuck behind a vengeful person, aggressively driving the speed limit, Virginia plates. I pointed the best way out of the park.

"The others. They were all able to perform?" I asked.

"Well . . . yes, most, remarkably."

"Even the Secretary of State?"

"Wendy . . ."

"Could you speed up a little, please?"

He drove to my curb. The National Guard had moved out of the neighborhood, responding to sightings in Tacoma Park. The human shields had moved on, too. Medley sat slumped on the roof drunk.

"It appears the chagwa has left us," Ben said.

"Thank God," I said.

"I'll be tied up in a conference for a day or so. But there's enough meat cut up from the other night should she return. Serve it alongside the Carnivore Diet with some clean fresh water and you're set."

"What kind of conference?"

"An absurd thing I get roped into each year. The hundred and twenty-five smartest people in the United States. We get together and say dumb things."

"I'm sure my invitation is in the mail."

I staggered up the walk, pushed the door with my shoulder and went directly to the bathroom, where I gave back the minibar in a fraction of the time it took to ingest.

INSOMNIA AGAIN. I lay in bed with a wrenching so deep I was paralyzed. Dylan was right. I had never been able to help him. A chair would have made a better mother. Peter was never mine. Matt had always been out of my reach. And, as anyone could have guessed, one week and no word from Ben. I called and hung up on his voice mail. I lay on my back, looking for shapes in the stucco ceiling. Soon the horrible birds of morning sang, *We slept, too bad for you.* I went to the window to look for the chagwa. Some crows picked at a bone she'd left. The paint from Matt's birdhouses had washed away in all the rain, a miniature industrial town where you didn't stand a chance of getting out. Even the birds were stuck.

No work. The government was closed for Invasive Weeds Awareness Day, a win for the gardening conservationist lobby. All morning long I searched for something to hold my interest. I picked up the paper, put it down. I turned on the radio, turned it off. Made toast, threw it away, made tea, forgot to drink it, the dead bag floating to the top.

I tried to call Ben again. The windowless room of waiting for a man to call, I felt disgusted with myself. I tried to conjure the image of the mole on his back, growing spores, leaking pus. But then for the mole I felt only love. I called the hospitals. I limped down to the store. A woman walking three Afghans gave me Kleenex, sobbing into her own.

Another night worse than the one before. I looked in the medicine cabinet, all of my hiding places. I drank. Calvados and Chianti. But it just made me a wide-awake drunk. He'd met someone at the 125 Smartest People convention. Someone cerebrally sexy. I imagined worse. He was home screening my calls, laughing with his mercenary friends as they packed parachutes and Stinger missiles, on their way to overthrow a dictatorship.

At five, I called Dr. Dave. Ashanni was not as friendly as usual. Dave's voice was grave.

"We could have used you at the Russian Mission, Wendy."

"Oh, gosh. I forgot. I'm so sorry. Auction me off at Struggle & Change."

"I can't prescribe anything else."

"My back has gone out . . ."

"There's a good outpatient program at Our Lady of Incumbency."

"You have the wrong idea." I hung up. I tried Ben again. I checked the obits. Driving over to his apartment was out of the question. I would never stoop so low. But the very next minute I was in the car. I looped the city, checking all five Crystal City Marriotts. I wrote a breezy note. I ripped it up. I wrote an angry note. I ripped that up. Then I wrote a note suggesting that it was both our faults for not being in touch. Then I thought I should be more passive.

Dylan came and went to school, to Andre's house, to the clothing drive at the Red Cross. I sold my pearls for groceries. Didn't get much. Apparently they lacked the delicate play of surface color and translucence I was told they had when we bought them. "Knowing pearls has ruined me because I *know*," the Cash for Your Jewels man said. "See how they're whitish and porcelaneous and wanting for luster?" As though anyone who wasn't buying pearls from a desperate woman would notice.

I called in sick to work, and then remembered it was Saturday. I called Dr. Dave and hung up on Ashanni. I got caller ID'd.

"I was wondering if you'd had a chance to go over to Incumbency," Dave said on the machine. I went outside for different scenery. When I saw Ben Sotterburg walking up the front path of the house I went to meet him halfway, collapsing in his arms, feeling the corrosive ache of need.

"I haven't been very reliable," he said. "I apologize."

"It's just that after last week and everything . . ."

"Let's sit down and talk for a minute." When they tell you to sit, you're dead. "I think I may have taken things too far with us. Your husband is a man I admire . . ."

"Ah, yes, this, it's been a while." I could have mouthed the words as he said them.

"You're so emotionally available and generous and sensitive and I am but an empty vessel and unworthy—"

"Could you please dump me and get it over with?"

"I'm not dumping you. I think you need some emotional distance from me."

"What else do I need, Mr. Sotterburg?"

"I don't blame you for being angry. I'm the Peter Principle in relationships. This is as high as I rise, working my way up to failure. But I want you to know that you, Wendy Dunleavy, are my absolute, utter, exquisite failure."

"You met somebody at the convention."

"No. I mean I didn't NOT meet someone."

"So you did?"

"That's not why I'm here, Wendy."

"It's not NOT why you're here. And if the chagwa returns?"

"If you think I loved you for the animal, then you don't know me. But I wanted to mention that Thanksgiving is a special time for my family and me. I have a method of cooking turkey. Butterfly it, then soak it in brine, then dry it out, then cook it flat."

"You back over it with the Jeep?"

"It crisps the whole bird. If you and Dylan could come it would be meaningful."

"Couldn't you just go somewhere and die?"

"If you need to discuss this, I'm available."

"Why? It's over."

"It's not over."

"It's not?"

"It's not NOT over. We're not going to *not* speak, are we?"

"What?"

"I'll leave it to you, Wendy. When you're ready to talk, I'll come to the table."

IF THE ice-cream truck plays "Jimmy Crack Corn" one more time . . .

✦ ✦ ✦ ✦

"THIS IS arsenic. You said you could give me strychnine."

"Mr. Preston says arsenic's just as good." The taxidermist's assistant laid a beaver in a freezer trunk. I stood behind a beige shower curtain that divided Preston Trapping into front and back. Mr. Preston worked at a square table building a form for a small brown bear. "Instead of putting it on the trap, mix it in with the food."

A buck no one came to claim lay stiff across an old washer.

"I don't want any mistakes," I said. "I don't want to just make her madder."

"His insides'll turn out with that, believe me," the assistant said. He knew Mr. Preston was annoyed at being distracted. I imagined the chagwa on the square table, Mr. Preston stripping the skin off its back, the bones pulled out, the brains scooped, the flesh cleared. "Channel 5 says it's a male again, btw."

"You're kidding," I said.

"She's a he. Hard to keep track."

"Not for me," I said.

Hard of hearing from having guns go off too close to his head, the assistant spoke too loudly. "If we had the animal problem you have, there wouldn't be a problem. We know how to take care of this type of pest. Over there in DC, nothing gets take care of," he said. "We're not a Republican store or anything, but that government can be cut in half and you'd still get cream in your coffee. 'Cept the cream would cost you lot less."

"All right, I'll take this," I said to Mr. Preston. "But I did ask for strychnine, so I think you could give me a break on the price."

"Cut the government in half and there'd already be a break on the price," the assistant said.

"I get the skin?" Mr. Preston asked in a gravelly whisper.

"You get the skin," I agreed. "Do you have any Solisan?" You never know.

"Wish I did, dear."

THE CROWS were exceptionally mischievous when I got home from Preston Trapping. There were arguments up in the beeches and a convention of birds on our roof. A crow landed on our front lamp.

"Well, hello, sir," I said to the crow. He had something resembling pink spaghetti hanging from his beak. I looked up at the roof. There were easily a hundred crows pecking away. New ones came in for a landing, screaming at the old ones to get out of the way. I felt happy for a second because West Nile had all but obliterated the population in our area. Penny and I had come across several dead ones in the woods. But now it seemed nature had turned around. Then the sky darkened as more flew overhead and touched down on the house. A chicken hawk flew up from the woods and forced many of the crows away. And three more hawks circled above. I then realized I hadn't seen Medley in a couple of days. A hawk flew over and dropped from his mouth a khaki button from the sleeve of a safari jacket. And then another let go of something that landed exactly an inch from my foot, a sleepy eye that appeared to wander.

✦　✦　✦　✦

I HANDED MY new friend Stuart the National Guardsman a mug of coffee and asked him to look after Dylan. Then I filled a thermos and headed south. Route 66 toward Colonial World.

A guard at a booth stopped every car that tried to enter the fenced-in lot. I'd never make it through. I cut out of line, made a U-turn on the grass and headed back to Route 1, leaving the car on the shoulder. Then I hoofed it over the crabgrass and shallow swampland that surrounded the Jamestown Settlement. The mud swallowed my sandals. A press release seemed to have gone out to every mosquito in the area that my ankles had arrived. I came to a thin evergreen forest where the ground dried. Crossing the needles to an electric fence that wrapped around as far as I could see, I walked along the perimeter looking for a way in. Up ahead I saw a group of people. One man was dressed in jeans and a T-shirt that read: LIKE MY DRIVING? 1-800-FUCKYOU. The other people wore filthy Colonial clothes. They stood around a hole in the fence. The group seemed surprised and bewildered to see me, but they went right back to negotiating. There was a disagreement about what the Colonials felt they should pay the man for freeing them. The Colonials, a man and woman, a young teenage boy and a younger girl, were emaciated and covered in bug bites. The girl had a rash around her mouth. They didn't have any money.

"You work for me two weeks, the kids too, I let you go. Plus you get the Nova," the fence keeper said. The Colonial man agreed. "And your wife gives me a blow job on the way out."

"Forget that part."

"Fine. Two weeks' work, I let you out the hole."

"Plus the Nova."

"The Nova was for the blow job."

I moved through the group and crouched down to get under the fence.

"Hold on, there, buckarette." The fence keeper wrapped his big fingers around my bicep. "Try the main gate, this is off-limits."

"I need to get through."

"You want to get through, you pay me two hundred dollars plus a blow job on the way out."

"I don't have two hundred dollars."

He let out an exasperated breath and looked up at the hazy sky. "How much do you have?"

"I have twenty dollars," I said.

He shook his head, more commiserating with the sky. "Fine. You can work for me ten hours. I need all that dirt moved over to the retaining wall. Give me the twenty. You can move the dirt on the way out." He put his cigarette between his lips, ash an inch long, and with two hands wrestled his back pocket for his wallet. I looked over at an eight-foot mound and some wheelbarrows and shovels.

"Can I bum a cigarette?" the Colonial man asked him.

The fence keeper took a pack of Kent from his front pocket, shook one out for the Colonial and gave him a light with a Bic. The Colonial sucked in the smoke, a first breath of air after drowning.

I handed the fence keeper a ball of eight ones and a five, ducking under the fence while he counted. "Wait, I gotta check that it's all here. Okay, it's all here." Moron. "Don't forget the blow job." Sure.

I walked through a muddy village of trailers. People read the paper or talked on the phone. Someone yakking about a flat-screen TV, another about the new school being worse than the old school, a man making airlines reservations to Orlando. The next trailer was a control room filled with monitors and switches. The next was a shop for broken cameras. No one worked. Everyone was on break. The break was permanent. Guys came together to talk and complain about—what else?—contracts and parking.

"I gotta drive from here to hell and back and I'm on a Work-On-Day-Off."

"Don't talk to me about a WODO, every six days I gotta WODO."

Everyone wore a name tag and a pass. Everyone was named DON. No one paid any attention to me. I wove my way through to a tent with a sign that read: PRODUCTION STAFF ONLY. I moved aside the plastic strips of a door and entered a large staging room. There was a lot of commotion, everyone complaining. A few weary production associates listened and nodded to complaint after complaint, said they'd take care of it, said they'd talk to so-and-so, that they'd place the order themselves, handle it personally. A French camera crew shot a documentary about the shooting of *Colonial World*. A Japanese crew shot a documentary about the French documentary. The French crew had overstayed their welcome, even though their film would be good publicity. They hovered over every conversation, shining Frezzi lamps in everyone's eyes. The production associates kept swatting them away. The Japanese crew managed to make themselves invisible. I tiptoed over to a sign that read: ONLY COLONIALS BEYOND THIS POINT. Stepping through the plastic strips, I got nabbed. "Wait! You can't go out there. You're not Colonial." One of the production associates stepped out from under the French cameraman and headed over to me, tapping the ONLY COLONIALS sign with his pen.

"I need to talk to Peter Allingham. It's urgent."

"No one in, no one out. Influenza outbreak. And if *you're* sick you'll infect everybody." He turned back to the French crew.

"Please," I begged.

The production associate slapped his clipboard against his thigh. "Lady, does the name *Jamestown* mean anything to you? I'm looking at five hundred people dying of malaria or flu. My morgue is filled to capacity—"

The French producer burst in. "So you are saying that the experiment is a failure?"

"I'm saying the experiment is a galloping success."

"My husband is Matt Dunleavy," I pleaded. "He introduced the matching fund program for the period experiments."

"Dunleavy-Morris," a voice said. "We're here because of Matt Dunleavy, it's true." I recognized Andy, the head writer from *Harlan*.

"How good to see you." Andy had done so much to help hide Dylan's voice in the final days.

"Paul and I came over after the age-discrimination suits. I'm writing the introductions."

Paul, the former executive producer of *Harlan*, stepped up next to Andy.

"Can you believe this shit? Discrimination suits. They've created a whole new order. How's the kid?"

"He's doing . . . I don't really know."

"*I* know." Andy was a former Harlan. "She wants to go in, Paul."

"Wendy." Paul shook his head. "It's bad in there. It's filthy.

People are sick. The meat is rotten. There's a war with the Croatans and talk of a slave uprising. Go home. Be with your son. Jamestown is hell." He then looked in my eyes, understanding there was no dissuading me.

"Suit her up," he told the production associate.

"We're fully populated. She'll tip the balance. If the Fifth Floor finds out—"

"She's going in." Paul headed back to the control room.

There was a flurry of activity as both camera crews turned their lenses on me.

"As what?" the production associate asked Paul.

"Beats me. How 'bout a slave?"

"She's white!"

"Send her in as a milliner," Paul yelled over his shoulder.

"We have, like, eighty milliners already. Every female in the colony's a fucking milliner."

"So what's another one?"

The PA flipped the bird behind Paul's back and whisked me over to costume, an alcove with a plastic shower curtain. A tired woman with white spiked hair told me to strip naked.

"What about underwear?" I asked.

"No underwear in the Colonies." She put a stained linen shift over my head, and over that a whalebone vest that laced up the front, back and shoulders. She tied a petticoat around my waist and then an apron. Pockets dangled from a string. I put on a hat and was told not to remove it. Then some scratchy stockings that wouldn't stay up. "Sorry about those," the costume woman said. "We're under fire about verisimilitude." Over the stockings, I put on a pair of ill-fitting shoes. I had to roll my feet inward in order to walk. As I stepped out from behind the curtain, the angry production associate eyed me up and down.

"Very Colonial." He put his hands on my back and pushed me to the entrance. "Don't sing to yourself or touch yourself." He spoke into my ear. "If you have to sneeze or cough, do it privately, and for God's sake, don't talk through a yawn. Remember this is a completely balanced ecosystem. One bad turn leads to another. If you sit down, keep your feet firm and even. Don't shake your head or roll your eyes or lift one eyebrow higher than the other. Let me see your nails. Let me see your teeth. One other thing. Don't spit in a fire. Got it?" We stepped out into Colonial World. It reeked of sewage. It was humid. Bugs descended. He pushed me up three steps into a wagon with a horse and a driver. "Lot Five, Jerry." He smacked the horse, then disappeared behind the plastic strips of the production tent.

Jamestown. Nothing could have prepared me for what I saw. How our present day could have emerged from this I cannot know, because Jamestown looked like the end of the world. Smoke rose from burned-out buildings. The air stank of human and animal excrement. People trudged through the street dazed and sick. But all my driver, Jerry, wanted to hear about was the chagwa.

"We heard he ate some children. Is this true? We've dug holes along the perimeter, covered them with straw, just in case he jumps the fence or tries to dig under. Our muskets are worthless on such a beast. What have you heard?"

I saw men pouring water and shoveling dirt over a place in the ground where smoke came up.

"What happened here?" I asked.

"Powhatans. At first we got along. Then they began to resent us. They burned down the commons two weeks ago and now we're on full alert, twenty-four-hour watch. Wattle and daub go right up if you get anywhere near them with a flame. We've had to rebuild the town twice. Who can blame them? Gold Street cancels *Indian Territory* after five episodes and builds Jamestown on top of the sacred ground." Men standing guard on the street with muskets eyed me suspiciously. Women looked at me blandly from thresholds of mud houses. Children labored in the fields, little boys in skirts carrying bundles of thatch, girls working by themselves in the gardens. A teenager defecated on the side of the road, if you could call it a road. I was thrown side to side in the wagon as the wheels jammed down into holes in the dirt. Everyone looked exhausted. Another cart passed. It was packed with African-American women. My driver stopped our cart to let them by.

"Where are they taking them?" I asked. "Are they slaves?" The women lowered their eyes. Jerry snapped his wrist and the horse moved on. I watched the cart of women until I could no longer see their faces.

"It's just work," Jerry said. "Nothing but work. Everybody's sick and the only thing for it is a blood bath or a pill made from deer shit. I want commerce and billboards and clean sheets and TV. I used to drink straight from a bottle of Maalox on my desk at Merrill Lynch. What I wouldn't give. This is your stop." He pulled the horse's reins. Then he turned around and whispered, "Tell me before you go. The Mets. How are they doing? And the Bulls. Did they win? Did McGwire get traded? The rumors here are crazy-making."

"I don't know."

"You have baseball and you have basketball and you don't follow them? What I wouldn't give for a Twinkie. My, your teeth are white. Kiss me."

I stood in a rut. Over the fields of dirt, I saw Peter, a yoke around his neck and reins in his hands. Two stout workhorses led him. I waved, but he didn't see. I lifted my skirts, stepping into the mud, and made my way across the field. I couldn't get to him fast enough. He tried to maintain his balance, but the horses were out of his control. He was thin, his cheeks caved in. All the physical work should have made him stronger, but he was malnourished. He finally managed to stop the horses. I stood before him. His hair was long. His skin was burned. He wiped his mouth on his wet sleeve.

"You shouldn't be here. There's malaria and dysentery."

"The chagwa killed a man on our roof. Dylan is a mess. We're broke. I can't sleep . . . Your hands." I saw he had deep gashes in his palms from handling the horses' leads.

"You should see Adrianne's from all the churning. We were told to callus ourselves before coming. We didn't take it seriously."

"You need to see a doctor. Off-campus, or whatever you call away from here."

"*Mapacha*. It's a Powhatan word. It means 'before.' I need to finish this field by sundown or I'll never get my crops to market."

"Just come home."

"We die without crops."

"It's a TV show."

He shook his head. "I signed a legally enforceable contract."

He tried to walk, but his ankles turned in and he fell to his knees in the mud. I tried to help him, but he was attached to the yoke. The horses pulled us along several feet before Peter took control.

"Good God," I said. "Why don't you have any help here?"

He squeezed out from the yoke and let the reins fall to the mud. The horses sniffed the bare ground.

"I don't believe in slavery."

"How are the other farmers getting their crops to market?"

"What others do is not my concern. I don't believe in slavery. Not now, not then. It's reprehensible. Red Light! Red Light!" He pointed to an oak tree, where a camera was hidden in the foliage. We were on the air. Peter forced himself up, struggling back into the yoke.

"Good lady," he said. "I would pay you handsomely for a hat." I curtsied and petted the horse. "Okay, we're off," Peter said. "It was just a whip-around."

"Peter. I want you back. Tell me what you want. I can't protect Dylan. Matt and I are so disconnected. It probably wouldn't faze him if I left. It doesn't make any sense, us being apart."

"Wendy—" He began to cough. I felt his forehead. He was hot. His eyes were yellow.

"You're sick. You have to get out of here."

"I'm signed on through sickness."

"There's a hole in the fence. My car is parked on Route 1."

"I can't leave Adrianne and Kevin here."

His life was with her, not me, and always had been. If I had left Matt like Peter said he wanted, he'd have headed for Timbuktu.

"You mean you can't leave Adrianne."

We fell to our knees, sinking into the mud, grabbing on to each other.

"Is this really over? After all this time? Is this really it, Peter?"

"I think so."

"I'll stay. I'll bring Dylan."

"You have to leave. Matt loves you. We're just going to die here." He started to choke again. "Go. Just go. Red Light is coming. I need to work."

I trudged back over the field to Jerry the wagon driver. I climbed up and sat, leaning against a barrel, a maimed soldier returning. Jerry drove and sang "You Shook Me" until he saw we were on Red Light and switched to a Colonial ditty about Mary and her little white muff. In the distance I heard gunshots and yelling.

The production associate met me at the door.

"I understand we have a little slave uprising on Lot Eight. And Powhatans from the west. Thanks for tipping the scales," he said sarcastically. I stormed through the tent toward costume, stripping off the dirty apron and skirts along the way.

"Wendy." Andy approached, beaming with gratitude. "For the uprising on Lot Eight. How can I ever thank you?" He kissed my hand.

Outside the production tent, I got a lift to the road from a soda machine vender.

"Thanks for the NuGrape." I waved good-bye, reentering the twenty-first century. I was well off 66 and onto 495 before I remembered the fence troll's blow job.

I FINALLY DID what I never wanted to have to do. I went to Fidge Ellers's house in Hinton. I'd gotten his number from the girl with the blond roots at the WTO sit-in. "Come on by!" He said on the phone as though I were an old friend who'd resurfaced. Fidge lived in one of the many split-level prefabs on desolate streets that shot up here in the early 1960s, back when Hinton was farmland. I found Fidge's house among the rest because of the gray Mercury Grand Marquis in the driveway. The lawn and garden were groomed. In fact, tied to stakes were some of the finest dahlias I'd ever seen and some of the healthiest azaleas, past their prime but sturdy. It didn't matter. The place said, *Run-down. Depressing as hell. Just get what you came for and flee.* I could hear dogs barking, lots of dogs, and a man yelling at them to stop. Fidge greeted me as I came up the walk. "Nuke's got a pretty bad cut on his hand and he takes blood thinners." He headed toward the trunk of the Mercury. "It's a mess in there."

"How did it happen?" I asked.

"He was holding Bailey's leash 'cause she wanted to get to the pups and Eric let down the gate." He slammed the Mercury trunk and came around the car with an old first-aid kit, a red cross on a dirty white case. Standing too close to me, sweating and short of breath, he drew a diagram in the palm of his hand with his finger. "Leash cut right through." He traced his lifeline. "You can see all the layers of skin, right down to the subcutaneous." He turned his attention to my car. "You like the Rover?" I felt ashamed, driving such a luxurious car. At least the bumper was attached with duct tape. "I got a nice leasing deal."

"I got to get rid of that." He nodded toward the Mercury. "I like the new Trooper. Comes in an off-red I like, understated."

If I go in this house, something awful will happen.

"So you got the beast down there?" he asked. "We don't got any of those problems out here." He was embarrassed of where he lived, I could tell. "We got Neighborhood Watch. The beast shows up here, you'd have nothing but dead beast."

"We have Neighborhood Watch," I said.

We headed toward the door.

"Like my dahlias?" He smiled proudly. "They're prize."

"They are exquisite," I said.

"I had them in the back, but the dogs and kids killed them."

"They are difficult," I said. "Dahlias, I mean."

He turned his mouth down. "Just time-consuming. And you got to use chemicals. I hate breathing the crap. I'm losing interest." He sniffed up some running mucus. I followed him into the smell of dog excrement and yesterday's cooking. Puppies squealed, dogs barked. In a cage under some coats that hung from pegs, a hefty yellow Lab panted and howled. An emaciated black Lab with nipples hanging nearly to the floor paced in a hallway outside the kitchen.

"We're trying to dry her off," Fidge said. "That's why she can't be with her pups. They always get thin like that when they're makin' milk." We climbed over a gate into the kitchen. Eleven puppies, some yellow, some black, crawled over one another in an area cordoned off with chicken wire. Fidge's daughter did homework at the table, drinking a Capri Sun juice bag, eating from a box of SnackWell's. The TV was on, a cop show from the eighties, gunshots and screeching tires. "TV rule." Fidge switched it off. His son, Eric, stood over the pen with his friend. They dropped in a vibrating ball. The puppies jumped on the ball, biting each other on the neck as it bounced haywire. The refrigerator was covered with the kids' artwork, good report cards, a contract between Eric and his parents about finishing his homework on time, a button photo of

Fidge's wife posing with a chocolate Lab, Red Cross certificates for Junior Lifesaving, a magnet with the number for Domino's. Fidge kicked aside socks and shoes in our path. "I'm getting tired of picking up. Everybody needs to pitch in." I looked back at the dog in the hallway. The smell and sound of her puppies kept her milk running.

The girl at the table mistook me for someone else. "Mom's working a double."

"I just came to—"

"Come on in here." Fidge motioned toward the dining room. "Finish your homework, Antonya."

"Your mom is a nurse?" I asked.

"Yep."

"Those are our real heroes, aren't they?" I said stupidly.

"Not so many cookies, Antonya," Fidge said.

"I'm hungry."

"Have something else."

"I don't know what to have."

"There's fruit, there's cheese. And dinner is soon. And—Hey! Hey! Eric, you are being too rough with those pups!"

"They like it."

"I don't like it. I told you it's time for those dogs to settle down. They are going to eat soon and you are going to have them puking all over each other. Miles, aren't you supposed to go home now?" he asked Eric's friend.

"I'm eating here. My mom's not home."

"Oh, right. When I'm finished with this lady I'm going to make coleslaw, so you boys take out the shredded cabbage and wash it in the spinner."

"Why isn't Antonya doing anything?" Eric asked.

"I have a project," she said.

"Do you think you could just do what I ask?" Fidge said.

"I'll get the cabbage." Miles hopped over to the refrigerator. "I didn't know Froot Loops made yogurt."

"What did you say your name was?" Fidge asked me.

"Wendy." I hated the sound of my name.

"That's right. Wendy. Wendy Wendy Wendy. I have to say a name three times if I want to remember it. And then I got to remember if it's in a song. *'And Wendy has dah-dah-dah.'* And then I got to use it in a sentence. Wendy Wendy Wendy. Can I get you some ice tea, Wendy?"

"No, thank you."

"You sure? I'm having some."

He picked up his wet glass of tea from the Formica counter. We walked into a dark dining room. It had an oblong maple table and six imitation Louis XIV chairs. A painting of a girl with a hoop hung above a silver tea set on a maple sideboard. It was a room that was never used, just passed through.

"And you wanted Robacette, Wendy? I mean, Dederall?"

"Solisan." I wished he would stop using my name.

"Oh, right. Solisan, Solisan, Solisan. Do I have any Solisan?"

"You said you did on the phone."

"Don't mind me. I'm talking to myself, what a nut. Didn't they find something wrong with Solisan?"

"In rats."

He led me into a tight smoky room where a man sat on a wooden rocker, clutching his hand in a towel, rocking side to side in pain. A cigarette burned in a standup ashtray. Blood seeped through the fingers of his good hand. He looked up at us, his mouth open but unable to speak. I recognized him immediately.

It was the guy from the gas mains and the waiter from the River Marriott. Mercifully, he didn't seem to know me.

"Let's have a look-see," Fidge said.

The man let out quick shallow breaths as Fidge pulled the towel away from his hand, fibers sticking to the wound. The cut was horrible. A fault opening in his palm. He would need medical attention.

"Damn, man." Fidge shook his head. "Those blood thinners. When was the last time you had your ProTime check?" He rewrapped the towel.

"He needs stitches," I said.

"Nuke won't go to the hospital. Will you, Nuke?" He spoke to him as though he were hard of hearing.

Miles popped up in the doorway. "Is this shredded cabbage?" He held a bag of spinach.

"What does the package say, Miles?" Fidge asked.

Miles read the package and retreated to the kitchen.

Fidge opened the first-aid kit.

"I'm going to clean it now, Nuke," Fidge yelled. Nuke let out a frightened moan and pulled his hand into his chest. "You're putting me in a bad position, Nuke, not going to the hospital. Now give me your damn hand." Nuke shook his head, bending over.

Miles appeared again. "We can't find the cabbage."

"In the crisper."

"We looked there."

"Move things around."

"We did."

Exasperated, Fidge headed out of the room to find the cabbage. He turned back and pointed at me.

"You wanted Tylenol with codeine?"

"Solisan."

"Solisan, Solisan, Solisan." He hit himself in the head over and over. "Find your brain, Fidge, find your brain," leaving me alone with Nuke. Nuke looked up at me, his eyes pleading.

"He'll be right back." I turned my mouth up into a ridiculous hostess smile. The TV was tuned to C-SPAN with the sound off. Congressman Yerolzinsky pounded his fist, making an impassioned plea to ... the show's director cut to the empty chamber ... no one. C-SPAN at its best. A runner across the bottom of the screen reported a chagwa sighting in Shirlington, Virginia. Far enough away from Dylan. Nuke groaned.

"Maybe I should go find him," I suggested.

I stepped quietly back toward the kitchen. The boys stood at the sink washing lettuce. The girl looked up at me from the table. I backed into the shadow of the unused dining room and returned to the den. Nuke appeared to have passed out or fallen asleep. I sat in a rocking chair with a dust ruffle, upholstered in scratchy red plaid. When I leaned back, a footstool popped out. The chair flattened into a bed. I tried to move the arms of the chair forward, but they were stuck. I slammed my feet down on the footrest. The chair wouldn't budge. All I could do was crawl out the side. But the chair was left in the reclined position and Fidge would be back any second. I shook the chair. I pressed down on the middle as though trying to give CPR to a dead man. It was no use. The chair would not right itself. Then I heard a voice I knew.

"*Mom?*" Dylan. "*Mom?*"

"Dylan?"

I ran through the dining room to the kitchen. *"I guess she's not here. Come on. I'll show you where Bobby hid the fireworks."*

Antonya, Miles and Eric were gathered around the TV watching *Harlan*, the episode where Harlan's friend Butch ignites a storage room. I had to get home. I turned toward the front door just as Fidge came up from the basement with a gallon-size Ziploc bag filled with white oblong pills in bubble wrap.

"You're in luck. This is my last three hundred. You can count them out on the table."

"I don't need to count them. Just tell me what I owe."

"Oh, you need to count them. Three hundred is just a guesstimate. I don't want to overcharge you. Go on. Count them."

I looked down at his ice tea on the maple dining room table. It would leave a ring. If his wife were here she would swat him for not using a coaster. I noticed I hadn't seen him have any of the tea. He had carried it room to room, never drinking. The FBI agent in the Armani suit had never touched his ice tea either, while Matt drank glass after glass, gulping it down before the sugar granules had a chance to snow to the bottom. CNN interviewed the cameraman who controlled the lipstick cams at the sting. He'd artistically supplied a tight shot of the agent's ice tea. It was the glass of tea that made the cover of *Time*, put through a star filter, beads of moisture sparkling like zircons. "For me," the cameraman said, "the condensation on the glass put into high relief the corruption, the arrogance, the complete lack of regard for the American people . . ." A few frames of ice tea had entitled him to wear a leather jacket in the interview and spike up his hair with mousse.

"Change your mind about the tea? I'll get you some. You take sugar?"

"I had no idea of the time. I have to go."

"The tea is made."

"Sorry, Dad."

"Lemon?" Fidge went to the kitchen.

"You were right in coming to me, Harlan."

"Is ReaLemon okay?"

"I don't need the tea. Tell me what I owe and I'll be on my way."

Fidge returned. "Well, all right." He placed the pitcher on the maple table. "Let's see. I don't know. I don't usually move these. What do you think? A dollar apiece? Fifty cents apiece?"

"I only have twenties, so here's one hundred sixty and that's just fine and thank you."

"Hold on, I'll get change."

"I don't need change. Thanks for everything." I picked up the pills and headed out.

"Well, all right," Fidge said. "But I owe you. You've got a ten-dollar credit with me, Wendy Wendy Wendy. Or I could pay for drinks one night."

"Thanks," I called from the path. Once inside my car I reveled in the silence, being away from where I'd just been. And my reward from such a disagreeable experience: a surplus bag of Solisan that sat in the front seat like a newly adopted pet. Peace and sleep were on the way. I prayed I'd be able to escape the maze of streets that all looked the same. As I pulled the shoulder strap across, there was a tap on my window. It was Fidge. Surely he'd discovered the reclining chair and wanted reparations. I lowered the window.

"Yeah, hi. You're going to need to take Nuke here. I can't get the bleeding to stop." Nuke stood on the curb, clutching his hand. "You don't got to go in with him. Just drop him off at Our Lady of Incumbency. You know where that is?"

"Not from here."

Fidge moved around the car and opened the passenger door. Nuke slid in. Fidge buckled him in as he gave me directions. "Panorama is one way, so you got to go down to Deal and double back. After you double back, there's a circle. You go 'round. The fourth spoke is Panorama. Everybody gets messed up on the rotary because they don't have faith and they look back and miss Panorama. But if you just stay on and trust that you'll get there, you will. Even if it feels like you won't. Once you're on Panorama you'll see Bonaventure. Incumbency's right there. It's got a circular drive up to Emergency. Leave him and be on your way." He patted Nuke's chest. Nuke moaned. His hand bled through a dish towel with a fleur de lis pattern. Fidge slammed the door and slapped the rear of the car.

I drove. There was no harm taking a hurt man to the hospital. He needed help. But now there was a new kind of silence, the worst, the kind between people. "They'll be able to give you some relief at Our Lady." I had to say something. My heart tapped Morse code against my chest. I thought of prisoners of war in solitary, attempting to communicate with the soldier in the cell next door.

Nuke whimpered as I drove down the street looking for Deal. I passed a one-way street named Pakoma, not Panorama. And then I came to where I needed to turn, which was Decalthan, not Deal. I was determined not to become flustered. I'd drop him off, take a half pill, enough to get home. Once home, I could take a couple more, shower, wash my clothes, nap, figure out dinner. Maybe tonight we'd order Chinese. Up ahead was the circle Fidge had mentioned. It seemed like a strange place for a circle. In this deserted deep-suburban community, there was no need to control the flow of traffic. It was gimmicky, the whimsy of a bored community planner. As we approached, I saw signs that read, YIELD TO TRAFFIC ON THE CIRCLE. A blinking red light hung over the street. And another sign: TRAFFIC ON CIRCLE HAS RIGHT OF WAY. Another sign with a diagram of how to drive on a circle, another showing how *not* to drive on a circle, a red line slashed through the picture. Such a fuss. But as I entered the circle I was nearly sideswiped by a man in a Thunderbird. He blared his horn. I waved an apology and pressed lightly on the brakes. A car behind me screeched its tires. I had to swerve left to avoid hitting a Toyota Sienna with two kids and a husky in back. A dry-cleaning van obscured my vision of the street signs. Cars coming in from one of the spokes didn't yield and I nearly collided with a Chevy Capri. I saw a sign hanging over the road that read, TRAFFIC FROM HATTIE STREET DOES *NOT* YIELD TO TRAFFIC ON THE CIRCLE. I started to panic about missing my turn. Nuke got thrown as I swerved and braked and sped up and slowed down. I tried hanging back to lose the dry-cleaning truck so I could read the street signs but got honked at by a kid in a Mustang. Someone yelled, "Go to hell." A young man in an orange MG with the top down pointed hard to a sign that read, MAINTAIN SPEED IN THE CIRCLE. Then he gave me the finger.

"Did we pass Panorama?" I asked Nuke. He didn't answer. He'd passed out. His head slumped on his chest. Finally, the dry-cleaning truck veered off and the circle cleared of all traffic. I saw a street sign that said Roanoke. I thought since *R* comes after *P* I must have missed Panorama. Then I did exactly what Fidge told me not to do. I turned around in my seat and looked back at the streets I'd passed. I nearly rear-ended a Pathfinder. I moved to the outside of the circle and I was going around again. Nuke woke, weeping, in more pain than before.

"We're on our way to get you help."

I must pay attention, go slowly, not worry who honks, just have faith that the street will come. But the cars from the second spoke didn't obey the yield signs and I was nearly hit by a Bronco. I leaned on my horn and hollered out the window, "I have right of way." The Bronco moved in front of me.

"You tell him." I looked over at Nuke. He smiled at me, his head leaning against the window. I swerved again to avoid a 4Runner. "I like your style," Nuke said.

"Well, thank you." We came to Roanoke and simultaneously we turned around in our seats, looking behind us. We missed the turnoff. "Damn!" Caught in the gravity of the circle, we flung around its axis again. Nearly crushed by an Excursion, pummeled by a Suburban, snapped in two by a Montego, around and around we went. "We must not look back," I shouted. "No matter what."

"But the truck. It's blocking our view," Nuke cried.

"Eyes forward." The truck hung back.

"Here's Roanoke," Nuke yelled. "We missed the turn."

We started to look back again. "NO!" I cried. We stared forward and just as Fidge said, we came to Panorama.

Panorama was shady and quiet and newly paved. It had become dark. I found Bonaventure. By the time I saw the signs to Our Lady of Incumbency, Nuke's breaths were coming slower. There didn't appear to be any new blood on the towel. The cut must have coagulated. I followed the signs to Emergency, up into a circular drive. Out front, the triage unit walked about, smoking, waiting for action. I stopped the car at the entrance. A pregnant woman in green scrubs came over and opened the passenger-side door.

"This man has a bad cut on his hand," I said.

She took one look at Nuke. "Oh, no. No way," she said. "Keep driving." She slammed the door and stepped back from the car.

"He's injured," I yelled through the window. "I need to leave him with you."

"Get out of here, lady." The woman walked away, holding up her hands.

A man in green scrubs saw there was trouble and came over to the car. "Move your vehicle out of the emergency lane."

"You don't understand—"

"No, you don't understand. Clear the emergency lane."

"Where should I take him?"

"The hell away from here. Move it." He slapped the car. We drove out onto the street, new territory. Now what? Nuke's hand was bleeding again. I felt like I was a hundred miles from home. I needed to call Dylan to tell him I'd be late. I drove around the streets, trying to think of what to do. I wanted to talk to Matt.

"Where do you live?" I asked. "I'll take you home."

"I was staying with Fidge and Carolee. But Carolee got mad. She was on nights. I was getting a beer from the fridge. The top broke and she didn't like that the dogs were out when they were trying to dry off the bitch . . ." He told some crazy story I couldn't follow that went on and on. The only information I could get was that Nuke had no place to go and that he was going to bleed to death in my car. ". . . and Shep had the storage padding—"

"I have a doctor friend," I interrupted. "He owes me a favor."
I pulled into a 7-Eleven to use the phone. I called home first
and got the machine. "Dylan . . ." I didn't know what to say.
There was no money for dinner. No food in the house. And
where was I? "Ask Stuart to take you to Andre's." Then I called
Dr. Dave. Ashanni didn't even return my greeting. It took Dave
a long time to come to the phone.

"I've got a problem," I said.

"Yes, you do."

"That's not why I'm calling."

"I think we should talk about your options, Wendy."

"I have a hurt man in my car. The hospital has refused to give
care. I need to bring him to your office."

"I know what you've been doing."

"No one is helping me." I started to cry.

"All right, Wendy. Bring him to the house."

Nuke looked at me closely when I got back to the car.
"You've been crying. Did someone hurt you?"

"I found a doctor." I wiped my nose on my sleeve and started
the car. The rag on his hand was soaked. I drove to Democracy
and down Old Crescent to Dave's house in Edgemoor. The last
time I was here I helped stuff envelopes for S.T.O.P. Famine.
Edgemoor was a beautiful neighborhood, flawless lawns, wide
paved streets. If events had been different, this could just as
easily have been my neighborhood. But now I was out of place.
Dave stood by the curb, his hands in the pockets of his Dockers,
the white stripes of his golf shirt lit up in the night. He saun-
tered over to the car. I lowered the window. He looked in at me,
but before I could speak he noticed Nuke.

"Oh, Christ, Wendy. Get him out of here. Go. Take this and

go." He flung a gray business card at me, turned his back and walked into his house. I looked down at the card. It read, *STAY AWAY FROM ME. DON'T COME BACK.*

"Asshole," Nuke said as we drifted down the silent street. "You don't need him. He's all wrong." I turned the car, right, left, right, left again. We came to a brick facility with a large field behind. Without the slightest care, I drove over the sidewalk and the top of the field. We bounced down a steep hill. Nuke whooped and slapped his leg with his good hand until we came to the center of the field. "DAMN! WOMAN! That was EX-CEEEE-LENT! You got juice!" I turned off the car. We listened to the crickets and frogs. "It's nice back here," Nuke said. "I heard what you said on the phone back at the 7-Eleven. About no one helping you."

"Yeah." I opened the bag of Solisan and took out three, swallowing them with some water from an old bottle of Dasani I found under the seat.

"Got one of those for me?" I gave him the bag of pills. He took four. "What are these?" He asked.

"Solisan. It's a stabilizer."

"Good. Don't like to be up."

"Neither do I."

"'Cept these don't look like Solisan." He popped another in his mouth anyway. I held a pill up to the interior light. He was right. It wasn't Solisan. It was Stimural. The choice of truck drivers and anorexics. My heart began to race.

"I think we're going on a little businessman's trip," Nuke laughed.

"I can't handle speed," I cried.

"You're going to have to ride with it. Damn, that Fidge, always ass-backward."

I dug through my purse searching for a pen and paper.

"What are you writing?" Nuke asked.

"A note. For us. If we are going to speed, I need some reminders." I jotted down three sentences and read them back. *"This is not a conspiracy. No one is trying to get you. You, Wendy Dunleavy, wrote this."* Nuke nodded his approval. "Sign here as witness." He wrote *Nuke* in long jagged letters. I clipped the note to the visor. Nuke started in on the nonsense about the fight with Carolee and the guy named Shep. Then he sensed that I found the story tedious so he shut up.

It was a muggy night. We could hear a stream nearby. We decided to go down to wash Nuke's hand, maybe by then the Stimural would kick in, then smooth out. We walked out into the field. A flock of birds lifted off the ground, turned black in the sky and swept over us. We slid down a muddy hill to the creek. The water was too shallow and rocky for washing, so we followed the creek downstream. We walked through pockets of heat, then cool, until the creek bed became airless and stultifying. My clothes felt sticky. A bug chewed my neck.

"Over here," I called to Nuke. I found a pool of clear water. He crouched on a rock next to me. I unwrapped the dish towel. He plunged both hands into the water. I found another small pool, where I dunked the towel over and over trying to clean it, scrubbing it on a rock.

The same flock of birds flew back over the ravine.

"You're very kind to me, ma'am," Nuke said.

"This is ready." I wrapped his hand in the towel. He winced as I tied off the ends. "The water's not clean. You'll need a fresh bandage."

We walked back, stepping over the footprints we'd left in the mud. But then I saw, superimposed on them and moving in the direction we were now heading, unmistakably, the prints of a chagwa. Birds in the trees began whistling like it was morning, squirrels and other animals shrieked through the woods, and then silence.

"We need to leave here," I said. "Immediately."

Nuke looked at the prints. Through the trees we saw a house lit up.

"Maybe we can get help," I said. "Follow me."

We crossed the creek, slipping into the water and soaking our shoes, and moved through the brush up the hill. As we neared, we could hear chamber music and smell good things to eat. I wasn't sure when I'd last eaten. We heard the low bass of people talking, the high notes of glasses, the triangle music of a fork dropping on brickwork. The woods stopped abruptly. A magnificent lawn stretched upward to a patio with a Venus de Milo fountain. People milled about eating hors d'oeuvres.

"Looks nice." Nuke sniffed the air. We marched up the lawn and stepped through a hedge onto the patio. A waiter stepped up with a tray of champagne flutes. We took one. "Good stuff," Nuke said. Then a waiter with a tray of flat round crab cakes came over. Nuke put a couple in his mouth. "Not bad." Another waiter offered ball-shaped crab cakes. Nuke taste-tested. "The balls are better." Then a tray of Gruyère quesadillas served alongside a mango citrus dip. "I'm more a crab cake man," Nuke said. He waved off the crudités waiter, but I took a few carrots for my pocket. As I reached for miniature corncobs I noticed my fingers were dirty. I pulled back my hand. Then I looked around. I knew everybody. In fact, I knew the house. I'd been to scores of parties here. It belonged to Trip Vernon, the former Secretary of Commerce. His wife Linney was a fabulous hostess. Her parties were famous. Though no President had ever attended, there was always a security check just in case he showed. In the center of the flagstone patio, I saw Birdwell McGrath, the former Labor chief, chatting away with Galloway Bradfield, the former Chairman of the Joint Chiefs. By the dog-shaped boxwood stood Mo Condon, former senator from New Hampshire. Blessed with below-average intelligence, he could maintain hours of superficial conversation. Annabelle Straub, the former senator from Wisconsin, was back to back with Manny Rice, the former White House Chief of Staff. Paul Winterson, the former congressman from Detroit, was held hostage in conversation with Goosey Keegan, the former wife of George Keegan, the former Secretary of State. Bill Lifton, the former Secretary of Defense, feigned interest in a waiter's point of view while it was clear he was just using him for his crab cakes, one after the other popping them into his mouth. "Look over there." I pointed out Sukey Van Hazen, the former correspondent from LMN. I'd admired her when she was on NPR, the toughest interviewer in the business who used her wiles to get anyone to hang himself by the cord of her magic mike. Then she went to TV. Then she went native, showing up at parties like this with the very people she spent a career vilifying. Harold Krane, the former senator from Maine who before running for office taught high school, was by the begonia patch telling anyone who would listen that when he taught Milton he did *Paradise Lost* backward so the kids would know where they were going with all that gobbledygook. Nuke and I edged through the crowd picking up rolled carpaccio and scraps of conversation.

"... no, no, they ship the bones from Egypt very carefully ..."

"... an executive VP who does nothing but write checks for people like us ..."

"... we did a superlative job defending the factories ..."

"... he got so damn emotional losing those planes ..."

"... just say you never met me ..."

"... military industrial complex: God love it ..."

"... the chagwa. You have a greater likelihood of winning a Cabinet position ..."

"... sold the ambassadorship to Belgium four times in the last election ..."

"... tack it on the end of the milk bill ..."

"Wendy!" It was Carmel Blossom, the PR flack from Goodman & Goodman.

"Carmel. It's good to see you."

She leaned close to my ear. "What is this party for?" Carmel got so many invitations she couldn't tell them apart.

"I don't know." An actor dressed in a chagwa suit pranced across the patio, shaking hands, miming imitations behind backs, having his picture taken with Heppy Malone, former White House attorney Jordan Malone's wife, patting behinds. Coolers of steaks lined the edge of the patio. Hunters in plaid shirts and orange vests and hats had been hired to stroll the perimeter of the house. Every so often a former senator would escort an attractive woman to the coolers so she could toss a steak. Smoke billowed from Webers, center lawn, in an attempt to bring out the chagwa.

"It's ... it seems to be a chagwa party." I was shocked.

Carmel rolled her eyes. "Say you never saw me."

"Will do."

I moved aside so that former Congressman Weisbach's wife could get to the steaks. Gigi Weisbach gave me a tea when Matt took office and said she wanted to be close. Former Senator Glock shoved right past me. At the inauguration ball we danced twice. He'd playfully nipped my shoulder when Matt broke in. Gigi flung a strip steak out on the grass and the crowd applauded. "Get that girl a contract!" Senator Glock cheered.

I looked for Nuke. I found him by the fish pond talking to Coco Bradfield, wife of the former Chairman of the Joint Chiefs. I moved over to break it up—God knows what kind of craziness he was spewing—when a scuffle broke out on the patio. Guests hovered around the former Defense Secretary, who had been knocked to the ground.

"For months I stayed up nights in the War Room going over those numbers again and again. I wept for every one of those boys," Secretary Lifton yelled. "Good God, I've got blood on my face. I think you broke my nose."

"You son-of-a-bitch, you've got blood on your hands!" Two waiters held back the former head of Common Cause. Secretary Lifton was moved to a chair. The former deputy secretary of Labor told him to squeeze a napkin tightly on his nose to stop the bleeding.

"I'm all right, I'm all right." He pushed his wife's hand away. "It's my feelings that are hurt, frankly."

"Try not to talk, just hold the napkin."

I rushed to Nuke. He had moved on to Bunny McGrath. She was on to him, looking at his hand and clothes, pulling back from his breath.

"So I had the broken bottle and Carolee was hyped about the dogs because they were trying to dry off the bitch—"

"Bunny, how terrific to see you," I broke in.

Not recognizing me, she darted into the house.

From the center of the patio came the booming voice of Coleman Burke, former deputy undersecretary of Money. Sycophants hanging on every word surrounded him. A man with nothing to say and plenty of airtime to say it, he kept the crowd enthralled. His secret of attracting attention and respect by stating the obvious suddenly dawned on me.

"With eaRRRly intervention," Coleman said, "we can arreSSSt problems befoRRRe they become cataSSStrophes."

"Do you hear what he's doing?" I whispered to Nuke. "Listen. He annunciates his consonants. It's brilliant."

"Wow," Nuke said. "I always thought that guy was smart. But you're right."

I decided to give it a try. I turned to Figgy Kates, the wife of the former anchor of *Newsroom*. "EXXXceLeNT CRRaB CaKeSS." She smiled and moved away. It didn't work for a woman. I came across lockjawed. But what about Nuke, standing here by the fountain, his good hand held open in anticipation of the next lime coconut shrimp? He got the waiter with the good crab cakes in his sights and stalked him. I grabbed him by the sleeve.

"What?" He was annoyed because the waiter had slipped through the California doors of the house.

"Annunciate your consonants." I wet my fingers and plastered down a piece of his hair. "Talk to me so that everyone can hear."

"What should I say?"

"Say you like the crab cakes."

"The CRaB CaKKeSS aRRe EXXceLLeNT. SSuPerrrB. FirST RaTe."

People quieted.

"Do you really think so?" Tokey Lifton asked.

"Say something about problems in the inner city," I whispered.

"WhaT we haVe in the inner CCCiTy is a laCK of CoMMerCe. ABle BoDied MeNNN on the STRReeT with NnothiNG To Do."

"And just what do you propose we do, sir?" Sheridan Yates, the former Secretary of HUD was indignant.

"INNNNDuSTRY!"

Everyone shouted questions. I slipped away to search for a new bandage for Nuke. I bypassed the front hall powder room, opting for the one off the library, since I knew it tended to be stocked with first aid. The library was dark and leather and filled with smoke from a cigar. I walked across the wide plank floor.

"You don't have a drink, my dear." It was a voice I knew, but that was impossible. Holman Greenly, the twenty-term senator, appeared from the smoke, sitting in a club chair. My old friend and enemy.

"Holman."

"Who's there?" he called.

"It's me. Wendy Dunleavy."

"Wendy. Is it really you?"

"Holman." I came close so that I could touch him. "It can't be true. I was at your funeral."

He waved me off with his lobster claw of a hand. "That was a funeral for my leg. Diabetes." He knocked three times on his new prosthesis.

"You had a funeral for your leg?"

"Santa Anna did. I wanted to see who'd show. And you did,

my darling. In a red suit. Shame, shame." He shook his finger, then began to cry.

"What is it, Holman? Don't cry."

"All your misfortune, Wendy. And I couldn't be there for you."

"No one could. Believe me, I know how this town works." I sat on the ottoman and brushed the dirt off my feet.

"How's Matty?"

I shrugged. "It's difficult. You know."

"I've always had a place in my heart for you, Wendy." He tapped against his chest. It made a hollow sound. "Have you seen the latest polls?" he asked.

"I don't read the papers."

"I'm leading."

"But you're not even running. Half the world thinks you're dead."

"They're writing me in. They won't accept my resignation. They like to watch me nod off during arguments. They think my hearing aid and colostomy bag are quaint. They want me to die right there in the chamber, to catch it on C-SPAN, and they will. They'll write me in after I'm dead." He wept quietly into his hand.

I combed his hair behind his ear. "Why not just let her have it, Holman?" I referred to his third wife, who'd been hovering in the wings for the seat since the seventies.

Holman turned firecracker-red. "That Lyme's-carrying tick? How dare you, Wendy Dunleavy? Never. Over my dead body. Not even then. You dykes out to de-limb me like a tree that needs pruning. Traitor! Bitch! Cunt!" I didn't flinch. The Holman Howl was a sign of affection. He took my hand and placed it on his crotch. He did this to all the congressional wives. No one ever complained because it was Holman, and Holman was Holman. It was part of his legacy to grope. "Your tits look good in that top."

"I need to go."

"Let me fuck you, Wendy. Would I still get a library if I died on top of the wife of a convicted felon?" He wrapped an arm around my hips in the Holman Hold, pulling me into his lap, then flung me out of the chair, landing on top of me. I'd been in this place before, on this Sultanabad rug, in fact. The Holman Roll. No one minded. Holman was harmless. I felt full Holman Wood against my pubic bone. He thrust his hips into mine, the Holman Hump. If you think that's harassment, you don't know Holman. Holman humped everybody. Just try to bring charges. You'd be laughed out of any courtroom in America. "Oh, that Holman!" The judge would split his sides on the bench.

"Hump back, Wendy. Just for goodwill." He tried to slip me the Holman Tongue, but I turned my head, took it in the ear. He pulled up my legs, shoved his hand down my pants and began rubbing me. "You can deny everything later." Then he collapsed. A thousand congressional wives, and he had to die on me. "No, I'm not dead." He was crying again. I rolled him off. That was simply not done. You let Holman hump until he made his point, then you let Holman roll off. He lay on his side, his prosthesis twisted into an unnatural pose, the foot turned inward, the knee facing out. We lay side by side looking up at the vaulted ceiling. He struggled into his front pocket and with a shaky hand brought out a baggie of white oblong pills. Solisan.

"A token, Wendy. Remember your dear Holman." I held the bag as though it were filled with thirty precious stones. "Imagine what you'd get for that on the black market."

"Is there a black market?" I asked.

"We're working on it."

"You are dear, Holman. Though I'm sure coming from you there's a price."

"I'm appointing you chairwoman of my library committee."

"Me, Holman? Why?"

"Because you'll get it done. You came to my funeral. You were the only one. I don't need anything elaborate. Just dignified. A place with some shade. An old knotted tree, some shrubs around the entrance. Do charge for parking, though. And require validation. People lose all sense of virtue when it comes to parking."

"I don't know, Holman. I'm honored. I'd have to talk it over with Matt."

"I doubt he'll applaud the idea. Especially when he learns I asked your forgiveness."

"For the gun bills? Who didn't oppose? We stood alone on our side of the room."

"The guns? Pshhhh. I vote no in my sleep. S.7475, Mrs. Dunleavy. Do you know what that bill would have done to my state?"

"I'm surprised you even remember. We knew you'd never let it pass the Senate."

"Matt had fifty-two percent, Wendy. Someone got to Brockmire and the Hawaiian. It would have passed were it not for Dunleavy-gate. And it would have buried me."

I perched myself up on my elbows. "What are you telling me, Holman?"

"That bill could not be permitted to go through. And that Student Council president husband of yours should have known. That's not how business gets done in this town. And the one who knows that better than anyone is you, Wendy Dunleavy."

I got to my feet.

"Needless to say, we never had this conversation," Holman continued. "And you never saw me."

"Holman. Is there documentation of this?"

"There always is, my dear. Good luck finding it. Nobody wants to talk about Matthew Dunleavy anymore. There's only one issue on the mound. The chagwa, the chagwa, the chagwa. I want to help you, Wendy. But I'll be dead within the week."

"You've been saying that for twenty years."

"It's time." He reached up a gnarled arm. "Now come back to bed, darling. You can run off with a conversation that never took place when the sun comes up."

I pulled a chenille throw off the couch and covered him.

"Where are you going?" Holman said. "You haven't been dismissed."

"To the U.S. attorney."

"He'll have you arrested for trespassing. I gave him the job. Don't leave me like this. At least help me reattach this leg. For old times' sake."

When I got to Nuke he was back on the Carolee/Shep/broken bottle story. I had to push my way through the crowd.

"Shep was trying to separate the bitch from the brood—"

"You're calling for a referendum to *dry out the dog,* as it were?" The former Secretary of Money, Carl Hershorts, confronted Nuke. "Why not come out and admit it?"

"Carolee says somebody's gonna pay for this—"

"Ohhhh, put the burden on the taxpayer." Carl Hershorts was livid.

"We need to get to your next *appointment,*" I said.

"What? Oh, yeah. That. Right. Gotcha."

"But you haven't answered the question," Carl said.

"He'll send his position papers in the morning." I moved Nuke from the crowd.

Once by the creek we started to run, our feet hitting the ground in unison, our breathing in sync. Sometimes I was in front. Sometimes I was looking at Nuke's ankles. The creek had risen, the mud covering over the chagwa prints. We sensed he was watching us. I doubt we were particularly appetizing, but meat is meat and we had no headgear, so we took turns running backward. We came to the divide in the trees where we'd entered the creek bank and climbed up the hill to the field, Nuke helping me up with his good hand.

"Feel anything from the Stimural?" Nuke asked.

"Nothing," I said.

"It must have been over the hill and lost potency. I wouldn't put it past Fidge to sell old stuff. Not that he meant to, but he's dumb enough." We climbed in the car and locked the doors.

Nuke caught his breath. "Everybody says you can't kill this animal. I think that's a lot of crap, just a way for the agencies to get their budgets." He gazed over the field.

I swallowed three of Holman's Solisan with the Dasani. Nuke took four. I saw a folded note sticking out of the visor.

"Look at this."

Nuke leaned over and examined the note. It read: *This is not a conspiracy. No one is trying to get you. You, Wendy Dunleavy, wrote this. Signed, Nuke.*

"Holy Ghost. That's not even my handwriting," Nuke said.

"And it's certainly not mine."

"Who would do such a thing?"

"People who want to hurt us."

We turned to face each other.

"The way those nurses treated us at Our Lady of Incumbency," I said. "I can't believe how badly Dave treated me. How could a doctor turn his back on his own patient? What about the Hippocratic oath?"

"That's just it. That guy is a hypocrite."

"All those people at that party who vanished when we needed them, just to protect themselves. All our hard work. We were expendable. They knew Matt was framed. I don't have a friend on the planet. I cannot go through another sleepless night." I took another Solisan. I offered another to Nuke, but when I looked over he'd gone to sleep. Blood dripped down from his finger. I found the card Dave had thrown at me. It didn't read *STAY AWAY* anywhere on it. It was an address and phone number for a hospital. The clinic was Our Lady of Incumbency. As soon as I decided to go to this clinic, I saw that I was parked on its grounds, in the back of its main facility. As soon as I drove up the hill and around to its entrance, a pregnant nurse and a man in green scrubs met me at the car. As I walked up the path, I looked back and didn't see Nuke.

"There was a man in the car," I said.

"We have him," the nurse told me.

As soon as I filled out some forms and signed my name, I saw Matt over by the drinking fountain.

"Darling, get to the U.S. attorney," I called over breezily. "Holman Greenly. S.7475."

"Holman Greenly's dead, Wendy." Matt's voice was underwater.

"You must be hungry." A nurse looked up and down my emaciated body in the elevator. From my pockets, I took some flat crab cakes and the vegetables I'd stolen from the crudités platter. I ate them up for her sake. Vanessa Duane and Kelsey Reisenfeld came running to the door of one of the rooms.

"Wendy! Are you with us in the Sotterburg wing?"

"I don't know." I waved as the nurse led me to the newer part of the building.

I asked about Nuke all the time. During morning run or kitchen detail I'd sidle up next to an orderly and ask what they knew. "Do you remember the night I came? There was a man in the car . . ." But no one had information. I wondered if he got out at the main entrance or if earlier he'd slipped into the field.

"How did it begin?" a doctor asked on Day One.

"S.7 . . . something . . . something."

"What's that, Wendy?"

"Vandals," I told him.

My room had a view of the street.

Book III: Dylan

RAIN AGAIN. I WATCHED IT splatter the steps from the left foot of Lincoln. The Lincoln was my favorite of the statue monuments. Unlike the wheelchair hidden beneath the cloak on the Roosevelt, Lincoln's sorrow is cut into the stone. He says, *I feel like hell, but I'm going to go abolish slavery and preserve the Union anyway.* A breeze pushed water across the concrete, then it rained so hard I thought it would make craters. Two men walked into the atrium with a pair of Jack Russell terriers. They dropped the leashes so the dogs could run. The dogs came over and sniffed and jumped up. The men rushed to me, pulling them back by their collars, apologizing. But I said I liked them. They let me play with the dogs for a while. I threw their tennis ball across the floor. They skittered after it, leashes clattering behind. Then I held both dogs on my lap. I asked one of the men to take my picture with my disposable camera. I wanted to remember the dogs. I held them up to either side of my face. One of the men took my picture. The dogs were squirming, so I held them tightly. The littler dog yelped. Hey, one of the men said. You're squeezing the dog too hard. He doesn't like that. They took the dogs out of my arms. I said I was sorry, that I just really liked dogs like that. They said it was okay, but they needed to get the dogs home for supper and that I should get to where I'm going too. Just last night the chagwa ran across the buried man statue at Haines Point. After all this rain, he'll be hungry, all right, they said. I followed them to the edge of the atrium. I asked if they could tell me where they got the dogs because I'd like to get one or two like them. They said from a breeder in Arlington, but the breeder had gotten out of the dog business, was now doing full-time carpentry and drywall. As they walked off under an umbrella holding the dogs inside their coats, I realized that the men must be gay because everything they said was *we* this and *we* that and I wondered if they thought I was trying to get picked up. Then I wondered, if they thought I was trying to get picked up, why they didn't try to pick me up. I then felt the pocket of my windbreaker to be sure the camera was there, that the men hadn't made off with it. The camera was there. But most of all, I missed the dogs, and despite all efforts to think of something cheerful, I felt only worse.

WAITING FOR her was interminable. Intolerable. I knew it would be a long while before I saw her again, but still I went to the Metro each day at 4:20 when she used to return from work.

I would wait there. Trains would go by, one after the other, and she wasn't on any of them . . .

That couldn't be true. She never rode the subway. I don't know if I was aware of missing her or not. I know I found certain tasks difficult. I could hardly feed myself. The house fell into disrepair. The computer broke and we hadn't paid the phone. There was no gas for the stove. We hadn't paid the water tax, so a man came with a wrench one day and turned it off. The electric company never shut us down, though. Dad had done too much for the utility. So there were lights and TV. I bathed in the creek behind the house. I drank Hawaiian Punch juice boxes, left over from a party years ago. All the sugar made me irritable and weepy. My side hurt from where the chagwa had taken me into his mouth. I didn't know what to have for dinner. I didn't know how to occupy my time or what to wear. My clothes were too warm for the season and I didn't know where she put my summer shirts. But the difficulties were better than a court liaison or foster home. When I heard the advancing footsteps of Family Outreach I hid beneath the couch until the heavy shoes of the counselor retreated on the slate. One day I found my old Magic 8 Ball.

"Should I get the Pizza Supreme?"

A triangle appeared in the little window. "Outlook good." Pizza Supreme it was.

"Do I do these dishes tonight?"

"My sources say no." The dishes remained in the sink.

"Should I wear this vest with these pants?"

"Signs point to yes." And I came up with a look that suited my slight frame.

✦　✦　✦　✦

MORE WIND. I was cold. I could see pairs of people crossing the Mall, grabbing on to one another beneath Stars & Stripes umbrellas, bought at one of the price-gouging concession trucks. The Lincoln was empty except for a man leaning against the statue looking out at the rain. He said something about being stuck, but hell, if it kept the animal away the rain was fine with him. There are tunnels under this building, he said. Built in WWII or during the Cold War, one of those, in case the city got bombed. I went through them when I was a kid. Well, no, maybe not. He put his index finger up to his temple and pretended to screw it into his head. I don't know what I'm remembering, he said. Then he asked if I visited the memorials much at night and if I appreciated how beautifully they were lit. His wife read the Gettysburg Address carved in the marble above, then came over and offered me a cherry Life Saver. I took one. Then they offered me a ride. I got into the back of the car, a Mercury Grand Marquis that smelled like dogs. The seat made a noise when I lowered myself into it, as though it were stuffed with hay. The woman pulled out another roll of Life Savers from the glove compartment. She told me to keep them, she had a whole box from Costco. I held the pack in my pocket, twirling the cylinder between my thumb and index finger. The man switched on the heat. I felt tired, so I leaned my head against the window, looking up at the streetlights that bent over Wisconsin Avenue like the town elders. I stared at the back of their heads, the flesh of his scalp squeezed into a ridge ear to ear. I thought about being married. I wondered what it could possibly be like to have someone you could have sex with whenever you wanted with no rigmarole. It didn't seem equitable that the rest of us had to plead and interpret the encrypted scramble of the porn channel.

We headed north. The man said, Let's stop at the Cathedral. We parked illegally and darted out of the car, running across the grass to get out of the open where the killer could be lurking. I showed them the gargoyle with the TV camera. They said they'd been to the Cathedral upwards of fifty times and never noticed. There's a space shuttle in one of the stained-glass windows, I told them. The man didn't believe me, so we tried to get into the nave, but it was locked. I kept saying it was true about the space shuttle and soon he believed me.

The man stayed outside to smoke while the woman and I sneaked into one of the tombs on the north side of the building. We sat close together on a stone pew and finished another roll of Life Savers, crunching away. I told her I liked the way she smelled, that I liked her perfume, that she smelled clean. She said what I was smelling wasn't perfume, it was soap, eucalyptus. I said, Ukulele? She laughed. I kept moving closer to her, because I liked the way she smelled. I told her it was one of those smells you want to roll up a twenty to snort. She said she'd never heard anything like that before and she thought that I was clever. I told her I was cold, especially my legs. I pushed against her to get closer. I said I liked her hair because it was brown and curled under and stayed in place. I said I hadn't noticed she wore glasses, but that she looked good in them and I mentioned the statistic that said people who wore glasses were smarter. She said she'd never heard that before either. I like brown hair better than blond hair, I said. And again, I said I was cold. I had my legs pressed up so hard against her that she sat sideways on the pew. I asked her if she had on a lot of layers, you know, under her coat, and what the layers were. She said she had on a sweater and a long sleeved crew-neck shirt from

Lands' End. For a few moments we listened to the sound of our breathing echoing in the chamber and watching our breath blow heat into the air, colliding. Then I asked her what she had on under the crew neck.

"That's all."

"That's all?"

"Well, you know . . ."

"What?"

"A bra."

My hand was balled up in my windbreaker. I tried to move her arm with my elbow. *If she would put her hand on it, just for a second.* I thought about kissing the side of her face, or putting my hand on her leg. My elbow was a stump, trying to hook the inside of her elbow. I began digging my arm into her side to get her to move her arm. She pulled her arm tight into her side. It was getting late. I didn't have time for this game. What was a hand job to her? She'd done a million hand jobs, who knows what else. Finally, she moved. But not how I wanted. She put her arm around my shoulders and rubbed my tricep to get me warm. Then she put both arms around me and rocked side to side. It made me furious. I put my chin on her arm, trying to push it down with my head. She held me tighter. I wrenched my hand from my pocket, grasped her arm, and pulled down like I was trying to do a chin-up on a bar. But she was strong. She lifted weights, probably. My skinny hands were nothing on her biceps.

We joined the man outside. He looked up at the building, admiring its flying buttresses, regarding them as great sentinels on duty around the church. The woman said she preferred classical architecture, that she objected to the verticality of Gothic, that the buttresses were ugly, looking as if the scaffolding were left in place. Well! The man said. Well, well! He asked me what I thought. But I was filled with such contempt for both of them. I just said I liked it fine.

We drove north on Connecticut Avenue. You should come out to the house, the man said. We know boys your age. Like dogs? He'd probably been watching me with the Jack Russells. Maybe he thought I was trying to get picked up by the men. I kept my hand on the door in case I'd need to jump out. We got eleven pups and they *allll* want to be held, he said. I said I was tired and needed to get home, that there were people waiting for me. My seat was damp, the smell of dogs so strong it was as though three wolfhounds sat on top of me, panting in my face. The man talked about how the Wizards were cursed, the coaching always bad, how if there was a wrong decision to be made they'd make it, a thirty-point lead to lose, they'd lost it. What were we being punished for? he wanted to know. The Red Sox traded Babe Ruth so, understandly, they were destined to have victory outside their grasp for eternity, but what had *we* done?

"We didn't fight the Jim Crow laws." The woman looked out her window at houses lit up at night.

The Jim Crow laws? The man said. At the stoplight he looked at her. This was the only town with Jim Crow laws? Then how do you explain the success of the Atlanta Braves or, for that matter, the Washington Redskins? The woman shrugged. The man pressed in the lighter. He lit his cigarette, rolled down his window and threw the lighter out. I can't believe I did that, he said. Am I the biggest idiot you ever saw? I just threw the lighter out the window. He stopped the car, backing up at thirty miles per hour. Pulling over, he turned on the emergency flashers and got out, running back to look for the lighter in the street. Cars shot by. Water splashed the windows. I looked out at the man searching the black street. He jumped up on the median to avoid a speeding Camry. The woman glanced over. He bent into the gutter, kicking around the ground with his foot. Can't see a thing, he said, getting back in the car. I'll have to come back in the day. We drove on. The woman reached over and pressed off the emergency flashers. After a pause the man said, I wish you wouldn't do that. You'll attract the police, she began. That's not the point, the man interrupted. *I'm* driving. They became silent. Eventually, everyone hates everyone.

The main street into my subdevelopment zipped past us, the National 4-H, Washingtonian County Club, Ruth Bay Lake. A kid drowned there in 1957. People say they've seen him. They say he walks around in flippers and a nose plug and a yellow towel and a ring. Always in the deepest snow, always in the dark of night. We passed some stores, a Starbucks, a Sunoco. Why don't you just try to relax? the man said. The car became airless. I moved around in the back seat. All these electronic stores, signs in Spanish and Vietnamese, stores threatening to go out of business, identical houses packed in, the strip malls and movie theaters with sixteen screens and not one of the films worth seeing. I moved side to side, door to door. Do you have to go bathroom? the man asked. I said yes. You can go at the house. Again I said I needed to get home, that my father was in law enforcement and strict about curfew. In that case, the man said, I will take you home.

"You can let me off here." We came back to the top of my subdevelopment.

"You don't worry about the beast?" The man asked. "I'm glad to take you to your door."

"Here's fine."

"Very well.

"Thanks."

"You're a terrific boy," the man said. "One of the finest."

The woman's face was wet.

Running down Hemlock the DeLucases' yellow lab, Pip, jumped out from the boxwoods and tried to bite me. He chased me all the way home, barking his head off, gaining on me, never tiring.

"WILL A GIRL love me?"

"Very doubtful."

I hadn't shaken properly or concentrated.

"A girl."

"You may rely on it."

"We're out of money."

"It is decidedly so."

"Should I take the mowing job?"

"Reply hazy. Ask again."

"I need a business plan. Lawns are out of the question. You mow them, you get paid, but then they gotta grow . . ." I should have thought of it before. "Gold Street."

It is said that every Harlan can find his way to Gold Street. I marched up to Connecticut Avenue and stuck out my thumb. One look and they'd take me in for sure, even for a morgue job. Gold Street took care of its people. They'd probably give me something high-profile, like tours. I made it in three rides, all from elderly ladies in air-conditioned luxury cars who said I shouldn't be hitchhiking and "if you're hungry I have Stella Dora cookies in that bag." My last ride drove over the Bay Bridge at eight miles an hour. Cars honked and passed on the right. I saw a bumper sticker that read: GET OUT OF THE LEFT LANE, GEEZER, AND TAKE OFF THAT STUPID HAT.

I arrived to a lot of activity at Gold Street. People moved boxes, exiting the building in tears, blaming and accusing. From the end of the hall I saw Marty Helpern, limping toward me, a cast up to his hip from a waterskiing accident, his face contorted into shock and grief. "They took my show. They took my show." Then I saw Bert, Harlan's father, push through the front doors.

"Dad! Bert! What happened?" I followed him into the parking lot. He carried the contents of his locker in a crate, the inverted Emmy, globe down.

"It's all the bottom line with these new people. You thought Gold Street was bad. I'm out of a job." A new sign was hammered onto a stake in the parking lot: KIRBY COMPANY EMPLOYEES. Kirby. They had amusement parks all over the world. They owned two television networks, beating back every antitrust and FCC challenge that stormed their gates. Recently they bought Machu Picchu. Though they retained the holy ground's beauty and mystery, they installed ramps and handrails, an information booth at the temple and natural snack huts along the way.

"But . . . but you're Dad."

"Not anymore. From now on, episodes take place while Dad's at work, or out playing cards, or on bowling night. They didn't want to negotiate my contract."

"What about the others?" I picked up photos of his real family that had fluttered down to the gravel.

"Little brother Bobby, gone. Sent off to boarding school."

"The Quages can't afford boarding school," I said.

"Full scholarship." Bert threw the crate into the back seat of his Pontiac. "Out of nowhere Bobby's an A student."

"Wait. Are you saying Nora's out?"

"Nah, promoted to Mom after Viveca failed her drug test. Lizzie's hanging in but not for long, the old lady's got heart problems. They won't replace her when she goes. Oh, and now only one Rough Rat for all the voices. And they cut his salary in half."

"Three-quarters of the cast gone? A girl as the rat? The show won't last a month."

Bert lit a cigarette and shook one out of the pack for me. "Don't count on it. You have no idea what the public will eat."

Some Harlans drifted over, Klemmer, Paco, Nat and Anton.

"You heard?" Paco took a Merit Ultra Light from Bert.

"Yeah."

"Marty Helpern. Gone. The McGregor Report. Gone. Chef Chino. Gone."

"Not Chino." I was dizzy from the news.

"*Harlan* took a lot of hits," Klemmer added. "Grandma and Gramps. Who needs 'em. No more bus driver. Crossing Guard: Gone."

"How are the rats supposed to cross the circle?" I asked.

"They just . . . have to take their chances." Bert kicked the gravel.

Unable to move, we hung around Bert's car in the parking lot all day, like those rabbits at the Denver airport who refused to believe their burrows had been poured over with cement, granite and asphalt and lived and bred in the terminals.

IT WAS Paco's idea, but I saw the potential. People wanted chagwa urine to rub on their bodies so the chagwa couldn't identify them as prey. Customers brought their own handkerchiefs. We took them in my back yard, pressed them against chagwa markings on the biga tree and handed them over for money. At five dollars a rag we did well. The day of the chagwa sighting near the Iwo Jima Memorial, we were overwhelmed with customers. They lined up the front walk all the way down to the street. We could barely keep up.

"What the hell's this?" A man held his monogrammed handkerchief to his nose. "It's bone-dry. It smells like popcorn."

"That's the way chagwa piss smells," Nat said.

"You trying to hustle me?"

People demanded wet cloths for their money. What the hell? We pissed on them ourselves. Human piss bore no resemblance to chagwa piss, but they didn't care. They wanted to feel safe. We must have drunk three gallons of Gatorade that day and were up half the night emptying ourselves into detergent bottles to saturate the next day's rags. In no time at all we had enough cash for food. It was Paco's idea to call the rags Chag-Away.

THROUGH THE porn scramble a room full of girls, ten of them lying on top of each other. Four on the bottom, three on top of them, then two, then one. Naked. As happens with these all-girl pyramids, guys come in. And one guy pours champagne over the girl on top. The champagne runs off to the two girls below. And then to the three below them and so on. The guys take turns holding their flutes beneath the runoff.

"To drink from that." Anton and the other Harlans were enchanted. "What I wouldn't give."

Five o'clock. We heard the theme music coming from houses up and down the street. Today, the new cast member. The end of an era: a woman as voice of rat boy. I clicked the remote to PBS. It was one of the too-many episodes about Lizzie wanting to grow up too fast. This time she deludes herself into thinking a group of teenage marsupials want her to hang around. Hardly any Harlan at all, they were trying to break in the new voice slowly. Harlan barges in on a heart-to-heart between Lizzie and Mom in the kitchen.

"Anybody seen my skates? They were under my bed this morning."

"Wow," Klemmer said. "Who goosed the rodent?"

"You're interrupting, Harlan."

"But I've got to meet Larry at the rink in six minutes. All the guys are waiting."

"Maybe if you put your things away like I tell you . . ."

"Mom . . ."

"She doesn't have any of the nuances or subtleties," Anton said.

"She doesn't sound clean," Paco added.

"What's so important that I can't be in here? Is it girrrrl talk or something?"

"Harlan in drag," Klemmer said. "Harlette."

The camera panned up to the window, where a snowstorm was raging.

Harlan's dad entered the kitchen for his last show. *"You're going skating in this weather?"*

"Imagine the hork before that line," Nat said.

"Daaaad, skating is a winter sport. It's supposed to be snowing."

"Daaaaaad," Nat mimicked.

The scene switched to the Rough Rats by the park. They hung around with an older Rat named Pitch and they were all trying to impress him. Larry stood by Pitch's pickup truck shivering, quietly reminding the other Rats he had to meet Harlan at the rink in six minutes. Pitch asked if they wanted a ride. Larry looked at the truck and shook his head. The Rough Rats called him a sissy and hopped in the cab. There was no room inside for Larry, so he climbed up on the flatbed. The scene cut back to Harlan's kitchen.

"I just don't want anyone driving in this weather." Dad looked out at the snow.

"I can walk to the rink, Dad. But first I have to find my skates."

"Don't look at me, Harlan. If you took care of your things you'd be on your way to the rink right now."

"Mom's right, Harlan. Skates are expensive. Why, when I was a boy—"

"Spare me. I'll look in the basement."

We were demoralized and betrayed. The new Harlan had the creamy voice of a porn queen.

The phone rang. Dad picked it up.

"Is it for me? Is it for me? Is it Marcie? Is it Janine?"

"Lizzie, hush . . . yes, this is Roger Quage, Harlan's dad. Well, yes, he's on his way . . . but . . . yes, he's meeting Larry . . . but no, that can't be true, Harlan was just on his way to the rink. No one would drive in this weather . . . but he just spoke with him this morning, I . . . I see . . . of course . . . I'll tell him but . . . it just can't be. Dad lowered the phone.

"What the fuck?" Paco slid forward on the couch.

"Lizzie," Dad said. *"Go upstairs and find your Dappy Doll."*

"I don't play with that stupid Dappy Doll anymore."

"What is it, Roger?" Mom stood up. *"Lizzie get upstairs. Now."*

"All right. But I sure don't like what's been going on around here lately." Lizzie left the kitchen. Mom waited for Dad to speak.

"It's Larry. He was . . ."

"What, Roger? Take it easy . . ."

"There's been a horrible accident, Marjory. Larry's been . . . that was Sheriff Peters. He says Larry is dead."

Harlan came in the room.

"Found my skates." His parents stared at him. *"What? I'm sorry I didn't put them away properly. Next time I will. What is it? Where's Lizzie? What did I do?"*

"What the fuck is this? They killed Larry?" Paco was off the couch, looking for something to hit. "They fucking killed somebody?"

"I can't believe Larry's dead, man," Nat said.

Everybody was up, pacing around, not knowing what to do or what to feel. We didn't know what had us so upset, that they killed Larry or that none of us had been chosen for the *special* show. This was Andy's best work and he'd spent it all on a woman.

"Usually kids don't die, Harlan. But sometimes they do. And it's terrible."

"Why did God let this happen?"

"Wow, Andy finally got God in the show," Anton said.

"God can't prevent accidents, Harlan. But he's there for us after they happen."

"How long did it take? Twenty-five years?" Nat said.

"Don't lie to me," Harlan said. *"There is no God. And if there is a God, He's evil."*

"He definitely had to trade *that* for his severance package," Paco said.

"Don't say these things, Harlan. You don't mean them. You're just horribly upset."

"They should put God on trial," Harlan cried. *"Like all the other criminals. And you know what would happen if God were put on trial?"*

"Harlan . . ."

"He'd lose, that's what would happen."

"How did Andy get *that* by the Fifth Floor?" Anton asked.

"I'm messed up over this." Klemmer was practically weeping. "Is anybody else messed up over this? I know it's a goddamn cartoon character, but is anybody out there messed up?"

No one said a word. We should have come together, gone around a circle and said how we felt, remembering the good things about Larry, but we each suffered silently. Anton curled in on himself on the couch. Paco stared into the distance. Nat pulled his thumb from his mouth when he saw me looking. Tears spilled from Klemmer's eyes. I didn't stick around for the funeral or the inevitable scene where Dad comes to the park to find Harlan on a snowy bench, or the cold credits over black. I went to the living room and stumbled around looking for a beer and a Little Debbie under a couch cushion. There was no longer any place for me. Annihilation swept over. I thought of dying. Then from somewhere deep in the house I heard the voice of my mother.

"Mom?" I called out. The counselor at Family Outreach said this was normal, hearing or seeing the absent person. Still, I went toward the voice and found it. It came from a panel of wall between the range and door to the kitchen. She had always said this was where she planned to have a mudroom built with a separate entrance, for boots and jackets and sleds. This was back when everyone remodeled their kitchens and added on for a family room, the living rooms becoming storage facilities for candelabras and hardcover books on Supreme Court judges and the Rothchilds to be read when things calm down around here and the kids don't want to be with us anymore. But she only wanted a mudroom. The wall gave slightly under my weight when I leaned on it, the drywall melting around me. Plaster encased my arms and held my side where the chagwa had taken me into his mouth. When I pulled back to see, the wall grew a relief of her face. I heard her voice again, but now it came from even deeper in the house, a place I'd never find.

I WENT TO panel nineteen and wept. It was summer. I had nothing to do. I was ugly and small and upset about Larry. The only thing that kept me busy was waiting. But someone to my left was weeping harder, holding back nothing. "WAAAAAAAAHHH," the kind of crying at some point in life we learn not to do anymore. I was amazed by his ability. I shut up immediately. Everyone else quit sniveling and glanced over. "WAAAAAAAAAHHHH." All my usual sympathizers defected. The Wheelchair Man rolled past me. The Kleenex Lady pulled out her stash, sucked right into the wailer's orbit. I stared at the guy, his back shaking from sobs, his face in his hands. Then I saw what I couldn't believe: the Hephaestus hammer tattoo on his bicep.

Rahim Wilson brought up his head, clasped his hands together and shook his fists at heaven. "Oh, Dad. Dad. Why, Dad, why?"

Who the hell was he kidding? His dad lived in Roslyn, came to every one of his games wearing the same fisherman's knit sweater for luck. He'd sit in the bleachers unflinching, his hands hidden inside the cuffs of his sleeves like Buddha. Did Rahim really think no one was going to recognize him? He was a two-time All-American, twice on the cover of *Sports Illustrated*. It was Rahim, all right. Chewing up every last bit of sympathy.

"Let it all out, baby," the Kleenex Lady said.

"Your dad would be proud to have a kid like you." The Wheelchair Man patted his hand.

Peeking through his fingers, he noticed me. He could tell I knew, so he limped over to the statue, sidling up to a guy with a camera bag.

"Look at that." The camera bag man was incensed by the bronze figures. "They got the white guy out in front. It was *our* war. We were the ones stepping on the mines, getting it in the head. I never put my hand on any white guy's shoulder." His wife held his arm. Then he recognized Rahim. "Hey, you're Rahim Wilson!" *Gotcha!* "I saw you against Damascus, playing on a sprained ankle, and you still walked away with thirty-nine points. How's the knee?" Rahim shrugged. "Bad beat about the draft, man."

Rahim started to sob again. The Kleenex Lady rushed over, the Wheelchair man trying to keep up. I could barely stand to watch him blow his nose in the camera bag man's handkerchief, take hugs from the camera bag man's wife. He signed an auto-graph, then slumped over to the POW/MIA booths, dragging his leg. I followed him, staying just inches behind.

"Can I get you some coffee or an egg roll?" he asked the guy selling patches in the south booth.

"Hey, Rahim." They never remembered my name. "Too bad about the draft. Here's some money." I always paid.

"My treat." Oh, big man.

"How ya doin', Rahim." Latticia, the woman in the booth across the sidewalk, leaned out like she was waving to sailors. "I ordered that patch you wanted. Don't know when it'll get here, but it'll get here."

He blew her a kiss. "Coffee and egg roll?"

"I could use it today. So sorry about the draft, baby."

He limped down the path to the concession trucks on Constitution Avenue. I stood behind him in line, staring at the bar code tattooed on the back of his neck, wanting to stab a pencil in it.

"You got some nerve," I whispered.

Pretending not to hear, he ordered two coffees, two egg rolls and a bag of powdered doughnut holes.

"No charge, Rahim." The vender threw in an extra bag of doughnut holes.

I ran alongside as he headed back to the booths. "You really think you can get away with this?"

"Get lost."

"Are there people dumb enough to believe you?" He walked faster. "Do you know how old you would have to be if your dad did die over there?"

"I thought I told you to disappear."

"Your dad goes to every one of your games. The camera cuts to him after every move you make. What if he knew you were here?"

"Get away from me." He started to run, coffee sloshing out of the cups into the cardboard tray. I ran up behind him, put my hand over the bar code and grabbed the back of his shirt. His neck yanked back. I worried I may have really hurt him. He pulled out of my grip, whipped around and kicked me in the knee. I kicked him back, in the good knee. "Piece of shit!" he screamed.

"You're a piece of shit."

He shoved into me. The coffee flew out of the box, the doughnuts bombarding the grass into mushroom clouds of powdered sugar. Then he began beating the daylight out of me. He banged a dent into my rib cage, but somehow I got him in the jaw with a right jab. He fell back. I thought that would end it, but he came back with a left cross to my head that put me on the ground. I rolled onto my side, leaping up just as he charged toward me, and knocked him in the chin with my head. We fell backward on the sidewalk. I saw that his chin was split. He touched his face and looked at the blood on his fingers. I put my hand on top of my head and felt a lump growing. My ribs were bruised if not broken. I had trouble getting air. We looked at one another and then we began to cry.

"How long have you been doing it?" We took the red line to Zenith Heights, each of us stretching out on a bench, despite resentful stares from people who had to stand.

He shrugged.

"Not long. Since the draft." His knee was now replaced with a metal composite prosthesis, his career over at seventeen. He pulled a ball of Kleenex away from his chin and looked at the blood.

"Think you'll need stitches?" I asked.

"Maybe just one of those butterfly bandages. Or if you have a needle and thread."

"Sew yourself up?"

"I've been cut so many times, it's no production. This chagwa. Does he do any tricks?"

"He's not that kind of chagwa." I couldn't stop looking at him. All the games I'd watched and the interviews I'd read, the nights I'd fallen asleep gazing at his team photo, and here he was in the subway seat behind me, bleeding from something I caused.

"He's more the man-eating type?"

"Yeah, more like that." I noticed a new tattoo on his wrist: a medical ID bracelet with RESUSCITATE written in blue.

"So you're the one he put on the refrigerator. Did he bite? What's he smell like? Your dad's in jail, right? How come you're not on that cartoon anymore?" I couldn't believe the person giving me the time of day was Rahim Wilson.

We got out at our stop and raced each other up the escalators. I held back so I wouldn't win. Outside we bought Slim Jims and walked toward my house, looking over our shoulders for a bus, though neither of us really wanted a ride. It was one of those warm late afternoons when the air gets in your clothes and fools with you and the light makes everybody look good. A Trans Am sped by. We pretended to admire it. Rahim looked at the wide porches that wrapped around clapboard houses in the old section of Ruth Bay.

"Why do they call it Ruth Bay if there's no bay? Did they name it after that actress?" He asked.

"She named herself after the town. And it's not bay as in the Chesapeake. It's *bay* as in being cornered and forced to fight. These were country houses in the 1800s and hunting with dogs was big. A guy with the last name Ruth backed a fox up to a barn. The fox put up a fight. For nothing. He should have just turned up his jugular and gotten it over with. Instead he got torn to bits."

"He just didn't want to be made into a coat. Pretty sorry town, if you ask me." I agreed, but it hurt my feelings to hear Rahim say it.

"Does your dad know you go to the Wall?" I asked.

"Hell, no."

"Mine does."

"No!" He was in awe. "If mine found out . . . I'd be dead."

We tore across Ruth Bay circle, cars blaring their horns, slamming on breaks to miss us, and stood in the center by the fountain, out of breath.

"That made jumping out an airplane look like rolling over in bed," he said.

"I thought for sure that Town & Country had us."

A mist of recycled water from the Ruth Bay Circle fountain fell over us, shooting straight into the air, resembling a broken pipe. I expected Rahim to comment. He didn't and I was glad. I wanted him to like everything.

"We can't stay on the circle for the rest of our lives." I motioned toward the most treacherous part, where the cars came in from DC and never obeyed the yield signs.

"Why not? We got running water."

We tore across, howling, leaving a pileup in our wake.

"Why'd they kill Larry?" We lay on the grass behind the All Saints Church. I couldn't remember the last time I'd lingered outside. Not since before the chagwa. The chagwa liked to stalk the backs of buildings, especially churches, where the ground was lush. But I felt safe in the company of Rahim. I looked up at the sky. A microbe limped across my iris.

"The writer always wanted to kill somebody," I said. "It was part of his severance package."

"Severance package. Nice."

"They should pay high school players," I said. "It's not right that the school gets it all, and the networks."

"That old debate. The fat Elvis of arguments. It should leave the building."

"Sorry."

"I just don't want to look back and think I made a mistake by pushing too hard, know what I mean? Larry. He shouldn't have gotten into that truck."

I turned onto my side to face him. "I don't want to think about Larry anymore," I said.

He rolled over and looked at me. "So let's not," he said. "Whoever thinks about him has to cut off the end of his pinky." He drew an invisible line across his little finger.

"Agreed." I felt self-conscious about my sweaty hand as I shook his. But he didn't wipe it off like the girls who got stuck with me square dancing. "What if someone else brings it up while we're around?" I asked.

"They will. That's all anyone's talking about. Larry, Larry, Larry."

"In one ear out the other," I insisted.

"You're sure you're up for this?" he asked. "I'm going to know if you're thinking about it."

I believed him. "I can do it," I said.

"You don't know what you're up against." I didn't. "Lord of the No-Look."

We shook on it again.

THE HOUSE was filled with Harlans.

"The oven doesn't work." Nat came from the kitchen eating a defrosted uncooked pizza.

"We've been waiting for you," Anton called from the dining room, drinking a diet Dr Pepper.

"Some kick-ass scramble," Klemmer called from the library, rubbing his hands in front of the campfire of the TV.

"How can we phone in a pizza?" Nat gave up on the raw Tombstone.

I had trouble getting my bearings amid the commotion. "You have to plug a set into Mr. Lanahan's box."

Blood dripped down Rahim's chin as he searched out the back window for a sign of the chagwa.

"Which Harlan were you?" Anton looked up from the dining room table, where he was reading a month-old paper.

"He was never a Harlan," I said.

Paco stepped up next to us, smoking a Tiparillo. "That's Rahim Wilson, you idiot," he said. "You're Rahim Wilson."

Klemmer came in to gawk.

"Yeah, he's Rahim Wilson," I said, like it was no big deal.

"Too bad about your knee, man," Paco said.

"You got that needle and thread?" Rahim asked. I headed upstairs. "And some matches," he called after me. "And peroxide if you got it."

I raced upstairs. Rahim Wilson was in my house. And he

seemed to like me. My parents' bathroom was a museum of old powder boxes, chalky combs, quarter-empty bottles of cologne, toothbrushes with their bristles bent back and a Pat Conroy book face down and open on the radiator just as my father had left it two years ago. Covering the scale was an old *Nation* with a cover that read "Break Dancing with Yeltsin." How many years ago was that? Bits of fish-shaped soap melted down to finless ovals, tails intact, lay on their side in the soap dish by the tub. The smell of Lily of the Valley, Crest, Oil of Olay and Lavoris saturated every crevice of memory. Everything was as it had been, like a roped-off room in a *How They Lived* theme park. I grabbed peroxide and a quarter bag of cotton balls.

I searched my mother's vanity through scores of old lipsticks, empty pill bottles, pearls that had broken off strands. A tooth. I didn't want to see any of it. Rahim was waiting. I found a quilted pouch filled with spools of thread and needles stuck into their paper tops. My mother sewed well, hems and seams with the tightest little stitches. I liked being with her when she sewed. It took her attention off me. In another drawer I found some matches, a stash of three-quarters-empty packs of Merit Ultra Light and many folded pieces of notebook paper. I opened one: *This is not a conspiracy. No one is trying to get you. There is no committee,* a note she must have written to my father after the indictment. The Magic 8 Ball bumped against my foot.

"Do you like Rahim?" I asked.

"Yes."

KLEMMER FOUND an old game of Chinese checkers that was missing most of its marbles. Paco made a queen out of Silly

Putty for the chess set. The white knight was a screw, a jumbo paper clip served as a black bishop. Nat pressed his face into a nail sculpture that was missing some of its nails, then tried to keep it steady while he turned it around to view his work. Anton worked sealing the Chag-Aways in Ziploc bags, but sales were bad since the chagwa moved south. Rahim came to the door of the library. He'd stitched his chin with chartreuse glow-in-the-dark thread. I followed him out of the room. We stood at the dining room window.

"Let's go out there." He motioned toward the yard.

"I don't know if that's a good idea."

"He's not there."

"He could be. At any moment," I said. We walked out on the deck. I looked all around to make sure the chagwa wasn't waiting for when we'd least expect him to attack. "If he comes back," I said, "don't look him in the eye or act like you care."

The air smelled of plumeria, even though there wasn't any plumeria anywhere near DC.

"You really sewed yourself." I looked at Rahim's chin in the light from the city. He shrugged. We sat on the steps. I thought I saw orange stripes in the woods, but it was just light from the street on some bushes. A breeze blew through, swaying the branches of the biga tree. Then everything became still.

"Have you thought about *it?*" *Larry.*

"Nope," he said. "You?"

"Not once."

I should have had a brother, someone to share the blame. I shouldn't have had to face my parents alone. The whole story would have been different. I was cold and moved closer to Rahim. He put his arm around me and rubbed the cool skin of my arm.

"You're the type who never wears enough clothes, who's always cold and still won't put on a jacket."

"That's me," I said.

The thread on his chin glowed in the dark. My mother used it for a Halloween costume the year I was a toad so I'd light up and not get hit by a car trick-or-treating.

"What are you looking at?" he asked.

"I was thinking I'd like to sew something on me with that thread."

"You're not cut."

"I like the way it looks."

He laughed, but I felt understood.

"Do you like where I live?" he asked.

"Only because you live here." For a while that was all I needed. Crickets chirped. Frogs croaked. A meteorite shot from the left horizon to the right. That could not have happened, I know. There was too much light from the city and shooting stars don't occupy the entire sky. There were no more frogs since the snakehead fish took over the Potomac, and it was too early in the season for crickets. But it was certainly that kind of a corny night.

I HEARD THE shower go on. The faucet in the kitchen sputtered. The doorbell. Someone obscured by packages.

"Dylan, you may not remember me. We met at a stressful time. I'm Ben Sotterburg. A friend of your parents'. May I come in?"

Two guys carrying bags of food followed. Ben directed them toward the kitchen. They ran back outside for another round of groceries. Ben and I unpacked. I hadn't seen this much food in years. There was something different for each meal. Three kinds of cereal plus frozen waffles and Entenmanns's coffee cake and eggs and butter and cream cheese and bagels and three flavors of yogurt. There was everything you could ever want for lunch. Top Ramen, Spaghetti-O's, Chicken Noodle-O's, Cream of Celery, Cream of Mushroom soup, sliced roast beef, honey-cured turkey, turkey pastrami, bologna, sliced Swiss and Lunchables. And dinner! A whole cooked ham, Kraft Macaroni & Cheese, tortellini, chicken tenders, chicken wings, drumsticks, beef potpies. Rocket pops, Chocolate Chip Cookie Dough ice cream, Cherry Garcia, Chunky Monkey, rainbow sherbet and Eskimo Pies. Cascade. Fantastic. Dove. Bounty.

The smell of groceries woke the Harlans. They floated into the kitchen, pulled by the nose on wafts of food air. They ate whatever was in their way. Nat slapped a handful of bologna between two ice-cream sandwiches. Klemmer poured chocolate syrup over Trix and cut off a hunk of ham.

"You're Ben Sotterburg." Paco dipped Sunchips into the blue cheese dressing, a dish of Honeycomb on the side, a burrito warming in the oven that we hadn't been able to use since we stopped paying the gas. Ben had paid for everything. "You wrote *Fourth Down, Time to Punt.* It's my favorite book. I've read it twenty times."

Ben was modest. "It was an essay for an expository writing class. I just kept going and going. Putting a cover around it was the instructor's idea." He liked watching us eat.

Like the other Harlans, I ate my way across the kitchen. I started with breakfast, a bowl of Apple Jacks and a banana muffin. Anton cooked scrambled eggs mixed with chopped-up pieces of turkey and mini-marshmallows. I helped myself to some of those and washed them down with a carton of Yoohoo! Then I ate over to the coffee cake, ripped off a chunk and spread it with horseradish sauce, stealing a bite of Paco's burrito. Klemmer fought for space at the stove to heat a can of Chunky Clam Chowder, changed his mind about heating it and drank directly from the can, asking if anyone minded if he finished the Bugles. I said I would have liked to have had at least one, but forgot immediately upon opening a Toblerone, dunking it into the salsa and wrapping it up in pita.

"Shall I slice the pineapple?" Ben asked.

Rahim was up. He stealthily glided into the kitchen, looked at all the food, daintily picked up the bag of Cheetos and went to sit in the dining room.

"Rahim Wilson, Lord of the No-Look, as I live and breath," Ben said. "Marymount, fourth quarter, five seconds, Our Lady of the Highways down by three. Westerly Hail Marys from the baseline. You throw back to McGurn, a pass so blind one would think you'd been dipped into the River Oubangui. Can you tell me? I know you're exhausted by the question, especially now with what happened . . . but how was it that you always knew?"

Rahim stared ahead, eating the Cheetos one by one in little hamster bites. "It's just having a sense of where you aren't."

Ben knew to stop asking questions.

"The fish sticks are ready," Anton announced. We grabbed them up, spread them with peanut butter and Boursin and put them between two pieces of raisin bread. We ate and ate, long past the point of hunger, morning to afternoon. Fritos with caramel fluff is an interesting blend of tastes and textures, the sweet mixed with the salt. Sardines and jam, I do not recom-

mend. But bologna and Cherry Garcia is sublime. Soon we collapsed on the kitchen floor wondering what had just happened.

"Don't worry." Ben stood over us. "I'll replenish the supply.
And these?" He picked up a high stack of Chag-Aways and
dropped them in the trash. He then unpacked a large bundle
wrapped in white paper from the butcher. "I only ask that you
do not touch this package." We rose up to peek over his arm as
he placed it on a shelf in the fridge.

That evening, we watched *Treasure of the Sierra Madre* in the
library. Ben carried in a tray of 7-UP cocktails and stuffed
mushroom caps. Then he cooked us a meal of short ribs,
creamed spinach, onion rings, home fries and sliced beefsteak
tomatoes.

"Are we eating the thing in the package?" Klemmer whispered.

"No," Nat answered. "It's still there."

"When do we get that?"

"Maybe tomorrow?"

An hour later we were back in the kitchen. Everybody
grabbed a carton of ice cream, Nat and Anton fighting over
Chunky Monkey. We fought over who got the nitrous hit in the
Reddi-wip. We fought over whose turn it was to use the toaster
for turnovers, for space at the stove for Jiffy Pop, for the last fun-
size Kit Kat, for the box of Ritz Bits. Then Paco opened up the
fridge to look at the package. We came over. Klemmer poked it.
Nat poked it. Ben cleared his throat from the dining room.

As we ate up Ben's blueberry buckle in front of the movie,
the chagwa slammed against the back door.

"It's him," I said.

We jumped up.

"I want to see." Rahim headed for the dining room.

"Rahim, don't," I called after.

"Someone needs to throw him what's in that package." Paco headed for the kitchen.

"Man, is he ugly," Rahim said.

"Everybody to the crawl space," I shouted.

"Boys, boys, sit down and finish your desserts." Ben stood at the head of the dining room table with his arms outstretched. "Tonight we feed ourselves, not the chagwa."

"He'll get in the house," Nat said.

"He'll kill us all," Paco said.

"He'll go find a dog," Klemmer said.

"Or me," I said.

"So we have to feed him." The chagwa slammed against the house again. Rahim backed off the window.

"No." Ben slapped the table. "No longer will we feed the chagwa when *he* wants. From now on, we feed the chagwa when *we* want." He made it clear he would tackle anyone who moved toward the package. We stared at Ben, Bogart and the Hustons duking it out for the gold.

No one could sleep that night worrying about the chagwa. We were going nuts wondering what Ben Sotterburg had in mind. Again and again the chagwa threw himself against the house, roared and knocked over the flower pots Ben had brought to spruce up the deck. We tried to distract one another with easy conversation, but everybody was scared and could think of nothing else. Ben suggested a chess tournament. Paco dragged out the table with the makeshift set, the paper clip, the screw and the Silly Putty filling in for missing pieces. It did nothing to calm us. Ben opened by moving his queen's pawn, a conventional opening suggesting a rational series of moves. But his system was anything but rational and conventional. Clearing the path for his bishop, his attack was relentless and savage. He came from all sides, the pieces individually animated and mighty. It unnerved any one of us who sat down across from him. We'd load up the center while he swooped in from the sides and killed us.

RAHIM PULLED BACK the covers on my parents' bed. I got in next to him.

"Try not to think about him," Rahim said.

A branch brushed the side of the house.

"What was that?"

"Don't be so jumpy."

"What's with that guy?" Nat scurried into the room and climbed in bed with us. "He's just sitting there." Ben stayed awake all night, watching the chagwa's every move.

"Why isn't the chagwa leaving?" It was the first time I'd ever heard fear in Paco's voice. He lay on the bed upside down with his feet to our heads.

"Why doesn't he go get a dog?" Anton squeezed in next to Nat.

"What the hell is that guy doing?" Paco said. "He's been watching him all night."

Klemmer burst into the room. "I'm scared! And I'm all messed up about Larry. Isn't anyone else messed up over Larry?"

"Go to sleep," Rahim said.

But no one slept. Every little noise sounded like the chagwa getting in the house. Rahim smelled like paper bags.

The next day was worse. The chagwa was hungry and furious. He broke windows. He paced over the broken glass and roared. He pissed on the house in scatological defiance.

"Why doesn't he go eat a deer?" Klemmer said. We ducked beneath the study window when the chagwa looked our way.

"There's a Bernese mountain dog who runs off the leash in the woods," I said. "That would hold him a few hours."

"What the hell is with that guy?" Nat whispered. Ben hadn't moved from the night before.

"I've had it." Paco stormed downstairs. "I'm getting the package. I can't stand it anymore."

"Oh, no, you're not, young man. That package belongs to me." Ben snapped out of his trance. "Go anywhere near it and you can include yourself in the buffet."

"Would you mind telling us what it is you are doing?" Rahim asked.

"Watching and waiting, just like him." Ben nodded toward the animal.

"Those are some big damn balls," Rahim said. "Shit, he just grew an eye."

"Try not to see him as exceptional, Mr. Wilson. See him as anything but ordinary and you give him his power."

"I'd like to see him with his chest ripped open. That's what I'd like to see."

All day minute things set us off. I accidentally brushed Paco's arm while carrying some laundry downstairs and he brought his fist within two inches of my face. Then he accused Nat of cheating at Indian poker by looking at the reflection of his cards in the window. Anton threw a metronome at Klemmer's head for singing the Lucite commercial over and over. Klemmer ducked or he would have been knocked unconscious. Then Nat said there were signs that Larry was going to die the whole previous season. Paco told him to shut up, he didn't know what he was talking about. Even Rahim lost his cool and said he could tell I'd been thinking about Larry. We couldn't go outside for air. Recriminations and accusations flew all around. Then an argument over who got the better scripts and whose voice cracked the most on his later shows. And still, Ben stayed by the window, never blinking.

The staring match between Ben and the chagwa went on and on. This was the most unnerving of all, the quiet. But it was Ben who held us hostage, not the chagwa. We wanted to do something about it, and we probably could have, the six of us, just stormed the dining room and subdued him. But we were too curious about what he had in mind.

"RAHIM." I MOVED over in my bed and put my head against his back.

"Hmmm?" He was floating around in a dream.

"You've never said my name."

"That's true?" He wore yellow boxers.

"Not once."

"Is that what you want?"

"I don't know." I lifted my head to look at him for a moment. His eyes were closed. It was four in the afternoon. The Harlans napped, exhausted from fear. I spread my hand out on his ribs.

"I'm going to get in a lot of trouble for this," he said.

"I would deny everything."

"You'll see."

"We haven't done anything," I said. Then I asked, "Do you want to do something?" He lay still.

"I don't want to be gay." He moved away from me, pulling up his legs, trying to cover up an erection.

"Neither do I." I looked at his picture in the Our Lady of the Highways photo before everything changed.

He moved so he was closer. We lay with our backs pressed together hard, curving ourselves so that between us there would be no spaces, not being gay or any of the other words for it.

DOWNSTAIRS THERE was commotion.

"He's going to feed him." The Harlans gathered in the dining room.

"Someone should stop him." Anton didn't mean it. We wanted to see what would happen. Ben came up from the basement with the handle of a broom and a piece of meat tied to it on a string. A bloody canvas sack hung from his waist.

"What are you going to do?" I asked.

"Teach him a few tricks." He put a whistle on a rope around his neck.

"I think you're going to die, that's what I think," Rahim said.

"Nothing is more tragic than a life without risks, Mr. Wilson. He'll lie down for us and sit up when we say. When I'm done you'll be able to ride him." Ben walked out the back door, across the deck and down into the yard.

"He's meat," Paco said. We fought for space at the window.

The chagwa ambled over, appearing almost tame, as if he were on the set of an adventure matinee. Ben met him halfway.

The chagwa dwarfed him. Ben held up the stick with the meat dangling. The chagwa sat back on his haunches, flicking his forked tail. Ben lifted the meat higher. The animal rose up on his hind legs.

"Ahhhhhhhh," we said.

Ben blew the whistle, which startled the chagwa, but then he threw him a chunk of meat from the canvas sack. The chagwa ate it up.

He held up the stick again. Again, the chagwa rose up on his hind legs, staying there for a longer period of time. Ben blew the whistle in a short, shrill burst and threw him another piece of meat. He repeated the routine for over two hours, each time enticing the chagwa to stay on his hind legs for a longer period of time. I began to relax for the first time since the chagwa came. Maybe he could be tamed. Ben brought us out of starvation, paid the bills and watched over us as we slept. If anyone could break the chagwa, it was Ben. Rahim and the Harlans felt it too, I could tell because we laughed and ribbed each other and went to the kitchen for snacks. We also discussed the possibilities of having a trained chagwa. Anton said we could put on shows and charge admission. Perhaps get more animals. We could have a program that taught kids about protecting wildlife. After we gave a talk on preservation we would demonstrate some of our techniques with the animals, sit, stay, jump through a burning hoop. Paco said he'd walk down 14th Street with the chagwa on a lead just to show he was a force to be reckoned with.

At the end of two hours, Ben took the chunk of meat that was attached to the stick by the string and fed it to the chagwa. And soon the chagwa rose up on his hind legs when only the stick was raised over his head. When he did this, he got two pieces of meat. Timidly, the boys and I stepped out on the back deck to get a closer look. Ben raised the stick higher. The chagwa did as he was expected and after Ben blew the whistle he was rewarded with a nice piece of raw roast. Then Ben made a circle in the air with the stick and blew two pulses on the whistle. The chagwa hesitated, then stood on his hind legs and rotated.

"Ohhhhhhh," we said.

But Ben did not like the hesitation and did not reward him. Again, he circled the stick above the chagwa's head and blew the whistle. This time, the chagwa spun around immediately. Ben threw him some meat and said, "Good chagwa." They did this several times until it was one smooth movement, the stick, the whistle, the chagwa spinning, the meat. And then, sensing the chagwa was ready to perform with only the whistle, Ben lay down the stick. He brought the whistle to his mouth, inhaled deeply, and let out a harsh blow. The chagwa jumped out at him, nailed him in the neck with his teeth, dug his claws into Ben's side and slammed him down on the ground. No one moved.

"Get the stick," Ben whispered. We sure as hell weren't going down there. Then the chagwa really went at him. Ben put up his leg. The chagwa ripped it off like separating chopsticks. Rahim grabbed the rest of the ham and flung it into the yard. I jumped off the porch and grabbed the stick, trying to bring it down on the chagwa's head. I missed and hit Ben. "In his mouth," Ben gasped. I shoved the stick into the chagwa's throat. He backed off Ben, shook the stick from his mouth, leapt over the fence and took off into the woods with the leg.

We dragged Ben up the steps of the deck. He was soaked in blood. Rahim whipped off his shirt and tied a tourniquet around what was left of his thigh. Paco called 911.

"I think he's dead," Klemmer cried.

"I'm not dead," Ben croaked. "Use my name," he told Paco.

"I need something more to stop the blood." Rahim stayed calm. "Get me a sheet and some towels."

I ran upstairs.

"What the fuck do we do?" I shook the Magic 8 Ball.

"Yes, definitely."

I flung open the linen closet, pulled out a sheet and an armload of towels and raced back to Ben. The Harlans tore around helplessly. We heard sirens in the distance. Rahim took the sheet and towels. I looked down at Ben. He stared at the sky.

"Is he dead?"

"I am still here." He'd become impatient with the question.

"Next time, get a flat sheet, not a fitted one, okay?" Rahim soberly struggled to find the corners. "Push right here as hard as you can," he told me.

"You're so calm," I whispered.

Rahim shrugged. "Stuff like this happens in my neighborhood all the time."

The medics came around back.

"Start an IV of Narcisillin immediately." Three medics loaded Ben on a gurney. We chased them around the house to the truck.

"I've been attacked by a chagwa." Ben closed his eyes.

"We're going to help you," a medic said. "Where's the leg," he demanded of me.

"The chagwa took it," I said.

They loaded Ben in the ambulance and drove off, sirens blaring. The cops and the fire marshal lingered a minute, each of them eyeing Rahim. They walked around the house once and left.

BEN HAD marooned us. We had no money. We were out of food. Night after night the chagwa came, expecting regular feedings. We had nothing to give. He bashed himself against the back door. He roared continuously and tore the back yard to shreds.

"I found some kind of chops," Klemmer called from the depths of the deep freeze.

"Bring 'em up!"

"Where's the National Guard?" Nat yelled. "Where are the cops?"

"Answering calls in Old Towne." Paco shoved the chops through the hole where a window had been. The chagwa swallowed them and smashed himself against the door. Putting the taste of meat on his tongue made him madder.

We crouched in the crawl space off the study, all six of us like smoked meat in the deli case. It was hot. There was no ventilation. Klemmer found the Magic 8 Ball and asked one stupid question after the other. Am I good-looking? Is Anton gay?

"Give me that." I swatted at him, trying to get the ball. He held it over his head and teased me by shaking it in my face when I pretended I didn't want it anymore.

"Move your feet," Paco snapped at Anton.

"My foot went to sleep because your leg wouldn't move," Anton shot back.

"I don't have enough room." Nat couldn't stay still.

"Quit moving around." Rahim elbowed Nat in the side.

We crammed our thumbs in our ears so as not to hear the chagwa rip the boards off the house.

"We're crow bait," Rahim said finally. When Rahim said we were done for, we believed it.

Paco popped out of the crawl space for air. He went to a painted-shut window by the desk and tried to force it open. Then he screamed bloody murder. Golden eyes appearing to shoot through the glass, the chagwa's face stared back at him. They both fell back.

"He climbed the fucking house."

We had to do something.

We decided to go to the Meadowcreek Stables to steal a pony. We had no choice. No one was helping us, the police and Animal Control responding to sightings on the opposite side of town. We drew straws. At three in the morning Anton, Nat, Rahim and I sneaked out the front, Paco and Klemmer distracting the chagwa with some scraps from Ben's roast. We headed down Western to Daniel. On Beech Drive, a car's headlights cut a hole in the darkness. We hid behind trees. Walking across the field of baseball diamonds, I thought of everything we were missing. We should have been doing cannonballs at the pool, popping wheelies and other things happy kids did in the summer, not on our way to kill a pony. Nothing ever worked out the way I expected.

Meadowcreek Stables was dark. Horses kicked the sides of their stalls in their sleep. We crept up to the building. Fear gripped us, but we had to press on. Feed or be eaten. Pick a pony and go.

"Here's a horse," Nat called. "He's awake. He looks like he'd go with us."

We joined Nat at the stall. He'd come across a black stallion with a star marking. But then we saw the sign with his name: NERVOUS.

"Probably not the best choice, a horse named Nervous," Anton pointed out.

We moved on. POPCORN was in her stall, eating. She was a plump, pretty brown and white pony. I whispered hello and petted her mane. She didn't rear up her head or kick. She kept eating. It had to be her. I stepped up next to her, holding a bridle like it was a garrote, and fixed the reins over her head.

"Come on, Popcorn," I made a clicking sound with my tongue.

We petted her and she came with us.

"Here we go, girl."

The sun was just pinking up the horizon. Steam rose from the trees. We walked through the park with a pony that would have done anything or gone anywhere we wanted. We certainly couldn't be seen on the street, so we took her into the woods. To avoid any do-gooder joggers, we stayed off the paths and moved into the brush. If we walked due west, we could stay in the forest the entire way except one street that crossed into the tributary that backed up to my house.

It got lighter. We could hear the garbage trucks and camp buses, kids rushing to their car pools, sounds we weren't a part of anymore. We knew to keep the noise to the right of us in order to continue west. It was difficult through the dense woods. We had to get Popcorn to step over fallen trees, make sure she didn't trip or that a twig didn't snap in her face the way it kept happening to me. *Fwak, fwak.* Nat and Anton stopped to sit on a rock and smoke. Rahim and I took the pony down to the creek. She wouldn't drink until I said, "Okay, Popcorn. Now you can have a drink." Then she drank quite a lot.

"Pretty pony," I said.

"I like her fur, or whatever you call it," Rahim said.

"I like her mane."

"She's nice. Look at her feet, or hooves or whatever you call them."

"Did you know that ponies sleep lying down for only a half hour and the rest of the time they sleep standing up?"

"I'm surprised they don't fall over." Rahim petted her side. "Dylan." He said my name. Heat spread from inside me.

"You can tell what a pony is thinking by her ears," I said. "When their ears are back they're mad or scared."

"She seems to like us," he said.

"I like her." We looked at each other. We knew we wouldn't be able to give her up to the chagwa.

We headed back up the hill to give Nat and Anton the bad news.

We found our footprints in the mud. But on top of our footprints and heading up the hill we saw, unmistakably, the prints of the chagwa. The sounds of the forest shut down. Rahim and I clung to the pony. Nat and Anton flipped out, trying to climb on top of each other.

We used the pony as a screen, shuffling in a huddle beside her, but on which side were we supposed to be?

"How did he find us?" Anton whimpered.

"He didn't find us," I said. "We came to him." That's the secret of the chagwa. He depends on the stupidity of his prey.

He'd been watching us the entire time. Why didn't he just come out and take us down by the creek or Nat and Anton while they smoked on the rock? Why does he wait? Because meat was tastier when marinated in fear. Fear was gravy to the chagwa.

"We give him the pony and run," Nat said. "I know everybody's in love with the damn pony, but we're turning her over. There's enough meat here for a week."

"I'm not giving him the pony," I said.

"I don't think any of us is going to have a choice," Rahim said. "He'll take what he wants to take."

Everywhere we looked, every turn we made, we saw him, the light and dark of the forest evolving into stripes, his outline blending, then spots coming into focus, then the whole animal, leaping out and charging.

He never came out that day, but we knew he was near. And here we were with this fine pony. But he didn't want her either. That was more frightening than the times he'd treed me on top of the fridge, or surrounded the house, or ate Ben's leg, or showed his face in the window. At least then I could see him and I knew what he was.

It was late morning when we came into Meadowcreek. Imagine being relieved to see cops waiting for you. And there certainly were a lot of them. Three cars, six cops, plus a crowd of civilians. Apparently, we had made a little girl unhappy when she came down to muck out her pony's stable. Waah, waah, waah. The mean stable girls stood shaking their heads, crossing their arms, satisfied.

The cops were roughest with Rahim. They bent him over the hood of one of the cars, demanding ID that he didn't have, convinced he had dreamed up the scheme, luring the rest of us from good homes. But then one of the cops recognized him and they started talking about the Wilkes-Barre game and how Jason Rabley was a crybaby and Coach Boyle was ruining the game. Still, they cuffed him and put him in the car. They were going on about player salaries as they slammed the doors. Anton, Nat and I went in the other car, but they didn't bother with the cuffs. The cops in our car thought the whole deal was kind of funny, stealing a pony. They'd done some crazy things when they were kids too. And when we told them we were Harlans they nearly jumped out of their blues. Their kids loved *Harlan*, hell, they watched it themselves, don't tell anybody. "For the family values," one cop said. It was a nice ride downtown. We were going to jail, but felt fine, lighthearted, in fact. It was the only safe place in town, after all. We'd get to jail, meet up with Rahim and they'd give us some lunch. For free. I turned around in my seat to give a thumbs-up to Rahim, but his car made a sharp turn left and our car kept straight.

"Where are they going?" I asked. But the cops stayed quiet all the way into the lot of the Noam County Juvenile Detention Center. Rahim was seventeen. He would be tried as an adult. This would trigger a competition among state's attorneys everywhere to see who could try the youngest person in adult court. The winner was Crike County, Virginia, where a nine-and-a-half-year-old boy was accused of grand theft auto. Rahim and I were going to different places.

"YOU BOYS are in luck." A stout cop, his forehead squeezed into permanent ridges from saying, "Next time I recommend the high road," every day, delivered the news. Someone had come for us. But what was so lucky about being sprung from well-lit rooms and a balanced lunch of pizza squares, green beans, apple juice and a granola bar? This was better than anything we had scraped up on our own. There was foosball and TV and there were well-meaning people who wanted to help set us on the right course. We even liked the classes.

"And what are some of the results you can expect from making poor choices? Nat?"

"Um, jail?"

"Good. How about you, Anton?"

"Not living up to your potential?"

"Superb. Dylan?"

"Uh . . . you don't get to vote?"

"Right on. Not being able to enjoy the liberties that others enjoy."

The chagwa was someone else's problem. The house would be taken by the state. So when the ridge-foreheaded cop came to say someone had bailed us out, our hearts sank.

He led us from the rec room down the corridor, past the cashier toward the waiting room and through a door with a glass window filled with chicken wire. When we saw who was waiting for us, we just about lost our hot lunch.

"Who called him?"

"Did you call him?"

"I didn't call him."

We tried climbing over each other to get back into the lockup, but the cop stretched out his arms to keep us going in the right direction. That face pasted together with spit and glue. That horrible smile reserved for driving off bridges. Billy. The Driver. The old feelings swept over us like an asbestos shower: vertigo, terror, hives.

"You boys don't look happy to see me."

"Oh, no, Bill," Nat said. "We're really happy to see you." We shuffled our feet toward freedom.

"It was decent of you to bail us out," Anton chimed in. "Gold Street really does take care of its people."

"I don't work for Gold Street no more." Billy had a way of smiling sometimes where he would turn his mouth down instead of up, all the dried riverbeds of his face emptying into his chin. "And I didn't bail you out."

"You didn't?"

"Nuuupe."

"Who did?"

He pointed to the men's room. The door opened. Out stepped a man in a bomber jacket, black boots, aviator sunglasses and a green shirt. My father. Released eight months early for a family emergency. What I wouldn't have given to be driving off a bridge right then with Bill.

"LINE UP, men." Paco and Klemmer dashed out of the house with several bags of garbage and stood side by side at attention. My nostrils burned from the smell of ammonia. Billy perched my old hockey stick on his shoulder like a crop. Anton, Nat and I took our places next to Paco and Klemmer, looking up and down the line for someone to explain what the hell was going on. But we had to stand in formation and wait. We waited for a long time. Then Dad walked up and down the line inspecting us. I didn't dare look directly at him. Billy tried to walk the line in the opposite direction. When they met in the middle, they stepped side to side trying to get around each other. Dad huffed in frustration.

"Any one of you have summer employment?" Dad asked.

"Yes, sir." Klemmer raised his hand.

"And what is your summer employment?"

"Mowing lawns, sir."

"And why aren't you mowing lawns today?"

Klemmer muttered something.

"What did you say?" Billy screamed in his face.

"Gotta wait for the grass to grow. Sir!"

"YOU GOTTA *WANT* THE GRASS TO GROW NOW, DON'T-CHA? DROP AND GIVE ME A HUNDRED," Billy yelled.

A hundred what?

Klemmer dropped to the grass, did three push-ups with his ass in the air, then fell to the earth.

"Good work," Dad said.

"Thank you, sir."

"You just bought your company one hundred push-ups," Billy said. "Drop." We looked at one another in shock and then did as we were told.

"In *unisom!*" Billy yelled.

"Do the ones we already did count?" Anton asked.

"NO," Billy shouted. "You gotta start from the beginning."

We began, everyone doing his own version of a push-up. Anton pushed his body up with his knees on the ground until Billy came around and kicked his arms out from under. Nat bent his body into an isosceles triangle. Paco managed to keep his toes curled under and his body off the ground, but he moved up and down only an inch. And Klemmer was just stuck, flat on the ground, his elbows pointing up like a cricket. I got to twenty when my arms began to shake. By twenty-six, I was paralyzed. Everyone writhed on the grass, clutching his arms.

"Pathetic," Billy said. Then he barked nonsense orders. We were completely confused, looking to one another to see if anyone understood, until Dad interrupted.

"Relax, boys. You won't be doing any more push-ups." We sighed. Dad would protect us from this sociopath.

"Yeah, no more push-ups," Billy repeated. "Roll over on your back and give me leg lifts."

We looked at Dad. He pushed his aviators up on his nose, turned and walked into the house. We were really in for it.

"WHAT DID I JUST SAY?" Billy put his face into each of ours. "TWELVE INCHES OFF THE GROUND, TWO INCHES OFF THE GROUND. TWELVE, TWO, TWELVE, TWO." Nat lifted his left foot, keeping his right on the ground. I thought Billy would take his limbs off. "DIRT BAG GOLD BRICK CHERRY! BOTH LEGS! ONE, TWO, ONE, TWO, ONE, TWO."

I saw Mr. Lanahan pull down a slat of his blind. We got through fifteen leg lifts before our stomach muscles gave out.

"Roll over and give me fifty," Billy yelled.

"I thought we weren't going to have to do any more push-ups," Klemmer said.

"One hundred," Billy said.

"But Mr. Dunleavy said—"

"One-fifty."

"Shut the hell up, Klemmer," Anton whispered.

"Two hundred. And this time you'll stay down until you've done two-fifty."

"What happened to two hundred?"

"Three hundred."

"You dumb fuck, Klemmer," Paco said.

Three hundred and fifty push-ups. It took over four hours to finish. Billy kicked Anton's knees and Klemmer's sides. He stepped on Nat's ass and Paco's back. And to me, just whisperings: "Got a bridge to show you, Rat Boy." When it was over we turned onto our backs, looking into the sun. Now would be a good time for the chagwa to take us, I thought. But he'd packed his things and headed out. We had nothing more to offer. Our bones and sinew didn't interest him.

Dad came out front. "What do you say, Bill? Next stop barbershop?"

We marched inside. A hard-backed chair was in the center of the living room, a broom and dustpan leaning against the wall and, plugged into an outlet, electric clipping sheers.

"When hell freezes." Anton touched his shoulder-length curls. "I'm going home." He turned to leave. Dad blocked the door.

"I'm afraid not. See, I've spoken with your parents and the judge of the Superior Eighth District Juvenile Court. You belong to me, now." Anton tried moving around him. "Go ahead. Give it a try. I promise you will be turned right around or taken back into custody. And this time it will not be so easy for you. No games, no classes. Atkin." Atkin Correctional. Nothing scared us like Atkin. Atkin was for the big guns. Everything unimaginable went on behind corroded bars and in underground laundry rooms. Our crime wasn't big enough for Atkin, but anyone could end up there on a technicality. And these days, technicalities came like junk mail.

Billy revved the clipping sheers engine.

"I almost forgot." Dad turned on the stairs. "Mr. Klemowitz. You are free to go."

"Me?" Klemmer asked.

"Tomorrow you turn eighteen."

"I do?"

Klemmer didn't try to figure out his good fortune. He got to keep his hair and never do another push-up. He dashed out, stopping only to pick up his lawn mower, parked in our driveway. Then he hopscotched his way into the yonder. The last we heard, he left the city and went south, following the endless lawn. By November he'd mowed his way down to Florida.

Nat went first. In three swipes his hair was gone. He looked like a big baby, with his puffy cheeks and little pig eyes. Then Paco, who looked better with a bald head, punk, in a way, and he had a nice scar above his left ear from cracking his skull on a diving board. Then me. I didn't look in the mirror. I knew I looked like a zucchini. That left Anton. He sulked over to the chair, his shoulders pulled all the way up.

"Can you leave a little in the back?" He asked.

"Sure," Billy said.

In less than a minute, he had no hair. Tears streamed down his face. For the rest of the day and well into the next, he kept putting his hand up to his ears, twirling his fingers around a ghost on his shoulder and squeezing phantom locks in his palms.

We got clothes. Billy handed out stacks of Gap T-shirts, Gap fatigues, Gap socks, Gap sneakers and hooded gray sweatshirts with GAP written across the chest.

"I hate the Gap," Nat said. That bought us two hundred more push-ups. And since we couldn't even vaguely do ten, we had to run in place for twenty minutes with our arms extended. Then it was time for dinner.

Dinner was good and there was a lot of it. Dad cooked steak and roasted potatoes, sautéed peas, mashed turnips, green salad, wheat bread and peach cobbler. We ate it all up. Nat worried he'd be hungry later, so he sneaked a handful of mashed turnips in his sweatshirt pocket. The rest of the night was spent learning how to make a bed properly, even if your bed was the couch or a sleeping bag. After that, we sat around my room comparing blisters while Dad and Billy went to bed.

"All this for stealing a pony." Flat-footed, the bottoms of Nat's feet were one large blister. "And the chagwa's not even here anymore."

"It's only going to get worse." Paco lay on the bed and smoked.

"Does my hair look bad?" Anton asked.

"Why do they make us run everywhere, and what's the deal with all the push-ups?" Nat said.

"Klemmer got off," Paco said.

"Where is Rahim?" I wanted to know.

"Your dad got mean in the clink, Dylan," Paco said. The Harlans looked at me as though it were my fault. I felt embarrassed to be related.

"The state's attorney would be overjoyed to try any one of you as an adult." My father stood at the door. "I understand they are reimplementing the chain gang." He balled up his hands in the pockets of his Gap sweatshirt. We thought we were really going to get it now. But he turned and went across the hall, into the room he had shared with my mother, the bed I had climbed into after nightmares.

The Harlans limped off. My side hurt.

"Will I survive this?" I asked the Magic 8 Ball.

"Very doubtful."

AT FOUR A.M. Billy woke us, screaming. He told us to get dressed, make our beds and meet him in front of the house. Double-time. We followed the orders, breathless from having risen up out of unresolved dreams, a girl just opening her legs, a dead relative in midsentence, "You must know—" Grandmother began, and never got to finish because Billy cut in.

"OUT OF THE SACK, RAGBAG." Right between the eyes. Why do some people have more spit than others?

The night had done nothing to cool off the day. It would be sweltering by noon. We shook out our feet to limber up. Then we had to run three miles with Billy chanting stupid rhymes that we would have to echo to keep us in rhythm, pushing himself along on a razor scooter.

"My girl's always on the rag."

"My girl's always on the rag."

"She's a honkin' mean old hag."

"She's a honkin' mean old hag."

Cursing the daylight, I dreaded the idea of anyone seeing us. But galloping up Cyprus Street was none other than the Lowry girls' cross-country team, ripping pieces of Kubic Kumquat from an orange rod of gum. An impression of a gang of sleek elk whisked by as we lowered our heads mumbling Billy's, "Two old ladies lyin' in bed. One rolled over to the other one said . . ."

Home from the three-mile run, breakfast was waiting. It was

good and there was a lot of it. Dad made scrambled eggs, sausage links, pancakes, Cream of Wheat and Danish pastries. We had to eat it all. I wasn't used to eating so much. And right after breakfast we had to do two hundred push-ups because Nat hadn't pulled his sheets tight enough.

"Sorry," Nat whispered to us.

"Sorry?" Billy wailed. "Sorry comes between shit and syphilis in the dictionary."

"Not right in between," Nat pointed out. "There are many other words too."

Three hundred push-ups.

Then we had to march. This time in broad daylight, ninety degrees, ninety percent humidity, singing Billy's preposterous rhymes.

"See the naked and the nude."

"See the naked and the nude."

"Dance in solemn solitude."

"Dance in whuh? What? Solemn what?"

Our rhythm destroyed, we had to drop for a hundred push-ups right down on the asphalt of Wyngate Road. Our hands ragged and bloody, Billy then marched us by Meadowcreek, where the stable girls had gathered to jeer.

After the run there was lunch. Again, it was good. Again, there was a lot of it. Over the next few days we came to dread the meals. Not just the food, which was too much and made us full and sleepy and the push-ups more demanding, but the whole atmosphere of *mess*. It was tense and strict. We weren't allowed to talk and we had to sit still and we had to eat every crumb on our plate. I made a decision that I would never call the dining room the mess. The dining room with its harvest table where my mother tossed her keys, losing them when they slid off the other side, where she threw her coat, never hanging it up, where the bills stacked up, where sometimes there was fruit in a bowl, would never be called the mess.

"Like it?" I reached out for Rahim in a black vinyl Our Lady of the Highways team uniform . . .

"GET YOUR LAZY ASS UP OUTSIDE O-FIVE-MINUTES SOLDIER!"

No, no, no. But finishing your dreams meant leg lifts, running in place, marches in the heat. And push-ups. More push-ups. We did them in the mud and on the hot cement. We did them when we did something wrong. We did them when we did everything right. Everything hurt. Swallowing hurt. Blinking hurt. My arms throbbed in constant pain. They hurt so much I couldn't raise them. In the shower, I couldn't lift them to wash myself. I had to pour liquid soap into the tub and roll in it. I couldn't jerk off. My dreams were feverish teases and Billy screaming it all away. In the middle of an airless night, I sneaked out.

I found the woman from the Cathedral at the Einstein monument, as incongruous as retrograde orbit. Sniffing the air for cigarettes, I could smell that the man was nowhere around. I moved right in, pushing her onto Einstein's shin. A marble horoscope spread out before him on the ground. I balanced myself atop his right foot that rested on Bootes and Hercules, a fold of his pants digging into my knee. I lifted her skirt, moving her underwear aside. She put her hands all over me, said, Oh, your body, oh, you're strong, which she couldn't have meant but said to keep my erection when I could not. She rubbed it between her palms like she was shaping onion rolls, she spit in her hands, she slid down the legs of the statue and opened her mouth. She even turned around, bending over a deck of papers on photoelectric effect. My dick turned and ran, up into the cavity of my body. Stepping back on an equation and zipping my pants, I told her she was beautiful but I had an early meeting.

"Rahim ..."
"SHIT SACK OUT OF BED DOUBLE-TIME TWO HUNDRED PUSH-UPS TWO-MILE RUN TEN-MILE MARCH."

ANOTHER ATTACK. Behind the old post office. Blood still oozed from gouges in the fresh kill of a concession truck owner. The body was still intact. The chagwa had dragged him into the alley, intending to come back later for the meal. SWAT teams stood ready. But the animal would know better than to show up where he was expected. Candy wrappers and empty doughnut hole packages fluttered above the city, some hovering high enough to ground planes at Reagan National. Some caught a wave that landed them in front yards as far away as Richmond.

WHEN THERE was down time in the evening, we were told to write letters to our families. I didn't want to write to my mother. But not doing something brought attention to yourself and the last thing you wanted to do was stick out. So I wrote. At first nothing more than how are you, I am fine, 'bye. But then I got a letter back and I saw her handwriting and I remembered her. Dad and I were told that we were not allowed to give my mother any bad news so as not to make her downhearted. And

Dad told her that while we were "training" she couldn't give me any bad news so as not to make me downhearted. The rules left little to say. So we came up with a code. We found that if we simply placed an exclamation point at the end of a sentence, even the dreariest topics came across as cheerful.

Dear Mom,
   The mail just came with your letter! And a lot of catalogs! So many! What a waste! What a colossal waste of time this is! I got a haircut! I am bald! I think you are really going to like it!
   Love, Dylan

Dearest Dylan,
   I adored your letter! I hung on every word! I am lonely as a castaway! Guess what?! Last night I had a fever! Like a little kid! Can you believe it?! After all this time I'm still detoxing! Of all the silly things! It's OK cuz there are a lot of friends from the old days right here at Incumbency! They liked Solisan too! What a mess I made of my life and yours! Dad cut off all your hair?! Your beautiful hair! He says, "I know what I'm doing, Wendy! I have good reasons for such training! I wish I'd had it at his age!" Can you believe he's a liberal Democrat?! Or was, who knows! But it all sounds like fun! Love you! Love you so much I can barely stand it! Any sign of the chagwa?! How is your side?!
   Smiles and kisses, Mom

Dear Mom,
   Last night Billy pulled us out of bed at 4 a.m. and had us do push-ups in the rain! Today we had to build a 20-foot-high wall in the back yard! Again, in the rain! You should have seen the pile of bricks dumped

in the driveway! Mr. Lanahan was furious! Dad took care of him! Anyhoo, we built the wall! It was lopsided and when we tried to climb it, it fell into a zillion pieces! Oh, you can imagine we got a few push-ups for that! Dad says we have to build it again and again until we get it right! My side still hurts! Save me! Can you?! Remember that game we used to play where I'd turn all around under the covers and you'd have to guess where I put my head?! How was it that you always knew?! No sign of the chagwa! But the police and Animal Control have begun searching door to door! No knock or warrant necessary! Cool, huh?!

Love, Dylan

Darling Son,

Push-ups at 4 a.m. in the rain! Heavens! I'm going to have a talk with that Dad of yours, you can be certain of that! And a brick wall in my yard! That ought to be a sight! I guess you're glad the chagwa's not there to pester you! I keep checking the papers and listening to the radio for sightings! My roommate, Ronnie (you remember Ronnie Presido, she taught calc one year at Lowry) let me keep her radio when she left! You'd think with all the intelligence and expertise in this country we could find one measly chagwa! It's not exactly like he blends! I think about the danger I put you in! I should have killed him myself! So many regrets, Dylan! I have to piece everything together! The hard part begins now, as the shrinks say when they've run out of answers!

Of course I remember the covers game! I'd give a limb and an organ to be able to play that game with you right now! How did I always know where your head was?! Let's begin with BECAUSE I'M YOUR MOTHER!

Only smiles, Mom

P.S. I'm doing everything in my power to save you!

Dear Mom,

The wall collapsed again in the storm last night! All that work! Boy, there's a lot of mud in the back yard! At least I think it's mud, I hope it's mud, because we've logged about a thousand hours of low crawl in it and don't forget, we did have a 500-pound animal living back there, if you know what I mean! Then chow! Eggs! Bacon! Help! Oatmeal! Danish! Help! Fruit! Toast! Cottage Cheese! Help! Today, the wall went back up! But this time, everybody helped everybody and we worked as a team! Nothing beats teamwork!

Love, Dylan

Precious Dylan,

You must be pleased about the wall! Fifty lashes to your lousy father for making you do calisthenics in the rain! You'd think he'd want to make up for lost time by taking you to a baseball game! Or out to lunch! Anything! I've written Social Services! I'm trying to get help! It's hard to work the system when you are in the system but I am doing all I can! Please believe me! Today in group we talked about something called the double bind! Apparently I'm in it! Amazing how your life can just go to hell. Boy, I've sure got some pent-up rage!

Love, Mom

That was the last letter. She left off the exclamation point after *hell*. Dad went back over the letters, broke the code and wouldn't give me any more. It was just as well. The letters made me feel worse. Sure, mail call was hard when everybody else got letters, but it was better to just not think of her at all. Dad stood over me as I wrote:

Dear Mom,

I'm keeping a positive attitude regarding the push-ups and leg lifts. They are making me stronger. You would be proud of how positive I am. We finally got the wall right and every day we try to climb over. None of us has made it over yet, but we will. The ropes have been wet with all the rain and that is hard on our hands but I remember that everything we do is designed to make us stronger.

Your son,

Dylan

The less we expected, the better. We could do nothing to please my father or Billy, so we just did as we were told. Nothing more. We were told there would be no more low crawl and the next day we'd be in the dirt with hoses pointed at our heads. We learned to never expect privileges even if they were promised because we would only be disappointed. If something good came, like a trip to Ben & Jerry's for banana splits, fine. If not, fine. They'd use the phone and desserts and movies as something to motivate us. Then they'd make up a reason not to let us have them. Don't be happy, don't be sad. Cry and you're dead. Which arm, how many.

Dear Mom,

We made it over the wall today. All of us. After that, we each carved our name into a brick. Mine is eight from the left, twelve from the bottom. I think you are really going to like it.

Yours,

Dylan

The image of my mother no longer existed. Only the image of the wall where she'd wanted the mudroom. I looked back as I left the house to go to the supercans one evening and saw Billy painting over it, smiling wide enough to blind me with a gold molar. So what? I had enough to keep me busy. I carried out the Hefty bags, enjoying the pink sky through the trees and the quiet. I was surprised to see Dad waiting for me at the supercans.

"The meetings with the woman at the memorials." He took the bags from my hands because I had suddenly become too weak to lift them. "They stop. Stop now and you get a pass. Continue and things will become very difficult for you."

I didn't know how much he knew, but *that* he knew made me want to die. And the thought of Billy watching. I wondered if he knew I was unsuccessful.

THE NEXT day we had a ten-mile march. The heat and humidity were off the charts. Mosquitoes chewed on our necks. Our blisters popped and reformed. Our chagwa headgear melted and stuck to our heads. There were no stupid songs from Billy to distract us. He wanted us to concentrate on how bad we felt.

"Fuck this," I heard Anton whisper.

"If you hadn't stolen that pony . . ." Paco shot me a look.

"And what? Let the chagwa swallow us whole?" Nat shot back.

"I wasn't even there," Paco snapped.

"Maybe if you had been a team player . . ." Anton said.

"Why didn't you just leave the pony?" Paco asked. "Why did you have to return it?"

"Because Dylan fell in love with the damn pony. I didn't want to keep the pony," Nat growled.

"Everybody shut up." I was irritated enough to kick someone. Billy heard us squabbling. *Oh, great,* we thought. Push-ups on top of marching. But we were not so lucky. Up ahead, where the median strip gets wide on Wisconsin Avenue, we saw guys in orange jumpsuits. We thought they were the gas company, forever fixing the mains, but printed on their backs was ATKIN CORRECTIONAL. Men cleared the growth on the median, cutting the tall grass and weeds as two guards hovered with rifles. One man had found a pit bull in the grass, starched with rigor mortis. The prisoner stood guard over the body, waiting for Animal Control. We slowed down to look at the dog. It looked freshly stuffed by a taxidermist. Billy shouted for us to keep moving. The prison guard tried to get the prisoners back into the bus, telling the guy to leave the dog, this was Animal Control jurisdiction. But the guy wouldn't move. The guard started yelling. Another guard yelled at the other prisoners to stay in line. Billy yelled at us to stay in line. Then Anton said, "Look who it is." Dragging his shackled feet on the asphalt was Rahim. I nearly didn't recognize him because his head was shaved like mine and his skin had a cloudy pallor. I pulled out of line.

"Rahim." I ran to him. "Rahim, it's me, Dylan." At first he didn't seem to know who I was, maybe because of my haircut. But soon he recognized me.

"Hey, man." He was dazed.

"Rahim. What happened to you?"

"The girls at the stable. They pressed charges. They pressed hard."

Billy was apoplectic, hollering for me to get back. He tore across the street after me.

"What can I do, Rahim?" I asked. "How can I help?"

"I'm okay, man. It's hard. It's just hard."

He climbed on the bus and moved to the back. The bus pulled away. I ran alongside. Billy seized me around the waist, lifting me off the ground.

STEPPING OUT of line cost the group five-hundred push-ups, running in place for an hour, three hundred leg lifts and, for me alone, an overnight in Marshall's Have-a-Heart Big Game Trap. The box was four feet wide and six feet long, just big enough to sit up. I was bitten by every kind of bug. Every living thing was frozen in fear from the chagwa except the mosquitoes and red ants. To keep the bugs from eating my hands, I shoved my hands into the pockets of my sweatpants, where I discovered some beetles that had made their nests. I didn't sleep the whole night. I was scared the chagwa would come back. This would be the one time he'd fall for a trap. I kept seeing him bending over me. So when the Harlans came out for morning run, I was already standing out front waiting. The day was tough. I fell asleep on my feet, waking to Billy's nonsense screaming and saliva bath. He rigged up hoses with metal guns ratcheted up to the hardest setting and sprayed them right over our heads during low crawl. If we lifted up, we'd get shot in the face.

At dinner we welcomed the gargantuan proportions. Dad made "21" burgers, a fat ball of meat cooked medium rare around a couple of tablespoons of butter. The buns were homemade. He served the burgers alongside homemade french fries, salad, broccoli Parmesan, corn on the cob and baked beans made with molasses and a brown sugar crust. He'd learned a great deal about cooking at Ainsville from chef and tax evader Alexander Mercier. Dad tried the recipes on us and we were only too happy to taste. For dessert, we had individual chocolate soufflés. Anton was allergic to chocolate, so Dad made him an orange soufflé. We tasted it and decided we preferred the orange to the chocolate. Dad promised to make orange soufflés for everyone soon. But we all knew that any promise meant we might get it and we might not, so best not to expect it. After dinner we had a liberty. Nat and Anton went to the Wim Wenders festival at the Avalon. Paco went to find a girl at the Meadowcreek Stables. I sat on the steps at the end of our walk, digging the mud out of the soles of my shoes with a stick. Dad came out and stood next to me. What had I done now? He smoked a cigar, a disagreeable habit that held no appeal for me. I felt nervous because he'd been nice to us for several days. He'd heaped praise on us. He'd given us a number of privileges. Now I waited for the worst. Dad looked at the street as though inspecting a battlefield.

"How are you?" he asked quietly.

I felt tears well up. It was his first sign of affection since he'd come out of Ainsville. Longer ago than that. Since the sentencing. Mom had hated public appearances, despised the hypocrisy of standing on the podium as the happy supportive family. But I'd lived for them, when he'd glance over and wink, tell the world how proud of me he was, and everyone believed him. Then he got busted and everyone stopped believing him. Me too. Now I felt sorry for him. Leaving the training and work orders to Billy, he had little to do but cook. I went overboard complimenting him on his meals. I forced myself to look enthusiastic about the tasks and calisthenics.

"I'm good," I said.

"Write to your mother?"

"Yes."

"Only pleasantries?"

"Of course."

"Let's play tennis." He may as well have said let's fly to Neptune. I looked around to see if anyone would be joining us.

Strapping myself into his old Mazda, I felt the colitis coming back, the lower GI hardening of constipation. He came out of the house with rackets, a bucket of balls and some video equipment.

"What's the camera for?"

We backed out of the driveway.

"We used video at Ainsville. I saw all the mistakes I'd been making my whole life."

I couldn't think of anything to say on the drive. It was the first time I'd been alone with him since the trip to Cooperstown to see the Baseball Hall of Fame. It was a fun trip. We took the bus, stopping in quaint towns. We met Yogi Berra . . . No. That was *Harlan*. Not me. We went to New York City. I spent the weekend in the bathroom.

Dad slowed the car as we passed the two-hundred-year-old Ruth Bay Club. We looked over longingly. "If you run for office you have to cancel your membership, if you know what I mean," he said. "The first Jew was Kissinger, the first Catholic a Kennedy. A later Kennedy. A John, Bobby or Ted would have been turned away." He went on to tell me how the golf course was flawless, the tennis courts immaculate and there was a room for cigars and a room that didn't allow women. Though he'd only been told, he winked, he hadn't actually seen.

The courts in Rock Creek Park were full, despite the latest chagwa attack at Fort McNair, and people were waiting. So we drove to a smaller park in Ruth Bay. It had a neglected cement court littered with leaves. Dad took hold of a weather-beaten broom and began to push the leaves. I rushed over to take it from him. I didn't want to see him sweep. I swept. Dad set up the camera on a tripod.

When the court was spotless, Dad dropped and hit. The first ball hit me in the head. The second, my face. But he kept hitting them, smashing them in my direction. Finally, I stepped back, swung and made contact. After that, I couldn't miss.

I jumped all around, skittering to the left, rushing the net, going by intuition. I knew where he was going to put the ball and went there. I knew when he was going to hit short before he even swung. I knew every slice backhand down the line, every overhead smash, every lob, which way he was going to spin the ball two strokes in advance, then three. Then I saw the entire set. And I knew my strokes were exquisite. Everything had top-spin, every shot perfectly placed. There was nothing I couldn't take on, nothing I couldn't keep on the court. I didn't have to watch the ball. I didn't have to see. I only had to think about him: Dad.

We shared a bottle of Poland Spring at the bench. "You've got a terrific arm," he said. "You connect. Good pace. If you were to get your footwork down you'd be something formidable." I'd never thought about my feet. "If you were to bend your knees"—he poured water into his hair, rubbing it into his scalp—"take smaller steps, position yourself a little farther from the ball. Everything is cramped because you crowd the ball. You have to respect the ball's space."

He rewound the video. I looked into the eyepiece. "See?" He said. "Look at those feet. They don't move." He was right. My legs were iron poles. I took huge lumbering steps toward the ball. And as for crowding the ball, molesting was more like it. He forwarded the tape. "Now I will show you something beautiful. That forehand. See how your arm goes over the ball? Exquisite. There it is again. How do you do it? Can you teach me?"

"I . . . I can try."

We walked back onto the court, trading sides. His first volley hit me in the face again.

"I wasn't ready." This time I put my hand over my nose, which began to swell.

He apologized and served again. I swung and missed. He hit another, which I barely got, too aware of what my feet were doing. I sent him a pathetic lob that dribbled into his court. He then smashed it so hard I moved out of the way.

"Keep your eye on the ball," he reminded.

I never took my eye off the ball, but still there was nothing I could hit. I remembered my footwork. I remembered that my forehand was perfect. What had he said about more topspin? I rushed the net, remembering to give the ball some room. I tripped over my feet, landing on my knees and elbows.

"Are you all right?" Dad rushed over.

"Yeah, fine."

"Remember, smaller steps. We're not running. We're scampering."

"Got it."

My game got worse and worse. My forehand sent balls

smashing into the net. My backhand sent 'em out of the park. My topspin stopped balls dead, rolling back on themselves, coming to rest at my feet.

"That was fun." He hung his arm over my shoulder as we walked off. "Something you and I can do together forever."

That was the last time I ever played tennis. Vile game.

THE CITY went on red alert. Chagwa sightings to the west. Dad took the Van Gogh Irises off the living room wall and put up a map of the greater Washington area, pressing pins into the reported sighting areas. The map got to be a confusing mess of colors as the chagwa was reported to be in two, sometimes three places at once. One expert on National Public Radio suggested the possibility of an infestation.

"Three chagwa doesn't make a population," the mayor shot back.

But all of the sightings described the chagwa's uniqueness: the ripped claw, the missing bicuspid, the eyebrows in the shapes of a sitting bull and Nova Scotia. One morning a photo appeared in the *Post* of a blurry chagwa stalking through the forest. The photographer was paid ten thousand dollars. But the picture was quickly deemed a hoax, a Beanie Baby shot at a distance. The man was charged and sentenced to three years.

Billy called us together during a late afternoon down period to tell us that we were entering the next phase of our training. Marksmanship.

"You mean actual guns?" Nat asked. We couldn't believe it. My father had his name on eight gun bills, the most contentious of which would have made guns completely inaccessible to civilians. He believed he went to jail for it. Still, we'd never been so excited. Billy said to get a lot of rest because in the morning we'd ship out to a firing range and we'd be required to pay close attention.

Chow that night was chicken drumsticks. Dad removed the meat, flattened it, stuffed it with chopped chicken liver and egg and wrapped it around the bone. An attractive dish and you could tell he was proud.

"Imagine someone ripping out your liver and stuffing it in your leg." Anton had been vegan before we began training. In the old days, a comment like that would have gotten us two hundred push-ups right there in the dining room and a mile of low crawl. But training had lightened up and punishments weren't so automatic. Even so, I could tell Dad's feelings were hurt. I was mad at Anton. I took a second helping even though I wasn't hungry, too excited about the next day's weapons training.

"These are the best drumsticks I've ever had." After dinner, we cleaned up and listened to the radio. A gutted deer was found on the railroad tracks behind McDonald's. Pugmarks were spotted nearby.

HANDS, LIPS and tongues disconnected from bodies on every part of me . . .

"GET UP GET UP GET UP." Billy bashed through the house, breaking into dreams, withering erections.

Dad stayed home, preferring to leave the machinery to Billy. He didn't like the idea, but he didn't put a stop to it either. Billy handed out hard hats. In the back of the van, we sat on them, alongside a long white metal box. Inside were guns, we knew.

Just as the van pulled out, Dad ran out of the house and said he needed to talk to me. I climbed out the back.

"Pay extra attention to safety procedures." He looked worried, the way he had just before the verdict came in.

We drove for a long time. There was a lot of laughter and bad penguin jokes, but then we drove over a bridge. It was just a small bridge, one lane, over a stream. We became quiet. Billy looked back at us in the rearview. The drive went on and on. We caught up on sleep.

Tires on rutted dirt and gravel woke us as we arrived at the shooting range. We spilled out the back, suffering the dismal disorientation of having slept on a hot day in the back of a van. The range was in a clearing in the woods. The woods were thick and dark, but the sun bludgeoned us in the clearing. Billy and Paco dragged the white case from the van and placed it on the gravel. We lined up.

"Gentlemen, meet your new friend. This is a friend designed to take a life. Never let your friend out of your sight. Do not ask someone to hold your friend. Do not put your friend down to eat. Your friend is the finest military rifle ever made. Keep your friend clean. We will now, uh . . . get to know your friend." Billy produced a key. But the padlock was rusted and the key got jammed. He turned it hard. He stood and kicked down on the top of the box. Then Paco stepped in and turned the key in the other direction. The padlock opened. Billy mumbled something about having loosened it, making it open easily for Paco.

We peered in the box. M-16s!

"Respect it, treat it right and it'll be there when you need it," he yelled over our excitement. Then he handed out the guns. We had expected handsome new rifles. These were dented and caked with mud. The barrel of my gun was clogged with dirt, the trigger and butt plate rusted. The weapons felt loose and decrepit. Nat's exactor and spring were worn and he had to trade the gun for another one, which was not much better than the first.

"Now, don't be bashful about asking for cleaning supplies if you need them," Billy said.

We spent the morning scraping the crud off our weapons. We dug mud from the muzzles, cleaned carbon and dirt from the barrel locking lugs, poked through the gas port with pipe cleaners. Dad showed up at noon with a picnic lunch of rare roast beef, homemade coleslaw, fruit and cappuccino brownies. He left immediately without giving my rifle a glance.

After lunch, we had to break down our rifles. But when we tried to put them back together the pieces didn't fit. Billy said it was because we hadn't cleaned our "friends" properly. By the time we reassembled, the range was closing and we had to head home for chow. But we were not too downhearted because we knew the next day we would get to shoot.

We sat in the back of the van on our hard hats.

"You want to aim right over the target." Paco held up his arms, pretending to shoot.

"That doesn't make any sense," Anton said.

"In skeet shooting you shoot in front of the target," Paco said. "Then the target walks into it. Boom." He jerked back from the pull of his imaginary rifle.

"You don't know what you are talking about." Anton's disagreement was reflexive. No one gave it a thought. Neither did he.

"I have an astigmatism," Nat said. "I'll have to shoot diagonal of the target."

"Oh, that makes all the sense in the world." Anton leaned back against the wall and fell asleep.

"Only eight percent of soldiers actually shoot at their target, anyway," Nat continued.

"Where'd you get that number?" Anton mumbled.

"What do the rest of the soldiers do?" Paco asked.

"Just close their eyes and shoot around, lose their shit all over the place," Nat said.

"Quiet back there, Mr. Hammerstein. I'll have none of my men endangering morale."

The van slowed down for some roadside construction. We groaned. It meant more time with Billy and we were carsick. We wanted to shower and wash our clothes. We were hungry.

"Look." Paco moved over to the back window. "A chain gang." A dozen or so men in orange jumpsuits dug and pickaxed on the side of the interstate, a new experiment in Maryland. Guards and German shepherds stood by. The prisoners had customized their jumpsuits. One rolled up a pant leg; one had an arm out of his sleeve, anything to make himself different from the guy standing next to him. "Hey, it's Rahim."

I slammed against the back window. He had his jumpsuit unzipped, the top half hanging from his waist. He'd bulked up, his muscles like gourds. I thought, it couldn't be him, but then I saw the hammer tattoo.

"Billy, let me out of the van," I shouted.

"Get back on your hat, soldier."

The van got past the construction and back up to speed. I opened the rear door, the asphalt a blur beneath me.

"You crazy scrap!" Billy pulled over on the shoulder. I jumped out. He slammed on the brakes. "Your weekend is in the brink and the next three liberties with me." He chased after me, but the running and calisthenics had made me fast.

"Rahim," I cried. "Rahim." He looked up from his shovel. He'd changed. His skin had baked to the color of red mud. Muscles pushed through the skin on his face from clenching his jaw. He had scores of new tattoos, a minarets design carved onto his chest with a light filament, black cats on each of his knuckles. And on his scalp, a brain tattooed. Each lobe was identified: LOVE, HATE, PAIN, REM, NIGHTMARE, YOU WILL NEVER BE FORGIVEN. A guard stepped in with a shotgun. Billy grabbed me like a football, an arm through my legs, another around my chest, and carried me back to the van shouting all the torture I could expect when we got home, how the rest of my life would be spent on my face in the dirt, how I'd have to low crawl my way down the aisle at my wedding, assuming any girl in the world could bear to look at me. I'd low crawl my way to the grave, he said. I'd low crawl my way down to hell.

"Rahim," I could only whisper as he slammed his foot down on the blade of a shovel, bending into the earth.

I WOKE TO the silhouette of Dad against the back-yard sky on a night full of red ants.

"I brought you some Off!"

I had so many mosquito bites I was already starting an allergic reaction. My nose ran, my throat began to close, I had chills. I sprayed the insecticide in my hands and rubbed it into my face and neck.

"I made some calls about your friend," he said. The news was bad.

"There has to be something we can do."

"I saw Ben Sotterburg over at Mercy. He says he'll make some calls."

"It was a pony. We were returning it."

He shook his head. "Sentencing in this country. I tried to make changes. They called me soft on crime. I went to jail for it. Rahim's lucky he didn't have his hands cut off."

I felt embarrassed for my father, still insisting he was innocent. He handed me a canteen of water. We listened to cicadas.

"I don't know what to do," he said. "I've been disbarred, I can never run for office again. I don't know how to do anything." I wanted to be alone again with the bugs. Listening to him was too much responsibility. "What would Harlan's father do?" He was serious.

"Well . . . Alistair's dad would offer you a job at the car dealership. All the neighbors would pitch in."

"Do we know any of our neighbors?"

"Did you ever . . . watch *Harlan*?" I asked.

"Did I ever watch *Harlan*? Every day. Never missed one. Only once when I was in the infirmary with food poisoning. Even then, Marshall had the tape sent over from Gold Street." I was stunned. "I got to hear your voice. I loved the show. So did the other guys. Little Gus Ambrose?"

"The extortionist?"

"Loooooved *Harlan*. Tough as nails, that guy, but threaten to take his *Harlan* privileges . . . And then Larry. When he died, I knew I had to get home. Somehow. The parole board saw the Larry episode too. Though they rejected my plea, they said, 'We didn't know Larry but we came to know him in his death.' I was proud to be your father, Dylan. Each time the credits rolled, I said, That's my son. I hope you're not embarrassed of me."

"Me? Embarrassed? Of you? Not a chance, Dad."

He put his hand on my forehead.

"You're burning up. I'm taking you inside." He slid his arms under my neck and thighs and pulled me out of the trap. He stood up with me in his arms and trudged across the dirt into the house. I tried to relax, to even enjoy the sensation of being held. But it had been too long. It felt strange. I was too big.

I woke after ten. The Harlans had left before dawn for the shooting range. There was a tray next to my bed. A piece of dry toast, crusts removed, a dish of homemade blueberry jam, soft butter, a pot of hot water and a mint tea bag in a mug.

"I'll heat up the water." My father stood at the door. He came over and felt my forehead. "You're still warm." He handed me some pills for the fever. I sat up. I was weak and the room went black for a second. "Careful. Not too quickly." The sky was overcast, the clouds low in a thick quilt. "Try to eat something?" He spread butter and jam on a piece of toast. It was delicious, but I had difficulty swallowing. He fixed the pillows and made the bed around me.

I woke again just after one. The tray next to my bed had a steaming bowl of homemade cream of potato soup, homemade saltines and ginger ale.

"I think you'll like the soup." Dad had pulled a rocking chair into the room and sat reading the *American Spectator*. He hadn't read in a long time, maybe the comics or sports, but certainly nothing on current affairs. I leaned over and took a bite of the soup. It was unlike any soup I had ever tasted. It was sweet and savory at the same time. The potatoes turned to cream in my mouth. For one second I felt rejuvenated. But then sleep found me again.

I could smell good things to eat when I woke again at five. I was disoriented, thinking it was morning, but the Harlans weren't back yet. I struggled up to go to the bathroom, then downstairs. My father was sitting out on the front stoop, taking a break from the kitchen. The sky was still overcast, enveloping the city. I stepped outside in my pajamas and sat next to him. He put his arm around me, then the other arm. I sank into his chest. He smelled like dinner.

A black Lincoln Town Car pulled up in front of the house. My father stood. We braced ourselves for bad news. The driver got out, dressed in a black suit. He opened the door to the back. A leg swung out, then another, then a cane. The driver leaned into the car and grasped a man around the waist, stretching him up onto his feet. It was Holman Greenly, the twenty-term senator. He started up the path, supported by the driver.

"But this is impossible." Dad's face turned ashen. "My wife was at your funeral."

His prosthetic leg was ill-fitting. He had to swing it out to the side by swiveling his hip like a golfer on the starting tee.

"Imbecile." He always despised my father. "That was a funeral for my leg. And the lady wore red. If you can't control your wife, Matty, you can't control your House."

"Dylan, get the senator some ice tea."

"No." He shook his cane, falling onto his driver. "I have more ice tea in my veins than blood. I gave my leg to ice tea. Thanks to the sugar it takes to make the sheep-dip drinkable." He tapped his prosthesis, then looked me up and down, unimpressed. "This is your boy?"

"This is Dylan. Dylan, meet the 'Honorable' Holman Greenly."

"Good to have your son near you. Mine hasn't spoken to me since *Brown v. Board of Education.*" He began to weep. We didn't know what to do.

"You're sure you don't want some ice tea?" Dad asked again.

"My ass is beat, Matty. I need to die. But they won't let me. The doctors are in on the collusion. They keep bringing me back to life. I've begged them to let me go." The driver produced a manila folder. "Here you are, Matthew. The documents proving your innocence, including testimony from both agents. All I ask in return is that you leave my name out of it. I want my library. Walk into the U.S. Attorney's Office, give it to that Mascotti bastard, get that kid from *The New Yorker*, you'll be back on your feet in a week. Run for Senate, if you like. You'll win. But understand, Mr. Student Council President, it is only my affection for your wife that leads me here today. Your gun bills were laughable. Your mandatory trigger locks. What arrogance. They said you were The One, Matty. But I knew the moment I laid eyes on you, parachuting into my state with your little tax rebellion, in my hometown, my constituents, that you would bring your own self down with your adorable enthusiasm. What did it buy you, Mr. Student Council President? An all-expenses-paid vacation in the brink." He began to choke.

"So, that's what I got clinked for?" Dad asked "The tax rebellion? Or the guns? Or was it the slots?"

"Taxes, guns, slots? You dare to think any of those microbes get past me, you arrogant cunt? S.7475. Your dirty bomb in my village. The Organic Hybrid Bill. I can barely say it without reflux. Do you know what that bill would have done to agriculture in my state? You'd have shut down my fertilizer and pesticide manufacturers in a day. Forty thousand jobs for a head of Bibb lettuce. I told you to let that business go. You didn't listen. But enough spitting across the aisle. I need to leave. Good-bye, Matty." He turned and limped back toward his car.

Dad flipped through the contents of the envelope, his eyes growing bigger, his face turning red.

"Three years of my life," he shouted at Holman. "I should kill you myself."

"I can handle that on my own." Holman waved good-bye.

"You'll be the last one standing. You'll never die, Senator." But he did. That night. Dad stormed over to the car. "The two hundred grand in the briefcase. I want every last cent deposited into Nowhere to Go by close of business tomorrow."

"Whatever you say, Matty."

"And I want you to make the gift in your third wife's name."

Senator Greenly choked and caught his breath. "A bit harsh, Matty, don't you think?" The driver lifted Holman's legs into the back of the car.

"Not if you want a library."

Chow that evening was pork.

"It didn't go so well." Paco sat on the end of my bed. "Nat kept shooting left. Anton, right. Me, all over the place. Not one of us could hit a target. Billy was bullshit. Made us run in place for an hour and then a ten-mile march down 270."

"Did you see the chain gang? Did you see Rahim?"

"Dylan." Paco shook his head. "You gotta forget about Rahim."

"I can't."

"The three of us made a pact. Nat, Anton and I. We agreed not to think about Rahim anymore. Whoever thinks about him has to cut off the end of his pinky. Are you in or out? Solo means 'so low.' That means no saying his name or thinking of him and what his life must be like. Shall I take care of this?" Paco took hold of the top of the Our Lady of the Highways team photo on my wall. I looked into Rahim's eyes and said I was sorry. He ripped the picture into exactly one hundred pieces, and we shook on it.

"So that's it about target practice?" I asked.

"I know the next task," Paco said. "I figured it out. I haven't told the others. You know it too."

"I do?"

"The target practice? The maps? The chagwa, Dylan. We're going to take him out." I fell back on the pillow. "Think about it. Nobody's been able to kill him. If your dad can make the city safe, he can come back. It's his only hope. What better way to show you're not soft than to put a gun in the hands of your own son?"

"I can do it." I laced my fingers behind my neck. On the white stucco of the ceiling, I projected killing the beast. "I could definitely take him out."

"Yeah? You haven't been to target practice yet. And those targets weren't even moving. Anyway, you're not listening to me. Don't you feel used? I feel used."

No. I felt I was about to do something great. Paco took his sweaty shirt off over his head and threw it on the floor. After all the torture, it was Paco's body that showed the greatest results, every inch of him defined by faults between muscles. His back looked like a relief map.

"You think you've been used?" I asked. "Look in the mirror." He moved in front of the full-length mirror inside my closet door. I rose up and stood next to him, removing my pajama shirt. From the neck down I was pretty impressive too. But not like Paco. "Who's been using who?" I moved closer so we could both fit in the mirror.

"Look at this." Paco shook his arm, then made a fist so that the veins would rise up against the skin. I tried to do it too, but my veins preferred to stay behind the scenes.

"Look." I pulled my arms back so that my shoulder blades touched.

"Gross," Paco said.

I turned my eyelid inside out.

He whispered, "Let's watch porn."

I flipped on the scramble. An infomercial for a mop that restored tile.

MORE CHAGWA sightings. We huddled around the radio. Dad updated the pin map. Black pins for delusional sightings by around the bend cases, red pins for more likely sightings by people with wits. This time by the canal, near the Boat House. He was in the water, swimming south. But he was also at Shops on the Boulevard, the same strip mall with all the Elvis sightings. That got a black pin. And, of course, never any pictures to go with the sightings. Animal Control managed to round up a golden retriever mistaken for the chagwa in Silver Spring. A

Newfoundland was contained in Manassas. The Harlans looked at one another nervously. But no one wanted to stick out by asking whether we were expected to kill the chagwa.

THERE WAS nothing I couldn't shoot. I nailed the stationary targets, turning the bull's-eyes to gaping wounds. As for the moving targets, I was even better. I imagined inside the circle was the chagwa. I switched to my weak side, puncturing the eye on the end of the mechanical arm again and again. Billy walked out to the field to remove the target paper, scratching his oddly shaped head, saying, Goddamn, goddamn, replacing it with fresh target. Then he dodged out of the way as though I were going to get the idea to shoot him. The Harlans laughed. The lunatic who had threatened our lives for so long now appeared pathetic and frail, impossible to despise. He served a new purpose. He was someone to have around to make fun of, to look down on in order to pump ourselves up even higher.

I sent the new target to heaven like the one that came before. The guys were awestruck. They laid their weapons in their laps and watched as I settled into each aiming area, zeroed my scope and let the target have it, needing only to envision the chagwa. I knew what I was doing was wrong, sticking out, showing off. It would mean more garbage detail, more cleanup, more push-ups, but I didn't give a damn.

My father showed up with lunch. Peanut butter and jelly and a bag of Ruffles. Not his usual elaborate fare. As we ate, Billy pondered whether crunchy peanut butter was better than smooth. We cleaned up and headed back to the course. Dad decided to stay and watch.

I reloaded, settling into a prone position, while Billy put a scorecard in the clip. He ratcheted up the target arm so that it moved faster and more unpredictably. The herky-jerky movements of the target didn't matter. I knew instinctively where the target would go. I didn't need to think. The gun was in control. Then my father said, "I've never seen such a marksman." And then, "If you were just a touch less tense. If you were to focus more on your front site. Keep your shoulders square. Use the pad of your finger, not the first joint. If you were to cant your left hand at an angle. Think sixty percent weak hand, forty percent strong hand. Pull the rifle back into your shoulder. You're strangling the gun. Don't jerk the trigger. Keep your strong hand relaxed. But, hey, don't listen to me. What do I know? You're a natural."

I rose up to my knees and sat cross-legged on the dirt, the gun across my lap. I knew better than to even attempt shooting again. My next shot would swerve left and the one after would whistle into the woods. Amid Dad's many compliments, my worthless side took over. No one knew it more than Billy, who, despite the Harlans' encouragement for me to keep shooting, stepped up and took the gun.

CHOW THAT NIGHT ... I skipped it. It would cost me liberties and privileges, but I needed to find the woman. I checked the Lincoln, the Jefferson, the War, the Roosevelt, even back at the Einstein.

I found her at the Washington Monument.

The wind whipped the flag ropes against the poles. We ran for cover in the shadow of the building. I moved right in, pushing her against it, our heads banging against the cool stone. We looked up to where the color of marble changed when the country ran out of cash and went with the cheaper brand of rock. She squeezed her legs around my hips. I pulled her knees to my chest. She weighed nothing. We followed the building up with our eyes, the obelisk piercing the sky, hell, yes.

HARLAN'S MOM sat on the edge of my bed. "Won't you even try the lugubrious liver, Dylan?" It slid around on the plate . . .

"GET UP GET UP GET UP GET UP GET UP." It had been a long while since Billy had awakened us, but that was the point. He'd been nicer lately just so he could terrorize us more when we expected it least. "IN FRONT OF THE HOUSE DOUBLE-TIME."

When I got outside I was the only Harlan. We would pay dearly for the others not getting out sooner. I should have slowed down so as not to stick out so much. Lugubrious liver. Wow. Billy told me to get in the back of Dad's Mazda. I got in and looked toward the door for the Harlans, but the house was quiet. Then Billy got in the front and pulled out of the driveway. I asked where we were going.

"The Billy retrospective." He looked at me in the rearview. "And I don't mean the Washington Monument." The old bad smile came back. He'd followed me downtown and watched the whole thing. I felt sick. He hadn't stopped me. He wanted me to get in trouble. And he was horny and wanted to watch. And worse, my father knew. Billy would run me twenty miles on I-95. I'd get push-ups until my arms turned liquid. I'd scrub latrines and get dishes and garbage detail for the rest of the month. The other Harlans would stand by helplessly, knowing that trying to pitch in would cost us all more hardship. They'd whisper, "We are with you, Dylan. Your garbage detail is our garbage detail." I'd lose liberty and TV and dessert. I could face any punishment Billy had in store, but I couldn't face Dad. We drove through the empty city and onto Route 50. I didn't need to ask what a Billy retrospective might be. The only place Route 50 went was the Bay Bridge.

I began seeing the seagull signs that signify you are on the right road. I moved around in the back seat. For a reason unclear to me, I took off my shoes. When we passed the fifth seagull, I looked for a way out of the car, inexplicably trying to wedge myself into the space above the back seat.

"Hey, I can't see. Get down."

I rolled back onto the seat.

"Can we stop?" My voice cracked. "I need to go to the bathroom."

"Yeah, we'll stop." But Billy didn't stop. *Relax into it. You are calm, unconcerned, carefree, peaceful.* We shot under the BAY BRIDGE 1 MILE sign.

"How you doing back there?" Billy asked. "Shaky? I brought a relaxation tape." He punched the cassette player. Led Zeppelin's "Immigrant Song" slammed out of the speakers.

"Billy," I said, my breaths getting shorter by the second. "Can't you give me latrine duty? For old times' sake? I'll do mess detail for the rest of the month. I'll wash out the supercans. Can you at least turn down the volume?"

"I gotta tell you, kid. If I hadn't followed my father's orders to the letter, he'd have thrown me off this very bridge. If you ask me, you're lucky."

Your calm spirit is growing stronger. What you don't see cannot hurt you. But all I could see was the surface of the water racing toward us. Billy passed through the SmartPass booth. We were over the water. Deep controlled breaths. Millions of people have driven over the bridge with no mishap.

"We are heading for the central span." Billy put his hand over his mouth and attempted making his voice sound like a pilot from the cockpit, blowing his nose in his hand to produce static. "We are going to approach in a slow, controlled manner." He sped up despite the blinking maintain-speed signs. "To the left side of the craft: water. To the right side of the craft: water." He began swerving all over the lanes.

"Can we take a break?" I begged.

"Sure. At a hundred and ninety-eight feet." It would be impossible to control the car at this speed. The body would break apart in midair. A wheel would crush the roof. I felt I needed to take off my clothes. I whipped off my sweatshirt. I began picking at the knotted string on my pants. For a second I must have passed out, because I was on the other side, stopping to pick some daisies for the guys. "These yellow ones are nice," Billy said, picking his own bouquet. When I opened my eyes we were beneath the central span. Billy scraped the tires against the right rail. The car shuffled left. Another scrape made the back of the car slip. Billy yelled and clenched the wheel, trying to straighten out. The car fishtailed smack into the guard wall. We spun. I slapped my hand onto my arm, digging my nails, trying to take off my skin. We stopped dead at a ninety-degree angle, waiting for impact. But the cars behind slowed and locked up.

Billy couldn't move. The cars on the bridge were still, no one honking or yelling out the window. I could hear nothing but

Billy's panting. "We're going to have to straighten out, Bill," I said softly. Billy couldn't figure out where he was. I moved up in my seat. "We're on the bridge."

"I'm okay, I'm okay." He turned the wheel right.

We passed the towers and headed downward. I was soaked in sweat. So was Billy. I expected him to make fun of me. But he slowed down to twenty, put his hand back and patted my knee. "It's okay, guy. We're done. No more." When we got to the landing, Billy pulled over. I got dressed. We opened the doors and got out. The ground felt like it wasn't there. We were by a swamp with wildflowers growing. I stepped into it, my sneakers sucked by mud. Billy came out and picked some flowers. We made two bouquets and tied them with stems. We put the bouquets in the back. I got in the front. The flowers would be nice for the mess.

"So the point's been made?" He wanted me to reassure him. "We can head back now, right?" He didn't want to drive over any more bridges either. We discussed an alternative route, wondering what people had to have done before the bridge was built. Maybe there was a ferry. But we had to get home. Breakfast would be waiting. We headed back. At the SmartPass booth, he took off his sweatshirt and gave it to me so that I could wear it over my head and not have to look.

WE LAZED about the front steps. Little was expected of us these days. We cleaned our shoes. We listened to the radio. A sighting was reported near the Wilson Bridge, heading north to the city. I often considered the possibility that the number of car accidents on the Wilson Bridge had something to do with the population's need to keep up with the status quo. A driver phoned the sighting into Oldies 100, then bashed into the car in front of him. Later that day, a golfer called in a sighting at Roosevelt Island. A jogger saw him dart across the Parkway. The police blamed the media for interfering with the investigation. The media blamed the police for not giving information. Elected officials told us to go about our normal lives. Stores had sales. Gas stations offered to pump at self-serve prices. We spent the whole day outside by the radio as people walked in and out of the house—Everett Feeney, my father's national security advisor and staff of one, lawyers from Wobley & Fowell, two men from the U.S. Attorney's Office, Speaker of the House Renny Mascotti and Carmel Blossom, the PR flak. Billy came and went to the deli for sandwiches.

"Any new reports?" Carmel kept poking her head out the door.

"The lot at Lady Bird Johnson Park," I said.

"If one more person tells me this is nothing compared to Israel, I'm going to scream."

Billy separated himself from us, sitting on the curb, drawing his name in the gravel and examining his feet.

"So what about you, Bill?" I called. "How are you going to fit into the new regime?" He smiled, genuinely happy. But this time it was a smile that was free of maliciousness, the stitch marks on his face looking more like bird tracks through mud.

"I'm going to be the driver."

We all said, well, hey, wow, isn't that great, then leaned back on the cement and closed our eyes to the blinding power of the sun. We slept until Everett Feeney and the others left. Then we were called into the house to discuss our third and final task.

◆ ◆ ◆ ◆

THE RAIN had stopped, but the air was still thick as I headed across the Mall toward the tent city. Everywhere was the turpentine scent of Def-11 as crop dusters blanketed the city with herbicide to defoliate the trees. The chagwa was running out of places to hide. Photographers brought low beach chairs and sat in the mist wearing bathing suits. They cooked on propane hot plates and read foreign papers. They listened to chagwa coverage from other countries, slapping their radios when bullets of static interfered. Angry wet people on walkie-talkies stomped by. Some tech guys from *Eyewitness* tried to drop cables across the lawn from their microwave truck on Constitution Avenue, but the police gave them problems. A producer ran out to talk to them. The police crossed their arms. The TV cables were coiled up and removed. Animal Control set up to the south, SWAT to the east, mounted police to the north. The National Guard took the streets. The Army took the air. The Navy, the Potomac River. The chagwa would come from the west, motorcycle cops corralling him into the Mall. And everywhere there were people camped who just wanted to have their picture taken with the chagwa, dead or alive. I recognized our camp by the igloo tents. The Harlans milled around on the grass by the Reflecting Pool, soaked from the rain. Billy stood guard over the white box that held our M-16s.

Paco greeted me halfway, his footprints behind him in the grass, water splashing up around his sneakers. "Someone saw him swimming under the Memorial Bridge. He's heading this way."

"How long?" I asked.

"Ten minutes. I was worried you wouldn't show. And that I wouldn't get to say good-bye."

"Where are you going?"

"It's my birthday. I'm eighteen. I'm free to go."

My side hurt from where I'd been held by the chagwa. The pain had moved into my hip. It would get worse over time, not better.

"But . . ." My throat closed. "Don't you want to neutralize the chagwa?"

"You know I can't shoot." He stepped up and gave me a hug. A guy hug. A hand on one shoulder, three hard pats on the back. Not worth a damn. "You're the one," he said. "You're going to kill him. I know it." His embrace left a wet print of his body on my T-shirt. He walked backward away from me, pointing his thumb and index finger like a pistol. "The naked and the nude."

"Dance in solemn solitude."

He shot me in the chest, blew out his finger, shoved it in his pocket and took off. Paco.

I moved down to the Wall, my old stomping grounds. Nodding to the regulars, I walked along the gravel path. The Wheelchair Man and the Kleenex Lady had moved on to the next boy, who leaned right up against the granite, his face wedged in the inside of his elbow. I thought, *Oh, I didn't do it that way, no no, all wrong.* He peeked out for one second and caught me looking. *Yeah, I know the drill.* He cried harder.

At the top of the incline, I glanced over the hill. Each chagwa unit had its own lieutenant, each appalled by the incompetence of the other. Only bits of information made their way out as the lieutenants shouted over one another on bull-horns. The park police were in over their heads trying to cordon off the area. Photographers got summonses for sneaking under the yellow tape. The mounted police raised a red flag meaning the chagwa was in the vicinity. I looked over at Billy. He tried every key on his chain, but none could open the box. He tried kicking down on it. He tried forcing it with his hands. I could see the weight of yet another failure bear down on him. Then I heard a voice I both knew and didn't.

"Look, Dylan," my mother pointed to a name on the Wall. "A boy named Mister Mister. Can you imagine naming a baby Mister?"

You get used to missing someone to the point where the missing replaces her. And then the missing has nothing to do with her. There was no room for her with all the space the missing took.

"That would make his formal name . . ." My voice tripped on the words.

"Mister Mister Mister," she said. It's right there. Mister Mister. Panel 17, six names from the left, fourteen from the top. Go see for yourself.

We walked along the Wall pretending to read the other names, but really looking at each other's reflection in the granite. She wore a silver coat. My eyes wiped across the stone like a rag cleaning a table.

"Look at me, Dylan." If I looked I'd never see again. I'd go myopic, then to black. And wasn't that just what she wanted, for me to be on her lead, unable to do for myself. "Look at me now." She took me in her hands and bent me backward. I hated the feeling, couldn't bear to be touched. She slapped her hand on my forehead. I had no choice. I looked. She then batted her eyes, perhaps twenty or thirty times. Her tears splashed onto my face and into my eyes. I tried to blink them away, wanting no part. But then my vision became clear, every grain in the granite, every story of every person on the wall. William Margolis, Rifleman, First Cavalry Division. Liked spiced gumdrops and surfing movies. A mine went off and killed the nine guys behind him first. James Andrew Lauder, Corpsman, Third Batallion, First Marines, took a bullet in his head during a human-wave attack. Captain Dennis Michael Montgomery saw a woman split in half, then turned his nightmares over to us.

Up on the hill a crowd began to form around my father. The *Post* and the *Times* had printed Holman Greenly's papers that morning. Dad looked over at me and waved.

"Dylan, come!" he called.

"Dylan, stay," Mom said.

They would tear me in half, these people, given the chance. Though in this chalk circle, the wise king would say, "Go ahead. Rip away." I stood on the grass, looking back at my mother and forward to my father, unable to move in either direction. And though I'd made a pact not to, I thought of Rahim. I said his name aloud, "Rahim." I saw him looking out his cell from across the water in an island jail, longing for nothing now, just longing without an object, because, like me, Rahim had made his own pact not to remember. But unlike me, Rahim could stick to a promise.

A crop duster flew too close to the Mall. Word spread that the chagwa had arrived. The Mall came under attack. Shots were fired from an Apache and then the bombs began dropping. A TV van right next to us blew up, mortars hitting just yards away. My father caught up to us. He and my mother grabbed me, lifting me off my feet. We headed toward the Lincoln Memorial. Panic began. Through the smoke I could see geese running across the lawn. People fled down Constitution Avenue.

"The Harlans," I said.

"Billy has them," Dad said.

The smoke and noise were terrible. A Marine waved his arm at us from an opening at the bottom of the monument just as a rocket cut a gouge in the Lincoln steps. When we got to the Marine, he was hopping on one foot. He shoved my mother and we slid down a dirt chute into a dimly lit tunnel beneath the building. Roots hung from the ceiling. Names were spray-painted on the walls.

"What if—" I began.

"Have faith," Dad said. My parents came together. I squeezed between. Dirt rained on our heads from a close hit. The Marine with the hurt foot found a deeper tunnel.

"This way," he told us. We crawled down.

Book IV: Wendy

THE NEWS REPORTED sightings three minutes apart. The governors closed the bridges. Traffic helicopters were grounded to clear space for the military. The chagwa moved in an easterly direction, getting closer to the center of the city. I sat on the yellow curb of the circular entrance to Our Lady waiting for Peter Allingham. Colonial World allowed him a four-hour liberty. He had to sign a legally binding contract to stay Colonial. He was late. Dooley the orderly sat beside me on the curb, listening to the radio my first roommate had left.

" 'Have You Ever Seen the Rain,' " I guessed the mystery oldie.

"I don't know how you do it."

To mark the time, I wore the same clothes I'd come in wearing. They were too light for the fall weather. I looked down at my pale feet in lime-green sandals.

"You should get a pedicure," Dooley said. "Do some nice things for yourself."

I began to cry.

"What is it?" Dooley asked.

"You and I . . . we've made this connection and now we're breaking it."

"You can always come back and visit."

"But you know I won't."

"You won't think about me once you're gone," he said.

"Oh, but I will."

"I've been doing this a long time, Wendy."

"Can't you say something that I want to hear?" I asked.

"What do you want to hear?"

I let out an exasperated breath. "You must run into this problem with your other female charges."

"All my charges are different."

"That's such an orderly thing to say."

A sky-blue cab pulled into the driveway. Peter sat in back. He wore the same clothes from that day in the mud field at Jamestown. His hair was past his shoulders and filthy, his skin beaten down by the sun and a bad diet, his smile revealing neglected teeth. I got in the cab.

Dooley leaned down. "Even if you hate me, you are going to feel worse later if you don't look at me and say my name and say good-bye."

I gave him the radio. "Good-bye, Dooley."

Dooley slapped the back of the cab.

"How are you, Peter?" I asked.

Peter had grown into his role as farmer. Fourteen hours a day of physical labor had made him strong. Praying at night and on weekends had made him at peace with himself. He leaned back, holding on to the strap above the window.

"Forgive me for not kissing you hello," he said. "I can't risk bringing back disease. And Lord only knows what I'm carrying."

"I didn't expect you in a cab," I said.

"I left the carriage on 66. All this . . . it overwhelmed the horse." Peter looked at sturdy houses, a grocery store, a drug store, clothing and electronics stores and restaurants and upscale hardware stores and banks. Everything in Colonial World had to be grown or made. A bandage on his thumb was concocted of fibers exhaustively scraped from dirty linen. And the noise. He kept putting his hands over his ears. "I'm afraid I'll have to ask you to pay for the cab. I have no money. Unless the driver is willing to barter for these squirrel pelts." He held up a string of gray and black furs.

"How is it there?" I asked.

"Adrianne is happier. We'll have a good harvest. We've built up immunities. Fewer people have died."

"And your slaves?"

"We've come to an understanding. I employ them as slaves— though I treat them as a kind owner would treat his slaves—as long as they agree to attend regular emancipation meetings."

"And Kevin?"

He shook his head. "I don't like who he's become, Wendy. He's cruel to the animals. He mistreats the slaves. It's all about *having* to him. What does he *get*. He has no sense of country."

"And with you and Adrianne as such good examples. You look handsome." He wore baggy purple trousers, fitted with a drawstring, a marigold blouse that laced up the front and a red doublet. He looked me over, not used to being with a clean woman. I recognized the spark in his eye.

"Tell me about you, Wendy. Did Our Lady help?"

"Well, I still don't sleep. But the good part is that now I have a whole community of nonsleepers and their phone numbers. We can just chat chat chat on the phone till all hours. Did you know we're called nonsleepers now? *Insomniac* is dead, buried in the word yard next to crippled."

The cab pulled in front of my house.

"I don't have to be back until tonight," he said. "I could come in and help you get settled." I was tempted. But there was no room in my life anymore for that kind of loss. I took twenty dollars from my pocket. The driver refused, preferring instead to barter for the pelts. When he waved off my money, I noticed his bandaged hand, a drop of blood leaking through.

"Wendy." Peter took my wrist as I started to leave the cab. "If you would ever consider it . . . if it doesn't work out here, there's a place for you at Jamestown."

I wouldn't last a minute in his world.

Time for a purge. The house looked clean but run-down. There was still the faint smell of chagwa urine and carrion. I made up my mind to toss every last piece of furniture, reface the cabinets and paint, paint, paint. Turquoise Dream, Electric Purple, Candy Pink, Tangerine. Let it clash, I don't care. I just wanted everything new. I'd lay down sod and lose that dreadful biga tree. I'd plant a thousand bulbs. I would cover the earth with daffodils. Let the neighbors stare. All my clothes would go to Goodwill. No more suits. No more black. Good-bye to mourning.

With Matt and Dylan camping on the Mall, I went to work. I rolled up the rugs, every last one, and dragged them out to the curb. On top of the mound I left a note: *FREE RUGS!* Then I carried out six dining chairs and took the table apart, leaf by leaf. Dragging out the sideboard was tricky because it didn't fit through the front door. How had we gotten it in? No bother. I found the saw and shaved down the legs. I threw some ancestral portraits that weren't really our ancestors onto the pile and on this I wrote: *FREE DINING SET!* I left the lamps so I could work through the night scouring every inch of the downstairs with ammonia and hot water. Wearing pink rubber gloves to protect my hands, I found a stash of old cloth diapers. They had been Dylan's. Protecting the environment was an issue in Matt's campaign, the overflowing landfills piled up with plastic. I was instructed to use cloth. They barely worked. Everything seeped through. The boy suffered eczema. I sneaked Pampers and lied to Channel 4. But they did make good rags. I scrubbed the walls, the molding, the floors. I got the ladder and washed the ceiling. When I dragged the ladder out to throw it in the pile as well, I saw the police had given me a ticket for putting out large refuse too many days in advance of Large Refuse Day. The ticket was for fifty dollars. It may as well have been five hundred dollars, we were so broke. In the reason-for-fine box, the officer had written: *FAILURE TO DO!*

I hit my closet hard, yanking out the suits, the black Tahari I wore when Matt announced he'd run, the black and gray plaid Chanel knockoff I wore for his acceptance speech. "The mind of the Dunleavy engine, my beautiful wife, Wendy." As though I had anything even vaguely to do with getting elected. Gone was the peach inaugural gown. Good-bye to the short black dress for cocktails and the red, white and blue paneled shift for the party at the French Embassy. Out with the light blue work shirts from RESTORE when we pounded nails and sanded and whittled and painted, smiling for the press as I missed my target and hammered my thumb. And what had we done by turning that dilapidated crack den into a Victorian townhouse? Encouraged developers to rocket up real estate prices, making refugees of the poor once again. Good-bye navy suit with brass buttons and red scarf. Good riddance circle pin and medium pumps. The gray suit for a hundred and one funerals, the pinstripes for lunch, the mint green for tea, the brown to be nondescript, the red for Holman Greenly.

Despite the strength I'd gained from aikido at the hospital, the mattresses were awkward and wobbly. I tried to manage them but tripped and fell. There was only one way to take them out. I had to ride them. I set them one at a time at the top of the stairs, sat in the middle on my knees, pulled up the sides and slid down. After the mattresses were neatly piled on the street, I rode the toboggan of the highboy down the stairs. I rode the chair-and-a-half from our room, its wheels slamming down the steps. Riding a TV is never a good idea. A vanity table with a mirror, I do not recommend. But a dresser drawer, especially on the last six steps when it becomes airborne, is what it must be like to fly. And then another ticket from the police for putting out more large refuse before Large Refuse Day, this time the reason box reading: *FAILURE TO BE!* One hundred dollars and I just had to laugh because I'd never come up with that kind of money, not in a thousand years.

I took a moment to rest by the curb. Looking to the east I saw that the sun would not rise. The sky would remain concealed for one hundred days. The neighborhood would sleep late. The few times that the sun sneaked through, people drove or ran to the spot where the clouds parted, only to have the sky close up the second they arrived.

"Welcome to October, Wendy." Toby Lapinsky waved from his door.

I went inside to make tea. There was only chamomile, left over from Dylan's futile attempts to keep his voice from changing. While I waited for the tea to cool, I looked around for a place to sit, but there was none. I should have saved a chair. I looked for a place to put the tea. I should have saved a table. So I stood by the window looking out back at the defoliated trees. Thankfully, the pines were impervious to the Def-11. The stripped-down poplars and beeches seemed to bend toward them for protection. The tea tasted like dirt. I drank it anyway, looking now at Dylan's wall. A brick monolith with ropes dangling, it stood twenty feet high and nine feet wide. A light rain fell as I went out the back. I pulled on one of the ropes. The wall was sturdy. I climbed up and over. It was a cinch after all the rubberized rock climbing I'd done at Our Lady. Then I looked for Dylan's name. It was exactly where he said it was. Eight from the left, twelve from the bottom.

Taking down a brick wall was harder than I had imagined. There's only one way to do it. With a sledgehammer. I pulled the ladder out of the trash. All the hammer-throwing I'd done at Our Lady, and I still couldn't wield one hard enough to knock off the first brick. But then I remembered how Matt had taught me to hit a nail on the sweet spot when we resurrected the house for RESTORE. For days I had smashed my fingers and pounded my thumb. I bent nails in half. They had to be yanked out of the boards by the Methodist boys. Matt came over to help. He smelled like pine and salt. He put his hand over mine.

I struck a brick. It loosened. Cracks spread down the mortar. I smacked it again. It tumbled to the ground, end over end. The second brick was easier. And the third even more so. Then I cleared my mind as I had been taught at Our Lady and thought only of the bricks: clay, water, sand, hit. Clay, water, sand, hit. Eight from the right, twenty-five from the bottom I came across PACO, etched into the brick. I tapped it carefully and put it aside for the handsome former Harlan. Just left of center, nineteen from the bottom was ANTON and up three diagonally was NAT. I stacked their bricks on the deck. Later in the day, I came to Dylan's. I broke off all the bricks surrounding and kept one long tower with his at the top. But the column began to list, so I wedged off his brick and added it to the others I'd saved. I piled the rest of the bricks atop the pyramid in the middle of the yard. On the street, I flagged down a contractor and offered him the bricks.

A sticky red gum dripped from the biga tree when the blade of my axe cut into it. I caught a few drops on my finger and rubbed it into a cut on the knuckle of my thumb. Within minutes the cut had faded. As I bowed in reverence to the tree and apologized for hurting it, I heard a dull bump of something landing in the woods. And then another. I walked to the edge of the yard. A crow fell from the sky. One by one, two by two, three at a time, West Nile hitting hard in our area again. I called an ornithologist that Matt knew from the Migratory Bird Act. He was a small, sad man who couldn't make eye contact, but he held my arm as we stepped over fallen trees and branches in the woods. The Park Service rarely cleared these woods and that was what I loved about it. A forest should be, doing what a forest should do, changing shape, rolling over itself.

There was no shortage of crows for the ornithologist to examine. He put on suede gloves, produced a small hunting knife and knelt to cut a bird from the breastbone to the top of the tail. He also made an incision at the crown of the head. Moving the flesh aside with the tip of the knife, he looked into the crow.

"If this was West Nile, I'd see swelling in the brain or infection in the spinal cord. I'll have to take him in to be tested, but this doesn't look like West Nile. The thinness and position of these birds suggests convulsions and vomiting. They're stiff but no rigor mortis, which suggests paralysis. Look at the eyes. They look burned. No, this isn't West Nile."

"Def-11?"

He shook his head.

"Def-11 takes years for symptoms to appear. We're not even certain that's what's causing coronary heart disease in birds. If I didn't know better, I'd say this was poison. There's plenty of arsenic around, in water, household items, apples. But how these birds came in contact with such a concentrated amount, I cannot know."

"The arsenic I put in the chagwa's food did nothing," I insisted.

"He must have poisoned the creek with his urine. And the berries for the deer. And the grubs . . ."

"What have I done?" I gasped. "There have been miscarriages. Three of my neighbors."

Now the ornithologist looked in my eyes. "It's all right. In time the land and water purges itself."

"What about the crows?"

"I can't say there's much we can do there. But maybe something good could come of it. Maybe this clears the way for something new. Remember the condor? What room is there for a bird with a twelve-foot wing span in today's world?"

I wept into my hands.

You'd think nothing unusual was taking place. Down on the Mall, people went about activities as though no chagwa roamed the city. A small group protested the treatment of prisoners at Guantánamo Bay. Six people shook signs and held banners, handing out flyers with photos of malnourished men. So few protesters came, they'd filled beach chairs with mannequins to strengthen their numbers.

I walked along the gravel path. It was National Pet Day. People walked animals that had no business as pets. I saw a woman walking a pig, a family with a crocodile. A man with a boa constrictor let a girl with an anteater put the snake around her neck for a photo. The flash of the camera made the snake nervous. The snake began to squeeze the girl's neck and had to be removed. A man climbed an elm after an orangutan. Where were the cats and dogs? A college student handed out anti-vivisection flyers.

"My wife wants me to get one of those," a man said.

"Vasectomy, idiot." His wife smacked him.

I wound my way through tent city, but the tents were empty so I headed toward the War Memorial. A man and a woman kissed on a bench. Not just kissing. Their tongues intertwined, twirling around each other. The man put his hand in her blouse, moving aside her bra. Passersby turned away. I looked. I saw them above the ground, their clothes dissolving, twisting around each other into a ball of weight so dense no light could escape their bodies.

"Wendy?" The woman disengaged, doing nothing to cover her breasts.

"Why, Nancy Price-Brundage." I felt ashamed for having stared.

"Nancy Price Brundage *Corbett*." She introduced her new husband.

"Well!" I said. "This is happy news.

"Tell Matt we got parking at Saint Peter's on Red Square. Two spaces. The Nowhere to Go Ball is the envy of the philanthropic world."

"He'll be ecstatic."

I waved to the bride and groom and moved along the path.

Women sobbed into lace and walked in their gray clothes. This could only mean Ben Sotterburg was nearby.

I found him partially reclined on a bench.

"There's not a lot left of you, Mr. Sotterburg."

His right pant leg was sewn shut just below his hip. He was accompanied by, surprisingly, a *male* nurse, who repeatedly took his blood pressure.

"It's the infection that's cutting me down. I do fine without the leg and hand." The left arm of his suede jacket had been tucked into the pocket. His silver hair had yellowed. His beard was coming in white. "Your husband, on the other hand, is making a remarkable recovery."

"So I've heard."

The cuff tightened around Ben's arm as the nurse pumped the ball. I remembered that arm around me.

"It's a great day for our party."

"He's going to take out your precious chagwa, Mr. Sotterburg."

"If we feel more secure from the outside, we can begin to change on the inside."

"How *right* you are. How *right* you've all become."

"I thought you despised the animal, Mrs. Dunleavy. Or perhaps you expect him to just disappear without our taking measures."

"Measures. I suppose you now say *neutralize* instead of *kill*."

"Semantics."

"You've gone over like the rest of them."

"We all need to evolve, Mrs. Dunleavy. Your husband has armed your son."

"As long as it's not your son, right?"

"There will always be a temple in my heart for you, Wendy."

"I've just come from a place that rendered me incapable of saying anything I don't mean."

"I see you're still capable of cruelty. But I do mean what I said."

"Well, then. There will always be a place in my heart for you too."

"You don't mean it, but it's what I want to hear." He looked sad. I felt pity. I still wanted him. The nurse scrambled to wrap the cuff around his arm. In a few seconds his pain subsided. "You don't realize, Wendy, I mourn every one of you." He motioned toward a woman on a bench near us, crying into Kleenex after Kleenex. A man in a wheelchair rolled over to help. "I don't even remember her name. But I miss her. Are you going to end this with 'not if you were the last man on earth, Ben Sotterburg'?"

"No. If you were the last man on earth, Ben Sotterburg, I would consider you."

"Wendy," he called after me when I turned to leave. The nurse pumped up the cuff. "Will I be seeing you on Thanksgiving?"

"Good-bye, Ben." I walked through a tidal wave of tears. Not one single drop was mine.

The press spread out in every direction. Helicopters were up in the air. SWAT practiced maneuvers from the trees. Animal Control dragged in a crate for remains. The mayor and the governors of Maryland and Virginia worked to settle a dispute between the police and the agencies over who would fire the first shot. The Attorney General would have the last say.

Men and women hovered in the MIA/POW booths, pointing out patches through fingerless gloves, shivering from being in the rain so long, casualties of lost causes. I brought them coffee, instructing them to keep warm. Then I looked for Dylan by the Wall. He wasn't there, but I walked along. I love the Wall, but it's too short, when you take into account the numbers of those affected. Each name has a hundred others attached. The Wall should surround the city. It should keep out invaders, keep in ghosts. All these memorials in a town that thrives on forgetfulness. I moved my eyes over a thousand names, seeing myself reflected among the dead, the reflections of those beside me and those no longer in this world. On Panel 4 was the reflection of a man bowing his head, crouching down. He touched the back of a name with his fingers. His hand was bandaged and bleeding through.

"Did you lose someone over there, Nuke?" I asked through the granite.

He dried his eyes on the gauze. "A lot," he said. I knelt and put my face against his.

I saw Matt as I walked back over the hill. A crowd began moving away from the mayor and the governors. Even the press had become bored waiting for the chagwa. I headed over the grass. I had to get to him before the throngs swallowed him. Everyone wanted to touch him. I broke into a sprint. He saw me coming and pushed aside two reporters, stomping his way toward me. I want to know which one of us broke the deal, at what point the mirroring stopped and our selves became majority shareholders. Staring each other down, enraged at being deserted, we charged at one another.

"I'm furious with you!" I yelled.

"I'm furious with you!" he yelled back. But this was said to overcome the entanglements of our reunion, to keep abandonment from ever happening again. He lifted me off the ground. One of us would have to concede.

"This beautiful woman . . ." Matt began, the press devouring every word. "Who stood by me every second of our nightmare . . ." I believed it too. Down by the reflecting pool, on the other side, I saw Dylan, walking along the edge, his Orioles hat shading his face. I could easily have not recognized him, he'd grown so much. He stepped heel to toe by the water. Matt looked up from a reporter. *Do not touch,* his gaze told me.

"Dylan," I called out and waved. But he didn't hear.

MATT SAID my daffodils reminded him of opiate poppies. He said that one night he'd come home from a lecture tour and I'd find him asleep amid one hundred Emperor's Goblets. And sleep was what we did around here most of the time. Dylan's blood infection medication doubled as a soporific. This morning he had drifted off during home teaching, the tutor waving good-bye as he tiptoed out. When he woke we spent a luxurious afternoon choosing designs for the new monuments that were printed in the *Washington Post.*

"I say build the War Memorial exactly as it was."

"Nah," Dylan said. "Leave it as a hole in the ground."

I scanned the proposals for the Jefferson.

"Rebuild to the letter but change the parking configuration."

"Jefferson owned slaves," Dylan said. "Build a slave memorial right on top."

"If you're going to count atrocities, you'll have to pave the Mall for an amusement park," I said. "What do you think of the new obelisk for the Washington Monument? I like the one with the glass." But he had gone back to sleep. I conked out too.

At six I looked over. His eyes were open.

"Are you awake?"

"I'm cold."

I covered him with a fleece throw. "Tomorrow we see Dr. Plessy," I said.

"I don't want to see Dr. Plessy."

"He has great hopes for the new antibiotic." Again, he closed his eyes. Dinner would be late. When I stood to go check that the parfaits had stiffened, I heard a creak and a footfall on the stairs.

"Penny, is that you?" Many times, I had called out for our lost dog like this. I heard another sound coming from deep within the house. I moved restlessly about, scanning the rooms. A March breeze came through the casement windows. The toaster fell. Then I heard nails clicking on the deck. I looked out the kitchen door. The air was still. Nothing moved. But then something smacked against the door, shattering the glass, filling my eyes with dust. A claw shot through an empty windowsill. I dropped and scurried on all fours to the phone.

"All our officers are downtown for the Million Guns March," the 911 operator said.

"The situation is here," I screamed, and hung up. When I looked up, a chagwa was balancing his tremendous weight on the rail of the deck like a gymnast on a beam. He then flung himself against the dining room window. The glass smashed, but the casement stopped him. He grabbed at the air, falling on his back in the yard. But he righted himself and padded around the house.

"Dylan." I shook him awake. "Get to the crawl space. Immediately."

"What?" He couldn't wake up.

"I know you're tired. Listen to me. Get to the crawl space."

He heard the chagwa's roar.

I placed him on the lift chair and sent him up the stairs.

"When you get to the top, roll off. Low crawl your way to the crawl space."

The beast roared again. Then there was a hush. I peered through the hole in the front door. A huge swollen eye stared back. His roar reverberated through the house. I called Dr. Jovanavich.

"Of course they didn't get him. He'd know better than to show himself in a crowd."

"They saw him enter the Mall," I insisted.

"People see what they want to see."

"He couldn't have escaped the bombs."

"They never found a body."

"The Mall was reduced to dust. There's an infestation. I've known it all along."

"There's no infestation, Wendy. He's the last one. They refused to breed. They lost their forests to roads, their skins to pelt, their bones to medicine. They made a decision to let their race die out. But not this one. This one refused."

The chagwa bashed against the door.

"What the hell does he want?" I screamed

"The boy, of course. If he kills the one who fed him, he will have made his point."

"I want you on a plane tonight," I shouted. "No one knows this animal but you."

"I wish I could."

Paint fell from the hinges of the front door as the chagwa butted it over and over. I ran to the other side of the house.

"Why is it that you have never been willing to help me?"

"I'm sick, Wendy. He gouged me as I dove into my truck in Butai. I've been fighting off infection for years. The pain is unbearable. Again and again this animal has defeated me, and now he's all through me. You don't know what it is to die without having gotten what you want."

"Could you just hang on a bit longer until I figure this out?" I heard an immense crash. He'd thrown himself against the window in the living room. Again, it was only the iron casings that kept him out. "He's trying to get in the house."

"Get a gun."

"I don't have a gun."

"Throw some meat. Get him sated until someone can come."

"We've gone vegetarian." I poured a pot of tomato stew out

the window onto the deck. I tossed the Eskimo parfaits, one at a time, spiraling into the yard. Then I slid down the wall, pulling my knees into my chest, and picked up the phone.

"He's not eating," I said.

"He's not a vegetarian."

"There's a chance I have chicken."

"He's beyond chicken, Wendy." It became quiet again. I crawled to the window and looked out. "What is he doing now?" Dr. Jovanavich asked.

"Sharpening his nails on the tree."

"I think we can work this out. But you have to trust me."

"Whatever you say."

"How sick is the boy?"

"It's unlikely he'll walk again."

The chagwa disappeared in a shadow. I stood and went to the living room. I saw the screen door fling into the yard. He then wedged the front door open. Infuriated by the chain, he shot his paw through the crack in the door. I grabbed a book and swatted the paw. His nails drew back into his skin, but then they pushed out longer and sharper.

Dr. Jovanavich was yelling my name. "Wendy, are you there?" Only the flimsy chain kept the door from opening.

"Oh, God, he's coming in."

"Bring the boy to the chagwa."

"Are you insane?"

"If he sees the boy is lame, we may be able to force a hermaphroditic episode. If the female sees the boy is dying, she won't want to harm him."

"He's not dying. There's a new antibiotic."

"Only the chagwa can revive the boy. Oyada Tanakpur

writes in *The Man-Eater of Raypong*, 'The father caresses the son with such fury that he kills him. The female then appears in despair so severe that she tears open her own breast, reviving the dead cub with her blood.' No pill will save him, Wendy. Give the chagwa your son."

"Never."

"Then he will kill you, Wendy. And the boy."

"And what if your experiment, your hermo-damaphrodite episode doesn't work? Then what?"

"Then you will have done nothing but tried."

The chagwa now had his forehead wedged into the door, bloodshot eyes opening all over his skull. Again, I hit him with the book. An eye was cut open and rolled back in his head.

"Good God, do as I say, Wendy."

"You're not even certain this will work," I cried.

"I'm doubtful, in fact."

The chain began to come loose from the molding. "He's getting in. Help me."

"I want you to find a rock or a large hard object," Dr. Jovanavich said calmly.

I rushed to the kitchen. "A pan? The toaster? And do what with it?"

"Find something he thinks he can eat. A rock. A rock the size of two men's fists."

"I do not have a goddamn rock."

"Open the back door. Go outside. Get a rock."

"He won't eat chicken, you think he's going to eat a rock?"

"It's your only chance. Go out the back."

I heard the door chain rattle to the floor. "He's in the house. Help us."

"Get out, Wendy. Get the rock." The chagwa appeared at the entrance to the kitchen. I backed out onto the deck. "Did you find a rock?"

"No." I saw the stack of bricks I'd left for the Harlans. "I have a brick." I picked one up.

"Do it, Wendy."

"I can't." I stepped backward. The animal charged. I tossed the brick in the air. He leapt right over me, catching it in his mouth. I heard his teeth break. He landed without a sound on the dirt. He then bent back his head and swallowed.

"Did you do it, Wendy? Wendy? Are you there?"

The animal looked up at me, surprised I would hurt him. As he turned away, I saw that indeed his testicles rose up into his body.

"Wendy?"

"It's changing." The chagwa's breathing became a whistle, then the sound of a sick man snoring, then a sputter. The brick was cutting off her windpipe, strangling her. "Do you hear?" I asked.

"Yes. I can hear. You did well, Wendy."

"Mom?" Dylan was crumpled behind me on the deck, his thin legs curled to one side. He grabbed hold of the banister and slid down the stairs into the yard. I took his hands. He rose to his knees. But then his head fell back. I caught him in my arms, lifting him up.

"Dylan." I shook him slightly. "Dylan, wake up. Look at me. Look at me now." I shook him hard. But no breath came up from his lungs. I shook him as hard as I could.

The chagwa came over to us, bleeding from the mouth. I saw that one end of the brick had punctured her neck from the inside. I laid Dylan on the ground. The chagwa stood over him.

Then she covered his entire body with hers. I tried pushing her off, but she looked up at me, her face pleading. So I stroked the hairless place on her back. She flicked her tail. We sat like this for a long time, longer than an hour, I'm sure. When finally she stood, I could see Dylan's chest begin to move. The chagwa backed off. Dylan sat up, covered in the animal's blood. He didn't know where he was.

"Am I in trouble?" he asked.

"Go inside now."

"I'm starving." He walked up the back steps. On the deck, he glanced down at his bloody clothes.

"Shower," I said.

He went in the house.

The chagwa tripped over her paws toward the fence, leaning against it. Her eyes cast downward, her jaw went slack. She looked ashamed to be dying. She reared back and, in a final gasp, leapt over the fence and galloped into the woods.

I picked the phone up off the ground.

"What's going on, Wendy?" Dr. Jovanavich said.

"She's gone into the forest."

"In search of a quiet place."

"I'm going after her."

"You stay where you are."

I climbed over the fence.

"It's not a game," Dr. Jovanavich continued. "Do you understand? I told you to stay where you are. Never stand near a dying chagwa, do you hear me? Wendy. Answer."

"I'm sorry we never met," I said.

Among the forsythia stems and brown grass of the forest, the chagwa was a blur. Even more so when she moved through the taxus and azaleas, the stalks of the kalmia, what little remained of the brush. There were so many shadows from the trees I couldn't tell if that was she up ahead. It was the chagwa bending into the water, but then it was a dam of twigs and leaves. It was the chagwa leaping off a stump, but then it was a poplar that had uprooted in the rain. She moved on. She faded. Each time I got close, she got farther away, reminding me of a mirage in the road on long drives in the summer when ahead the asphalt looks wet but you never arrive. There she was, lying in the ajuga like a lazy shepherd. No, it was a branch that broke in the Def-11. There, going over the hill to the gated storm sewer on the other side. I went over too. I saw her. She slowed down. She was just ahead in the aspens. Just up there by the oaks. Inches away in the poplars. Ten o'clock from the birch. Soon she became indistinguishable from the rhododendron and the vines, but I kept moving until I came to a place in the woods where I was lost.

About the Author

Julia Slavin is the author of a collection of stories, *The Woman Who Cut Off Her Leg at the Maidstone Club*, which was a *New York Times* Notable Book. Her fiction has won the Pushcart Prize, *GQ*'s coveted Frederick Exley Fiction Competition, and the Rona Jaffe Foundation Writers' Award. *Carnivore Diet* is her first novel. She lives with her family in Washington, DC.